A SNOWSTORM, A SCANDAL, AND A SECRET IDENTITY BLOW

INTO A WRITING RETREAT...

Meade Godwin knew the new chef was trouble when he rescued her from a snowy ditch. All the ingredients were there.

He should have remembered: if you can't stand the heat, get out of her kitchen.

Snowed In: Heat Rises

A Write Place Retreat Romance

MJ Compton

Comptonplations Publishing

Copyright

Cover designed by 100 Covers

Developmental Edit by Susan Bischoff, Bisch Please

Published in the United States of America by Comptonplations Publishing

www.comptonplations.com

EBOOK ISBN: 978-1-959923-19-0

PAPERBACK ISBN:

Julie Compton Ryder

Sister Extraordinaire

ACKNOWLEDGEMENTS

Micaela Compton for chef details and insights to millennial language

Carol Lombardo, chef and Whiteface Mt details

Kristine Kipers, Attorney

Rebecca Herwood-Mussen, Crystal Clifford, and Hollyanne Compton for insights to millennial language.

Cops & Writers Facebook group: Frank Carson, Itsa Merb, Angel Giacomo

The BFA Patreon morning office crew (You know who you are!)

The Purples (Carol Lombardo, Christine Wenger, Gayle Callen, Kris Fletcher)

The Ghostwriters of Thistledew (ALee Drake, Holly Weedon, Janina Grey, Elizabeth Doherty, Kat Morrissey, Christie Logan)

The members of the collective formerly known as CNYRW (I miss our monthly meetings!)

CONTENTS

CHAPTER 1

Lazlo brushed the pads of his fingers along the lovely Araminta's soft white shoulder. Her warm, satiny flesh tempted him to do more than touch.

JUSTINE MACKO WINCED AT the romance novel playing on her phone. She ought to turn off the book and focus on her driving instead of steaming up the windshield. The author, Andromeda Zeus, one of Justine's favorites, was a *New York Times* bestseller and winner of multiple awards, but *Desire's Revenge* was Zeus's first book and contained every overblown cliché that invited mockery from snobs who didn't understand the romance genre.

Ms. Zeus was one of the authors she'd be feeding as the chef at The Write Place Retreat, and in a fan-girl moment, she'd downloaded a couple of audio books from the library. She hadn't expected to get through even one of the books on what was supposed to be a five-hour trip from Brooklyn to the High Peaks region of the Adirondack Mountains, but here she was, five hours long past, her subcompact car struggling through snow that just kept falling. Meanwhile, Lazlo just kept putting the moves on his innocent heroine.

"One taste," Lazlo begged, his lips hovering over Araminta's. "That's all I ask."

"One taste leads to another," Justine warned the naïve Araminta. "Just say no."

"No," Araminta moaned. "We must stop."

"Right," Justine muttered. "Wish I could." Except she was in the middle of nowhere, with no stopping place in sight.

Snow toppled in drifts from the sky like broken 50-pound bags of flour, battling the fading sunlight this late afternoon in mid-February. Her windshield wipers failed to keep pace with the cascading white stuff that acted like glue once it hit the pavement and her windshield.

Her subcompact car preferred city streets, not interstates, and definitely not roads cutting through evergreens and mountains. And she'd had no money to address her mechanic's warning about bald tires that wouldn't pass a safety inspection, so she'd been white-knuckling it for the last couple hours.

A wind gust buffeted the car, pushing her into the oncoming lane. Justine yanked the steering wheel to return to her own side of the road, thanking her personal holy trinity of Julia Child, Wolfgang Puck, and Gordon Ramsey that no one was approaching. The car spun. Her phone fell. She jammed her foot on the brake, which only increased the wintery whirlpool. Gray, white, and dark, dark green blurred. Her stomach eddied in the opposite direction.

She eased off the brake pedal. The spin slowed. She pumped the brakes until the car stopped.

The highway remained deserted. Nothing in the countryside stirred except for the unrelenting snowfall.

Araminta tossed her head, sending an avalanche of sable curls tumbling down her back.

Justine took a moment to calm her racing heart. Her phone had landed on the passenger side floor, burrowing into a nest of gas receipts, reusable shopping bags, and the cache of plastic bags she'd repurposed as improvised gloves for pumping gas. So much for silencing Lazlo and Araminta. She'd have to ignore them and their now-muffled passions.

"Okay, back on the road. You can do it," she murmured, as if the car possessed ears. She tapped the gas pedal. The little car whined. Jerked forward a few inches. The driving conditions amplified the twitchiness of the overly sensitive steering wheel. She refused to let something as trivial as weather deter her. The snow scraping the bottom of her low-riding vehicle worried her, but wasn't she still standing after Lenny's betrayal? Moving away from the city wasn't accepting defeat. She was regrouping, which included dealing with the *oeuf*ing snow.

After several moments spent tapping and inching, the car finally pointed in the right direction. In the correct lane. She hoped. If highway markers existed on this stretch of the road, the snow hid them. If rumble strips grooved the pavement, her tires couldn't find them beneath the snowpack.

She checked the trip odometer—only a few more miles to The Write Place.

Even her skid marks were rapidly vanishing. Her headlights failed to pierce the decreasing visibility surrounding her. She switched on the four-way flashers.

She debated a moment before going out to check the rest of her lights. Snow tumbled over the tops of her ankle boots. The two-inch heels didn't offer much traction. She teetered to the front end of her car and cleaned off the headlights. Using fingerholds wherever she found them, she made her way to the rear. Her leather gloves weren't meant for extreme weather or practical function, but she'd piled her suitcases on the snowbrush in the trunk. She repeated her actions on the taillights.

Only a few more miles, she reminded herself. She lost her grip on the fender and slipped, twisting her right knee. "Puck!" She stumbled to the driver's door and crawled inside. Heat enveloped her.

Lazlo prayed Araminta would be moist with desire when he finally groped beneath her voluminous skirts.

"Give the snow a minute to melt," Justine suggested to the narrator. She held her frozen fingers to the heater vents. She needed them to thaw only enough to control the steering wheel as she drove the last stretch.

Clammy denim numbed the ache in her knee as the snow coating her jeans turned icy wet. She clenched her teeth to keep them from chattering.

"Okay," she told Saint Lawrence, patron saint of chefs and comics, whose medallion hung from her rearview mirror. Lazlo and Araminta weren't listening to her. They must have taken lessons from Lenny. "The joke's over. Let's do this."

She clutched the steering wheel and shifted into drive. She cautiously pressed the gas pedal. The tires whined as they dug for purchase. The car jerked forward. Justine released her breath.

"I want to protect you," Lazlo vowed. "Keep you safe."

"Don't trust anything coming out of his lying, cheating mouth," Justine advised. She spoke from experience. "You'll only end up stranded in a blizzard in the back of beyond."

The falling snow mesmerized her. She blinked several times to dispel the hypnotic effect. She risked a glance at the speedometer. A whopping five miles per hour.

"You're too desirable," Lazlo murmured as he slipped scarlet silk from Araminta's shoulder. "You are enough to tempt a saint."

"No! Don't let him see—"

A sudden movement ahead silenced her. A dark silhouette. Massive. In the middle of the road. Tree branches balanced on an enormous head.

Justine slammed on the brakes. Cuisinart had nothing on a subcompact car fishtailing on a snow-slick road when it came to whirling its contents. The world dissolved to black.

MEADE GODWIN PEERED OUT his windshield at the falling snow and cursed the delay at his attorney's office that had prevented him from leaving Manhattan in a timelier manner. When he'd called Darby Winehouse at The Write Place Retreat to give her his return ETA, she'd promised to have his cabin ready. He'd been gone only two nights, but long enough for the chill of the Adirondack High Peaks to invade his quarters.

"We're expecting heavy weather, so be careful," Darby had warned.

Heavy weather? In the city, they'd call the current snowfall a blizzard. Thank God for his Hummer. The vehicle was old, a gas-guzzler, and a pain in the ass to park. He kept it for his treks to the Adirondacks. Otherwise, he paid outrageous fees for a spot in his apartment building's garage, an expense his ex-wife continued to bitch about, although they'd finalized their divorce two years ago.

"Your agent is here, settled in the Crown Suite," Darby continued. "The new chef is on her way, too."

Chef. One reason The Write Place remained his favorite retreat. Darby Winehouse excelled in taking care of her guests. The staff at the retreat handled everything from meals to laundry. The experience was worth every penny Elaine-his-Ex bitched about him spending.

And he'd spun right back to fuming about his former wife and her greedy, grasping ways. Well, she was in for one hell of a shock once she learned his new strategy.

The windshield wipers slapping the glass applauded him. Meade's lawyer had assured him that his plan stayed within the parameters of his spousal support agreement, and Elaine still couldn't reveal his secret identity to the world without losing her share of his royalties.

Now to convince his agent, who didn't realize her Adirondack meeting with Meade included renegotiating with her favorite client. She believed Meade wanted to brainstorm the final book of his current contract, writing with the pseudonym that had made them both extremely well off. She wouldn't want to relinquish her guaranteed income any more than Elaine-his-Ex would.

Tough shit.

Penning romantic sex scenes bored him. His new ideas were better. Big. Bigger than the monster cocks and voluptuous tits on which Elaine insisted he'd built his career.

And speaking of racks, was that a *moose* blocking the road?

Meade jammed on the brakes. The Hummer fishtailed. The moose vanished behind a curtain of snow.

Holy shit! In all the times he'd driven from Manhattan to St. Huberts he'd never spotted a moose, much less come close to hitting one.

The Hummer slid sideways before stopping in the middle of New York Route 73. He thrust the transmission into park. He regrouped for a minute. The pavement proved slicker than he'd assumed. The snow resembled a conniving woman, soft and pretty to look at, yet secretive and dangerous.

I can use the image in a book, he thought, as he shifted his vehicle into low gear and eased into his lane. He scanned both sides of the road for movement as he crept forward. Broadsiding a moose, even at low speed in his mighty Hummer, could be a disaster.

No sign of the creature.

But what the hell was that?

He pulled to the side of the highway and stopped. Tire tracks in the snow resembled the scribbles he made when checking a pen for ink. Dim flashing orange lights caught his eye.

Damn. A car rested in the ditch.

He grabbed his cell phone before climbing out of the Hummer. Snow nipped at his exposed skin as he drew his hood over his head. The wind chewed through his jacket with icy teeth. "Hey, Siri. Lumos!"

The flashlight on his iPhone penetrated the descending darkness.

A tin can of a car tilted nose-first in the ditch, the engine still running. Not good. At least the blowing snow hadn't blocked the exhaust pipe, so no danger of carbon monoxide poisoning ... yet. The car hadn't been stuck long—a scant inch of snow coated the emergency flashers. No visible footprints meant the occupants were still inside.

Damn. Meade only wrote heroes.

Still, he had to help. He made his way down the steep slope of the ditch. He directed his flashlight through the driver's window and tapped on the glass.

The woman behind the wheel shrieked. She was alone and conscious.

"Are you hurt?" Meade asked.

"I don't think so," the woman replied, her voice muffled by the glass.

Meade jerked open the door.

"Wait a minute! What are you doing?"

Outrage instead of gratitude. Women were all the same.

Araminta slapped his hands. "Lazlo, please. You mustn't touch me like that."

"Fuck." Of all the women in the world Meade Godwin was destined to rescue, she would have to be one of his fans. Or rather, an Andromeda Zeus fan. "Shut off the book, will you?"

"I can't," the accident victim said. "My phone fell in with the trash, and I can't reach it. You'll have to plug your ears."

Trash? An echo of his ex-wife's slurs. Meade retained enough ego to resent relegation to the garbage. He opted to ignore the insult, despite agreeing that this book, his first, was not one of his better efforts.

Ten million readers *could* be wrong.

"I only want a chance with you," Lazlo declared.

"Can you get out?" Ice crunched beneath his soles as Meade stomped his feet in an effort to stay warm.

"I don't know," the woman admitted. "I'm waiting for my head to stop hurting and my fingers to thaw before I retrieve my phone and call a tow truck."

Great. She probably had a concussion.

"Not the best weather to wait in your car," Meade pointed out. "Let me give you a ride to the resort where I'm staying, and you can deal with whatever from the lodge."

"I don't know you. I don't get into cars with strangers."

"You happen to know a local tow truck operator?" He didn't bother to conceal his sarcasm. This woman was as annoying as any other he'd met. He wished she'd do what he suggested so he—they—could escape the weather before exposure did them in.

"You're so cold to me," Lazlo complained. "Have I offended you?"

"There is that," she admitted. "What's the resort?"

Finally. A smattering of common sense. "The Write Place."

"Oh." She peered at him. "That's where I'm going. I'm the new chef."

Her revelation simplified matters. "Hey, Siri, call The Write Place."

The phone at the lodge rang several times before Darby answered. "Are you okay?" she asked after he'd identified himself. She sounded harassed. "The county closed the roads due to the weather. Emergency vehicles only."

"I'm fine, but I found your new employee in a ditch about five miles from my cabin. Shaken, but visibly unharmed. We should be there in a few minutes."

"Oh, thank goodness. I've been worried about her. Chef Justine isn't used to our weather. Is she really okay?"

"She says she is, but she's worried I'm a serial killer."

"You?" Darby laughed. "Put her on. I'll vouch for you."

As much as he would rather be sheltered in his Hummer's heated cab, experience assured him pandering to feminine whims would be quicker. He thrust the phone at the woman. "The Write Place owner will confirm I rape and pillage only when the temperature is above sixty-eight degrees and sunny."

Chapter 2

WHOEVER THIS PERSON WAS—MEADE something-or-other, not that he'd introduced himself—he was cranky. Justine's new boss, Darby Winehouse, had assured Justine that Meade was harmless. Clearly Darby had never encountered the man in a snit.

He'd been peeved about the audio book. He'd been peeved while she searched for her phone. He'd been peeved when she swatted his hand as he reached in to turn off her flashers and because she'd hesitated to climb into a vehicle with a strange man.

Peeved morphed to cantankerous when he'd asked if she owned a hat, and she'd pulled a chef's toque from her tote.

But cranky was nothing compared to how ornery he got when she'd tried to stand on her twisted knee and fell into the snow with a shriek. Not due to the cold, but from the pain.

He'd ended up tossing her over his shoulder like a fifty-pound bag of rice, muttering f-bombs and other curses as he scrambled out of the ditch.

At least he'd gone back to fetch her tote and a suitcase when she'd asked.

"Thank you." She'd snatched her tote bag from him.

"Put your seatbelt on," he'd demanded, as he tossed her luggage in the back seat.

The icicles formerly known as fingers inside her gloves didn't want to cooperate.

More curses as he fastened the locking mechanism for her, punctuated with disparaging insults about wearing leather gloves in a snowstorm.

"The weather was fine when I left Brooklyn," she'd informed him.

Only to be lambasted for not checking the Adirondack weather report instead of listening to a trashy romance novel. "'Trashy' was your word, not mine," he reminded her.

What? She loved romance novels. Okay, the one playing as she drove wasn't the greatest, but who was he to sneer at any writer? He probably wrote depressing, gritty *literature,* if he wrote anything at all.

Now he stayed silent. Tense. Hunched over the steering wheel. Justine wasn't about to break his concentration. One ditch a night was enough.

Five miles, he'd told Darby. *His cabin.*

Justine had done her research on The Write Place before applying for the position. She'd learned there were four suites in the main lodge and three cabins scattered in the woods surrounding Nippletop Lake. Authors and other literary types traipsed to the mountains for peace, quiet, and no distractions. The former Great Camp offered no internet, cable or satellite television, and unreliable cell phone service. Guests escaped civilization in order to work.

Isolation didn't mean bad food. The retreat promised to feed its guests well—the reason Justine had been hired. She could manage the new job with one hand tied behind her back—as long as she retained the use of her knife hand. Oh, and access to ingredients. The storm might create an issue with supplies.

Snow, darkness, evergreens, more snow. This version of New York State was alien to her. Where were the skyscrapers? The street and traffic lights? If not the urban version, she'd settle for the rolling vineyards of the Finger Lakes or the majesty of Niagara Falls—anything other than this bleak landscape.

Meade swore and hit the brakes at the same time he yanked on the steering wheel. The oversized vehicle teetered. "I missed the damn turnoff to the cabin."

Justine learned it was possible for a human to actually growl.

He shifted into reverse and tried to back up.

The engine echoed his growl. The gargantuan tires spun as uselessly as her car's tiny ones had, proving that bigger wasn't necessarily better.

He tried rocking the SUV—reverse, drive, reverse, drive—the oversized man mobile wouldn't budge. After a few minutes of going nowhere, he put the transmission in park. His thumbs beat a tattoo on the steering wheel. "We're stuck."

She bit back her *you think* response. After all, he'd rescued her. She could be civil. In fact, she had good reasons to be civil. She needed him to enjoy her cooking. Her much-needed job depended on pleasing the guests.

Insecurity in the kitchen had never been an issue for her until recently.

No. Don't dwell on the past. The Write Place offered her a chance to reclaim herself. Get back on her feet. Recapture her culinary mojo. She refused to squander the opportunity by pitying herself.

"Want me to drive while you get out and push?" she offered.

He snorted. "What part of stuck don't you get?"

She said nothing—a hard-learned lesson for her.

Meade instructed his phone to dial Darby. "We're stuck at the turnoff. Any way Heath can meet us with a sled to help your new cook?"

Justine bristled. She was a classically trained chef, not a cook. Not that she would expect a person who growled and snorted to understand the difference.

"That bad, huh? Okay." He disconnected and resumed tapping the steering wheel. "The groundskeeper is picking up a guest from the bus stop in Keene. We're on our own. We're approximately a mile from my place. The lodge is a mile beyond my cabin. Think you can walk a couple miles?"

"Sure," she chirped, then cringed. She wasn't a chirpy woman.

As far as hiking a mile in deep snow, her knee throbbed like a boiling pot on a burner. Her toes weren't doing much better. Her head hurt as if struck by a meat mallet. But long hours on her feet in the kitchen had made her tough.

"What about my luggage?" She could manage her tote. In fact, she wouldn't leave without it. The suitcase was another story.

"It stays. Too much of a struggle in deep snow."

"All right."

See? She could be agreeable, despite rumors to the contrary.

She grabbed the handles of her tote and secured them on her shoulder. "All set." Not quite a chirp, but still too perky.

"Then let's go." He switched off the ignition.

Justine tumbled out of the SUV into knee high snow. The only way she could plunge through the drifts was in someone's wake—if her twisted knee would support her weight.

She was so screwed.

"I'll follow you," she shouted, but the wind whisked her words in the opposite direction.

Meade rounded the hood of his vehicle. "Hold on to the back of my coat."

Justine hoisted the straps of her tote higher on her shoulder. They slid into the crook of her elbow. She fumbled against

Meade's back until she found a belt loop to clutch. Her knuckles ached as she forced them to bend.

Pain flashed in her right knee. She stumbled against Meade, who uttered another colorful, creative curse. Her vision blurred. Or the snow created an optical illusion. The wind snatched at her hair and scarf and tried to invade her lungs. She would never make it to shelter. Stepping in Meade's tracks didn't help. She tugged on his coat.

"What?"

Even when he shouted, the wind whistling in her ears blocked his words. "I can't do this. I'll go back and wait for you in your car."

Instead of arguing with her, he simply upended her again and tossed her over his shoulder.

Now you have a plot for Andromeda's final book. The story is practically writing itself. Snowed-in is a popular trope. Forced proximity. Ought to sell millions.

Not that Meade planned on seducing Darby's new cook.

He found telling himself the story helped with the physical challenge of trudging through calf-high snow with a woman hanging over his shoulder. As long as he kept moving, he'd be okay.

The going was slow. The mile from the road to his cabin was a finite measurement. He wasn't wandering into uncharted Adirondack wilderness. The clear-cut trail guided him. Yeah, a few people had vanished forever in the six-million-acre park, but not him. Not tonight. Unless he strayed from the trail, he'd arrive at his cabin. Eventually.

Frostbite and hypothermia were still concerns.

After what seemed like an hour battling the weather, a light flickering between snowflakes and trees beckoned him. *His porch.* The usually annoying solar security light marked the end of his trek.

His legs and shoulders ached. The cold had turned his bones to icicles. His bundle hadn't stirred or made a sound in a while.

He stomped his feet as he crossed the porch and managed to punch the date his divorce was finalized onto the keypad lock. A blast of heat and the scent of burning wood welcomed them into the cabin. Meade lowered Justine to the bench to the right of the door before flicking on the light.

She collapsed against the wall. Meade wasn't sure she was conscious until she lifted her head and brushed her snow-mottled hair away from her face. Red cheeks indicated frostnip, not the more serious frostbite. The bluish lump growing from one side of her forehead, however, presented another matter.

"What happened to your head?" he asked as he tugged off his gloves.

Justine blinked amber-colored eyes at him. Or were her eyes a shade of topaz? He'd have to consult his inner romance hero. Later.

She winced as she prodded the bump with one finger. "I must have hit it when the car went into the ditch."

The lucid answer didn't ease his concern. He had no idea how long she'd been stranded. He dropped his jacket to the floor.

"We need to get out of these wet clothes," he said. "I'll lend you something until you get your suitcase. I'll try to call Darby and let her know you're okay."

Justine clutched her brown leather bag to her chest, staring at him as if he were crazy.

He remembered the silly chef hat she'd tried to pass off as winter wear. "Unless you have a change of clothes in your bag?"

"I don't." She sounded pissy.

"Then take off those ridiculous boots while I scrounge up something for you."

He unlaced his boots and toed them off, feeling smug because he'd worn winter-sensible clothing for his trip north, unlike the waif shivering on his bench.

When he emerged from his bedroom wearing fresh jeans, a white fisherman's sweater, and thick socks to protect his feet from the cold floorboards, he found Justine still on the bench. She'd removed her useless boots, coat, and scarf. Her skinny jeans were wet from ankle to crotch. Her cabernet-colored velour top might have been substantial enough for a sunny

September day in Central Park; February in the Adirondacks required more.

But the garment did look touchable, especially where the fabric cupped her breasts.

Take notes later, Meade reminded himself. Andromeda's readers loved his detailed descriptions. Women—except the ones he wrote—confused him. As long as he considered Justine a character in one of his books, he'd be okay.

Justine's cheeks weren't quite as red as they'd been, which he took as a good sign. The lump on her forehead appeared bluer, though, and the skin that wasn't red or blue was decidedly paler. Then he noticed she was asleep.

Not good. Between a possible concussion and hypothermia, his scanty knowledge of first aid suggested she needed to be awake. He jostled her shoulder. She mumbled a response. Gripping her arm, he shook her again.

"What?" She glared at him. "Don't touch me."

"Here." He handed her a blue and black buffalo plaid flannel shirt and a pair of black sweatpants with a drawstring waist. She could roll up the cuffs so she wouldn't trip. "You can change in the bathroom."

Her wet, skin-tight denim jeans would be a challenge to remove. Not his problem.

"I can't," she muttered, her glare fading a touch.

"Do you need help?" The words clogged his throat. Undressing her was not a place he wanted to go, yet his imagination persisted in providing indecent details.

"I can't stand," she admitted, her tone glum.

She'd not only removed her outerwear and boots, but also her socks. Cherry-colored polish on her tiny toes gleamed in the dim light. Her left foot was slender and delicate, while the right was swollen to twice the size of the other.

No wonder he'd had to carry her to the cabin. "What the hell?"

"I twisted my knee when I brushed the snow off my lights."

"You brushed snow off your lights after your accident?"

Justine narrowed her eyes. "Before, wise guy."

She needed help to get those jeans off. "You can't stay in wet clothes."

Panic flared in Justine's eyes.

Meade laid the facts out for her. "Right now, you're at risk for hypothermia, a concussion, and I'm not counting whatever you did to your leg. We're talking basic first aid here. And if your leg is as swollen as your foot, your jeans may need to be cut off you."

He needed a drink. He should have started a pot of coffee as soon as he'd changed. Too bad he'd left his Knob Creek in his Hummer, but his hands had been full.

Justine snatched the flannel shirt from him. Two of her could have fit inside the garment. She pulled it on, rolling the sleeves until her fingers emerged before she buttoned the front from collar to hem. Then she plunged her hand into her leather bag and pulled out a knife.

CHAPTER 3

Justine gripped her chef's knife. The eight-inch carbon steel blade glinted in the dim light of the room. Caring for one's knives was one of the first lessons taught in culinary school, and she kept hers sharp. Her custom-made tote contained special compartments for her collection, which is why she refused to leave it behind when Meade insisted on carrying her through the snow.

"Whoa." Meade took a step back. "Wait. Right. Cutting off your jeans. Isn't that knife a little big?"

What did he think she was doing? Attacking him?

Unfortunately, he was right about the size of the blade. Between the wet fabric and the swelling in her knee, there wasn't much space to maneuver a large knife.

She located a paring knife and handed it to Meade. "I can't reach, so you'll have to help. Start at the hem."

What a waste. She loved these jeans, but the wet denim leeched heat from her body. Even worse, slicing the heavy fabric would ruin one of her beloved knives, and she couldn't afford a replacement.

"Scissors would work better," he said as he hacked at the hem.

"Too difficult to resharpen," Justine explained. "And please pay attention to what you're doing. I don't need my leg sliced open. My knives are sharp."

He grunted.

What was it with this man and his animal sounds?

He notched the double layer of denim before setting aside the knife. He gripped the material in both hands. The fabric separated parallel to the seam.

The warmth of his fingers against her chilled flesh startled her. She jerked as he yanked, needing to escape the contact. Her unnatural reaction to his big, strong hands made her nervous. She'd sworn off men after Lenny. Even worse, Meade was one of the retreat's guests. Forbidden fruit.

His hands fell away from her leg. She didn't dare look at him, not wanting to know if he'd been affected by the contact or if the zing had been one sided.

Justine pulled apart the edges of the pant leg. Her knee was swollen. No wonder she hurt. "How am I supposed to stand on this? My knee looks like a cantaloupe."

"Nah. It's smoother, like a honeydew," Meade said.

"Very funny." Justine did not sound amused, although she'd made the joke first. Or maybe she wasn't joking. The size of her knee wasn't a laughing matter.

No wonder he'd had to carry her. The aches in his arms and legs from hauling her through the deep snow were insignificant in comparison.

"Hey. You're the cook. You're supposed to know the differences between melons. I'm not a doctor, either, but I'm gonna say you need medical attention."

Justine brushed a long hank of hair off her cheek. Vivid pink no longer stained her face. Meade had no idea if her pallor was natural or frostbite white.

"Can you get your jeans off now? I'll give you some privacy."

He set the knife on the coffee table, patted his pocket to make sure he had his phone, and climbed the steep stairs to the upper level.

The second story loft, open to the first floor, contained an office complete with desk, rolling chair, and a futon. A quilted curtain hanging on a rod could close the opening to the lower level. Cell phone service, if available, tended to be better closest to the roof.

His phone showed one bar. He hoped the signal was enough to call the main lodge.

Darby answered, sounding more stressed than she had before.

"Is there anyone around with medical experience?" Meade asked. "Your new employee isn't in as good a shape as I thought."

"Cam is working the storm. Heath was a medic in the army, but he isn't back from the bus stop yet." Darby's husband, Cameron, was a forest ranger. Heath was the groundskeeper for the retreat. "Where are you?"

"My cabin." Meade lowered his voice and detailed Justine's condition, along with his limited grasp of contradictory first aid treatments: ice here, heat elsewhere.

"I guess she won't be reporting for work tonight." Darby sounded resigned. "Keep her warm and don't let her fall asleep. As soon as Cam or Heath get back, I'll have one of them get in touch." She ended the call.

Meade's muse begged to write this scenario, except his editor would never buy the premise. She'd call it unrealistic and far-fetched while ignoring the hundreds of dukes populating historical romance fiction bookstore shelves.

As he descended the stairs, cooler air hit his face. The loft always hoarded the heat from the woodstove. He'd have to remember to keep the privacy curtain closed. Too bad Justine couldn't climb the stairs.

He paused midway to make sure she was decent. Her jeans were a sodden pile on the orange rug. His sweatpants were a loose fit on her, except for her right leg.

He continued to the main floor.

Justine's head rested awkwardly against the wall, her throat exposed, and eyes closed. If he were a vampire—or wrote vampire books—he would take the pose as an invitation. Her white-knuckled fingers remained curled around the haft of her knife.

He supposed he should wake her. He didn't have a thermometer to take her temperature, but he did have hot coffee. Or there was always the popular romance trope of relieving hypothermia by sharing naked body heat.

Yeah. Sure, if he wanted to be deboned.

At least he could move her from the bench to a more comfortable spot.

She didn't stir when he lifted her, which concerned him almost as much as the knife he didn't dare pluck from her grip. The sweatpants sagged against her slim hips. There wasn't very much of her. Shouldn't a chef have more meat on her bones?

He forced his thoughts away from the slender body in his arms and tried to forget the tingle that had surged straight to his groin when he'd touched her bare calf—not even an interesting body part. The real priority was the bump on her head that ought to be iced. Her knee, too. His horniness had no place in the scene.

Once he'd settled her on the couch, he checked the freezer while the coffee maker burbled. The kitchen had been stocked with personalized emergency rations, all part of the retreat's service. Meade always requested coffee, pasta, jars of tomato sauce, various cheeses, and crackers. Otherwise, meals were delivered three times a day by the staff chef—who currently languished in his cabin.

Sure enough, only a solitary tray of cubes meant for his whiskey populated the freezer. Not one bag of frozen vegetables was available to act as an icepack.

His stomach echoed the gurgling coffee maker. Between the blizzard and the injured cook, Meade doubted a meal would magically materialize tonight. That meant pasta and sauce for supper, same as if he were home, and didn't want food delivered. He put a pot of water on to boil.

The coffee maker sputtered to the end of its cycle. Freshly brewed java had to be one of the best aromas in the world. Meade pulled two mugs from the cupboard. He drank his black, but Justine might want cream or sweetener. He thought he'd seen sugar and fake creamer powder in the condiment cupboard.

She'd slept long enough. He rounded the corner to the living area. As he set her mug on the table in front of the couch, he noticed her lips were slightly parted. Drool trickled from one corner of her mouth. More importantly, her fingers were loose on the giant knife. He reached in to pluck the weapon from her grasp.

She lurched upright. She yanked the knife toward the back of the couch. "What the Puck?"

Puck? Was she a hockey fan? A Shakespearean scholar?

Thank goodness she hadn't lunged. "I needed to wake you and didn't want you to skewer me," he explained. "You might have a concussion. You might have hypothermia. Both conditions require the victim to be awake."

"I am not a victim." Justine bit out the words between clenched teeth.

"Right. The weather and your leg are conspiring against you."

She slumped in her seat and wiped her mouth with her free hand.

"I made coffee. Might help with the cold." Meade gestured toward the steaming mug.

Her fingers brushed the lump on her forehead. She winced. "Thanks. I don't feel frozen, so I'm going to take being thawed as a positive sign."

She set her knife on the table and lifted the mug, holding it to her nose. She closed her eyes, sniffed, sipped, and groaned. Her eyes opened, and her lips curved upward. "Thank you for the rescue."

Her smile was deadlier than her knife, shredding Meade's defenses with a precision that stunned him. "I'm fixing spaghetti and sauce for dinner, if you want to eat," he offered, grateful his voice didn't betray his less-than-gentlemanly thoughts.

The softness in her face dissolved. "What kind of sauce?"

"Whatever jar they stocked for me."

"No. You will not eat sauce from a jar." Justine lurched upright. "*I* will not eat sauce from a jar."

"It's not bad stuff for emergency rations."

She responded with a sound he wouldn't dare replicate on the page. Andromeda's heroines exhibited a full range of emotional outbursts; Justine created a new one.

She set her mug on the coffee table and wriggled into an upright position. "I'll fix a fresh sauce for your pasta." She tried to stand. Instead, she toppled onto the couch with a whimper.

"As I said, spaghetti with sauce from a jar." Meade struggled to hide his amusement.

"Help me to the kitchen." Authority rang in her voice.

He recognized the tone. Elaine-his-ex devoured television cooking shows despite her aversion to kitchens. Watching gave her a topic to discuss with her friends. All the chefs spoke in the same commanding manner: "Do as I say or suffer the consequences." Moving would keep Justine awake, although it might further damage her leg.

Yet he hesitated to assist her to the kitchen. Yes, the journey was only a few feet, but he didn't want to touch her. Not now. Outside, in the deep snow, had been one thing. She'd been bundled in her city-style winter wear. He'd been focused on his footing in the treacherous snow and worried about dropping her. Now she wore his clothes next to her skin, which he found disturbingly intimate. He'd already noticed too much about her: the texture of her complexion; the way her velvet sweater cupped her nice-sized breasts; the honey color of her hair as strands dribbled over her shoulders.

He tried to blame his reactions on concern about frostbite. She was an attractive woman with a refreshing attitude.

And off limits. She was *staff*, for God's sake.

Now he sounded like a Regency rake considering a tumble with the queen's chamber maid.

"Hello?" Justine interrupted his musings. "Kitchen."

The woman had threatened to gut him. Her actions should have dampened any residual lust flickering through his body, not intrigued him. And certainly not aroused him.

Chapter 4

Justine wavered between outrage and pity. Pasta sauce from a jar indeed. Not while she had life in her body.

The meat-mallet-to-the-head pain had morphed into a cleaver embedded in her skull. Her stomach roiled from the pain—or from Meade's terrible coffee.

Pasta would quell the nausea. A nice spaghetti *aglio e olio*, using ingredients found in any kitchen: olive oil, garlic, and red pepper flakes. Oh, the recipe loved being fancied up with Parmesan, lemon, fresh parsley, and so on, but the dish's beauty lay in its simplicity. Justine could prepare the entrée in her sleep. Once she got to the *oeuf*ing kitchen.

She grabbed the sofa arm and tried to stand again, making sure most of her weight settled on her uninjured left leg. The pain in her knee bit in with poisoned fangs. She bumped into the table. Coffee sloshed from the mug to the wood. She limped to the end of the sofa.

"Oh, for..." Meade finally moved to assist her.

The top of her head barely reached his armpit. He splayed the fingers of his massive hands across her ribs as he propelled her toward the kitchen. He gave off so much heat she wondered why he bothered with the woodstove in the corner and why his touch sent shivers through her anyway.

"I'm a pro at cooking spaghetti," he muttered as he guided her. "The water is boiling."

"I am a cooking pro," Justine reminded him. She tried not to lean into his body. "Did you salt the water?"

"No." Meade guided her around a chair. "I try not to eat extra sodium."

"Yet you eat sauce from a jar. Have you ever read the label?"

He grunted something unintelligible.

The kitchen was little more than a cupboard sized galley. The stove resembled a two-burner hotplate. An apartment-sized fridge, toaster oven, coffee maker, and half-sized microwave made up the rest of the appliances. Counter space was practically nonexistent.

Naturally the cabin kitchenettes would barely be functional. She was the retreat's chef. She wouldn't be prepping meals in the individual cabins. Darby had emailed photos of the kitchen in the main lodge, a more-than adequate facility. The kitchenettes were a just-in-case plan. This snowy night proved the point.

Meade propped her against the counter. "How much salt?"

Normally, Justine would have measured with her hand, but she hadn't washed them since using the bathroom at a thruway rest area. She eyed the pan rocking on the burner. "Tablespoon. I also need a skillet, extra virgin olive oil, a head of garlic, and a few red pepper flakes. Oh, and my knives to slice the garlic."

Meade snorted as he rummaged through a bottom cupboard. "Head of garlic? You're not at the supermarket. There might be a shaker of garlic salt. If you're lucky."

Not a true kitchen, she reminded herself. *Emergency facilities.*

Meade dropped a battered skillet on the free burner, then opened another cupboard. "No olive oil, only vegetable. You're in luck, though. There's garlic powder and red pepper flakes." He placed the spices and oil on the counter.

Justine washed her hands before making quick work of the sauce. Even questionable vegetable oil and garlic powder were better than jarred red chemicals. She leaned against the counter, keeping her weight off her injured leg. She improvised the lack of a ladle with a heavy mug to scoop pasta water from the boiling pot to stir into the oil and garlic mixture.

"Pasta is done. Can you drain it?" She didn't dare try to lift the heavy pot with her knee hurting the way it did. Besides, if she didn't keep yanking up the sweatpants, they'd puddle at her feet and trip her.

Her hands trembled as she stirred the contents of the skillet with a tablespoon. How would she cook for an entire resort when she couldn't stand? She was going to lose her job. A job she desperately needed—not only due to her debt, but because the location took her way from the city, away from the gossip and innuendo about why she'd lost Just Food. Away from Lenny.

MEADE COULDN'T LATCH ONTO a single thought from the whirlwind in his head. Elaine-the-ex would have asked what else was new. His confusion this time was different. Why was he catering to a snippy woman? If Justine wasn't being snippy, she was hostile. She'd pulled a knife on him, for Christ's sake.

Steam from the boiling spaghetti water blasted his face as he dumped the contents of the pot into the drainer in the sink.

Justine might be surly, but she didn't whine. She hadn't uttered a single complaint.

Her stoicism was refreshing. Elaine grumbled and criticized everything. Justine—improvised. He'd seen her swollen knee and figured she had to be hurting. Yet she'd hauled herself off the couch to the kitchen to cook dinner. Sure, she'd condemned his choice of sauce, but she'd presented an immediate solution. Meade reluctantly respected her determination.

"Shake the colander a few times, then pour the pasta into the skillet," Justine instructed. "I don't suppose you have Parmesan cheese."

"Sure do," he said, as he followed her directions.

He pulled plates from the cupboard while she coated the spaghetti with her fantastic-smelling concoction.

The only thing Elaine ever made for dinner was phone calls for meal delivery or reservations.

He found the familiar Astroturf green shaker of grated cheese in the refrigerator.

"Do you have a serving bowl?" Justine turned off the stove.

"Why dirty another dish?" Meade figured he was on cleanup duty, not one of his favorite places to be. The fewer items they used the better.

Justine made a neutral sound, neither agreeing nor disagreeing with him. Then she spied the tube in his hand. "That's not Parmesan."

"The label says different."

"The label lies. In fact, it's not even one-hundred percent cheese."

"According to the label it is."

"The label says one-hundred-percent grated, not one-hundred percent cheese. What you have is a Parmesan *style* cheese containing additives and preservatives. Cellulose powder, which is refined wood pulp. Genuine Parmesan is like Champagne. Parmesan comes from Parma in Italy. Champagne is an area of France. Only products from those regions can be called genuine."

Meade had been eating this grated cheese his whole life. "It's fine. Trust me."

Justine froze.

Okay. She had trust issues. He should have recognized her paranoia sooner. When she'd pulled the knife on him would have been a good time.

"Let's get you to the table," he said. "I'll handle dinner from here."

She closed her eyes once she was seated. The dark lump on her forehead intensified the paleness of her face.

He plated the spaghetti and brought their meals to the table. "Dinner smells better than it looks."

She opened one eye. "It would be better with fresh garlic, olive oil, and genuine Parmesan."

"I'm not a gourmet." He added plenty of cheese to the anemic-looking strands on his plate. Spaghetti, in his opinion, required tomato sauce.

"I never would have guessed." She opened her other eye and twirled her fork in the pile of pasta on her plate.

Food snob.

He lifted his fork to his mouth. Flavor exploded on his tongue. He swallowed. "This is amazing."

"Thanks." She barely acknowledged him, her focus on eating.

Her silence was strangely comfortable. The woodstove creaked and occasionally popped. Forks scraped against glass plates. Snow tapped at the windows. Coyotes howled in the distance.

Elaine would want high-brow instrumental music playing softly in the background. A fancy wine to accompany the simple meal. Imported-from-Italy Parmesan, once she learned the difference. No pasta on the menu, though. She'd banished gluten and carbs from her diet years ago. Meade didn't care for wine or fancy food. Sauce from a jar suited him because he didn't have to think to cook it. Simply toss a cup in the microwave for a couple minutes while the spaghetti boiled, and voila! Dinner.

Justine's creation was an agreeable change.

A pounding on the door interrupted his musings.

Justine jumped. She must have been in her zone, too.

Meade found Heath Remington, groundskeeper, and all-around maintenance worker at The Write Place on the porch. He uselessly stomped his feet on the snow-covered planks. "Darby said you've got the new cook, and she's injured."

"I'm not a cook. I am a chef," Justine called from the table.

"She's a chef," Meade repeated, as he stepped aside to let Heath enter.

"Right." One corner of Heath's mouth crooked up as he slid a backpack off his shoulder. He sat on the bench to unlace his boots. "Darby wanted me to take a look at her."

Meade didn't know Heath well, but something about the other man irritated Meade, more so tonight than usual.

"What's wrong with her?" Heath pulled off one boot.

Meade listed the possibilities. When he mentioned her knee resembled a honeydew melon, Heath arched one eyebrow.

Did people practice facial calisthenics in a mirror?

God. Now he was channeling one of his book heroes obsessing about the heroine.

Heath's second boot dropped to the doormat. He snagged his backpack and headed toward Justine. Kneeling on the floor next to her, he introduced himself. "Heath Remington, groundskeeper."

"Justine Macko, the new chef." She offered her hand. "You have a name straight out of a romance novel."

Meade made a mental note to never give the name "Heath" to a character. Except for a villain, he amended.

Heath grimaced. "Not a hero. Former Army medic. Let's start with the golf ball on your forehead." He fished a penlight from his backpack and shone the narrow beam in Justine's eyes. He asked her a few questions in a gentle tone.

Justine quietly responded. No sniping. No threats. Why didn't she sharpen her wit on Heath? Even worse, why did Meade even care?

"You might have a mild concussion," Heath diagnosed. "You should ice the lump."

"What about frostbite?" Meade barely contained his testiness.

"No sign on her face." Heath's thumb brushed Justine's forehead. "If you don't have ice, grab a bowl of snow from your porch. Okay, now for your honeydew melon knee. Loop your arms around my neck so I can carry you to the couch."

Annoyance skittered in Meade's gut, as Justine meekly complied. Heath lifted her as if she were an armful of firewood. Meade knew better. He'd carried her over a mile, battling drifts and howling wind, which was a lot harder than walking a few paces in a warm, cozy cabin. Her indifference to his feat irked him.

Why was she so cooperative with Heath? Unless she had a penchant for soldiers—even former soldiers. The romance genre loved men in uniform. He should know. Andromeda had written a lucrative Navy SEAL series.

He needed to busy himself, so he opened the woodstove door and poked at the fire. Sparks snapped. One burning log disintegrated beneath his prodding. He shoved another hunk of wood in the firebox. Smoke counterattacked and polluted the air.

"You need help?" Heath asked.

"No." Meade slammed the door and latched it.

The leftover spaghetti should be refrigerated, and the dishes needed washing, but he didn't want to leave Justine alone with Heath.

"Let's get these sweatpants off you," Heath told Justine.

"Roll up the leg," Meade grumbled.

"Turn your backs," Justine said. "Both of you."

Meade signaled Heath to join him in the kitchen.

Heath smirked. "She should take ibuprofen or acetaminophen for her headache. Ibuprofen would be better, to help with any swelling," he said, as he followed Meade. He checked out the leftovers in the skillet. "Dinner smells good. Testing the new chef's skills?"

Meade didn't want to discuss Justine with Heath. All the talk about lumps and swelling had his inner romance author snickering. His logic had flown up the stove pipe with the sparks and smoke. Instead, he focused on listening to the rustle of clothing. Was that hiss an inhale between clenched teeth or gas escaping a burning log? If he offered to assist her, would she come at him with one of her knives?

He didn't want to consider her reaction if Heath had made the offer.

CHAPTER 5

JUSTINE'S HANDS TREMBLED AS she tucked the rust-colored throw from the back of the sofa across her lap. Her injury terrified her. What if she couldn't work? She needed this job. Darby Winehouse wouldn't pay her to laze around.

She let the men know she was ready.

Meade's scowl could have frightened away the storm. He stood in front of the woodstove, arms crossed over his chest, as Heath knelt next to the sofa.

Heath's fingers prodded the side of her knee. She flinched. Pain wasn't the only reason. She tried to tell herself the injury caused the shivers skating around her body. Not good shivers, either, not like with Meade. The gleam in Heath's green eyes, his icy hand wandering as he carried her, the way his thumb meandered across her bare inner thigh all made her long for her boning knife. His touch wasn't inappropriate, but she still didn't have to like it. *He's my co-worker,* she reminded herself. She was going to have to get along with him.

"Might be a sprain, might be more serious." Heath kept his hand on her leg. "Stay off it. Keep it elevated. Ice for ten minutes every hour. Ibuprofen for swelling. As soon as the roads open, you should go to the medical center for pictures."

As if she could afford a doctor's visit, much less a CAT scan or MRI.

She jerked away from Heath's probing fingers and flipped the blanket across her leg. "What about my car? It's in a ditch. I need my clothes."

Meade interrupted with the details of the specific ditch from which he'd kidnapped her, then added, "One of her bags is in my Hummer, which is stuck at the turnoff to the back entrance."

Heath sat back on his heels. "Can't do anything until the storm ends. I'll take Justine to her quarters. Sal can help keep an eye on her. You can get back to work."

"I'm sitting right here." Justine waved her fingers. She'd endured being the invisible woman with Lenny. No more. "Who is Sal?"

"Justine can't walk," Meade said, finally uncrossing his arms.

Heath responded to Meade first. Naturally. "By snowmobile. Sal—Salome—is the assistant manager and in charge of other services."

"Bouncing around on the back of a snowmobile won't do her concussion any good," Meade pointed out.

A gust of wind rattled the windows as if to emphasize his point.

"Any concussion she has is a mild one," Heath replied. "She'll be better off in staff quarters than here."

"How do you figure?" Meade narrowed his eyes at Heath.

Heath returned the glare. "More people to keep an eye on her. Darby's worried."

Justine struggled to sit up. She wasn't vacationing at The Write Place. She couldn't cook for all the guests tonight, but come morning, she had no choice. "If you'll give me some privacy, I'll get dressed and ready to go."

"Wearing what?"

Meade had a point. The sodden lump of denim previously serving as her jeans still lay on the floor at the foot of the sofa. On the other hand, what was his objection? He ought to be doing a happy dance at no longer having to fake heroism.

Justine swallowed her pride. "May I borrow your sweatpants?"

"You can barely keep them up," Meade pointed out. "You won't be able to hold onto them and the grips on the back of a snowmobile at the same time. I won't elaborate about what bumping along for a mile will do for your headache."

She didn't understand why Meade didn't want her to leave but the thought of facing the cold on the back of an open vehicle sickened her. She was grateful for the excuses he provided. "I do have a headache."

"Any concussion you have is mild," Heath repeated. "Sal can lend you something to wear. It might be a day or two until I can get to every ditch in the county, which is where most of the guests parked this weekend, and guests have priority over staff."

"I'm a guest," Meade reminded Heath. "And one of her suitcases is in my truck."

Heath stared at Meade for a long moment before switching his gaze to Justine, then shrugged. "Hey, I'm only the groundskeeper. What you guys do is your business."

"What's that supposed to mean?" Justine asked. The last thing she needed was for anyone on staff thinking she was involved with one of the guests even before she started working. "If you're going to start rumors about me if I stay here, I'll go to the lodge with you."

She swung her feet to the floor and tried to stand, but the pain from putting her weight on her injured leg nauseated her. She sank back on the sofa and closed her eyes.

Meade wadded his fingers into his palms. He resisted the impulse to rush to her side. The lack of color in her face worried him. Logically, he accepted she was an employee. Heath was obligated to deliver her to the lodge. Justine should report for duty and start cooking.

Part of his reluctance to see Justine go was his distrust of Heath. The man hadn't done anything wrong, but he struck Meade as being unstable. Darby had once mentioned that Heath had served two tours in Afghanistan, returning to the Adirondacks after his discharge from the Army. *His mountains,* he'd allegedly said, *gentler mountains*. Darby hired her shirt-tail relative because he needed a job where he didn't have to interact with people. War had played havoc with his head. Time and space would heal him, or so Darby claimed. The groundskeeper position at The Write Place was a good fit.

Meade was the last person to trash-talk anyone who volunteered to serve their country. He respected the people willing to die to protect freedom. Besides, military heroes sold romance novels. His royalty spreadsheet proved their popularity.

Still, he resented the way Heath touched Justine while he examined her.

Meade wasn't jealous. He was being... gallant. He'd rescued her from the ditch, lugged her over a mile in blizzard conditions, tended to her in her vulnerability while she held him at knifepoint. Okay, that last part was a slight exaggeration, but still.

Meade read Heath's actions as sexual. He could practically smell the pheromones, and he recognized the signs. His livelihood depended on writing—and defeating—lecherous villains. His male protagonists were always revealed as good guys in disguise. Heath embodied the opposite: a pervert camouflaged as a hero.

Calm down. Meade had seen Justine evade Heath's wandering hand, as if she sensed lewd intent in his touch. Justine was well-armed with her knives.

Still, he was glad she'd decided to remain with him rather than risk the trip to the lodge on the back of a snowmobile. After all, he'd been the one to rescue Darby's new chef, not Heath. He wanted to be the one to deliver her.

Until then, Meade had a book to write. Meeting Justine sparked a plot, with her, along with Heath and himself in a love triangle. Fiction, of course.

The only problem was that in romance novels, the wounded soldier always got the girl.

Chapter 6

Justine's eyelids were as heavy and gritty as five-pound bags of salt. She was about to doze off when Meade slapped a garbage bag filled with snow on her knee. She nearly levitated off the sofa.

"Sorry," he mumbled. "Heath said to apply ice for ten minutes every hour."

He was awfully diligent for a man with an unwanted house guest. He'd been sweet to her, though, offering his bed, stating he'd sleep on the futon in the office loft. She opted for the sofa. She'd never crawled into a strange man's bed in her life, and she wasn't about to start. Now neither one of them was getting any sleep.

"Thank you for helping me out," Justine said.

"No worries," Meade replied. "I respect a woman who carries her own knives."

"Smart man." Her smile faded as she fumbled to say the right thing without sounding ungrateful. "Not that I don't appreciate what you're doing, but I don't need babysitting."

Meade picked up the mug of coffee she'd abandoned when she rescued dinner. "No worries. I frequently pull all-nighters when I'm on deadline."

"You're on deadline now? What do you write? I don't recall seeing your name on the list of authors who've worked at The Write Place."

"You checked me out?" he asked over his shoulder as he padded to the kitchen.

"No. I checked out the retreat before I applied for the job." She heard him spill the cold coffee into the sink. "I wanted to make sure I wasn't headed for a tacky repurposed motor court or haunted camping trailer."

As if she'd had a choice. The scandal had ruined her reputation. The job opening at The Write Place presented a path to recovery and included cooking, room and board, and a salary. She couldn't screw up the opportunity. That started with being nice to Meade.

"I use a pen name," Meade admitted, rejoining her. He nudged her chef's knife to the side and perched on the table in front of the sofa.

"What do you write?" she asked again. "I listen to books while I work. Are any of yours on audio?"

"I heard your taste in books when I pulled you from your car."

"How did you know it was a book?"

"It sounded like one." He seemed to dare her to argue.

"*Desire's Revenge* isn't the best example of a romance novel," she admitted. "I borrowed the audio book from the library because the author is one who writes here. Andromeda Zeus books is one of my favorite authors. Lazlo and Araminta's story is one of her earlier efforts. The newer stuff isn't quite as..."

"Trashy?" Meade bared his teeth. "Your word, not mine."

"I was going to say poorly executed. I happen to enjoy romance novels."

Meade made the same face most people donned when sneering at the romance genre.

"I eat greasy spoon food, too," Justine continued. "It's honest about what it is."

"Unlike fake Parmesan cheese."

"Anything genuine is okay by me. I wouldn't find your green tube of cheese as offensive if the label was clear about the ingredients."

"Who gets to define genuine? Or honesty?" he countered.

Those were questions she often asked herself, especially after being burned so badly by Lenny.

But this wasn't about her or Lenny. She was curious about Meade.

"Are you going to make me guess your pen name?"

"You'll never get it." He sounded smug.

"I can name that author in three guesses," she insisted.

Laughter burst from him. His chin lifted, exposing his throat. The corners of his eyes crinkled. Dimples drilled his beard-scruffed cheeks. "You think so? Give it your best shot."

His laugh triggered something she hadn't felt in a long time. She wanted to laugh, too, or so she told herself. The forgotten sensation was the urge to giggle and be silly, not launch herself at an attractive man.

She settled back to study him. Based on his appearance and behavior, she figured he wrote manly books. Moss Crockett, who penned best-selling action-adventure novels, was a frequent Write Place guest. She could easily picture Meade leading a safari, wrestling bears, and climbing mountains. Hadn't he combatted deep snow and howling winds to haul her to safety? The man had muscles. Stamina. Endurance. You'd never guess he sat in front of a computer to earn a living. He even drove a Hummer, a vehicle she considered an emblem of toxic masculinity, right after oversized pickup trucks.

Rescued by Moss Crockett. What a great story she'd have to tell the friends who'd cautioned her against taking a job in such a remote location. She'd cooked for famous people in the city, they'd reminded her. She'd fed plenty of celebrities at Just Food before the scandal. Why did she need to hide in the wilderness?

She remembered the fairy tale she'd begged Gran to read to her over and over. "Rumpelstiltskin."

Meade's blue eyes twinkled. His dimples deepened. "Good one, but nope."

She tried to recall the listing of authors on the retreat's website for a real name to throw him off balance; another ridiculous guess to make him laugh again. "Lacey Dover."

"Who?" His grin didn't fade as he leaned forward and waggled his forefinger close to her face. "One guess left. You should be careful. Otherwise, you lose, and I might claim a penalty."

His action triggered a spasm of wanting.

Their gazes met. Justine's nipples tightened, which could have been embarrassing but Meade's eyes were on her face, not her breasts.

Outside, an animal howled. Meade dropped his hand.

"Is that a wolf?" Justine asked, embarrassed that her voice came out so husky. No one mentioned wolves when she applied for the job.

"Coyotes," Meade replied.

She cleared her throat. "Are they dangerous?"

Meade heaved himself off the couch and went to the window. He tugged aside the pumpkin-colored curtains. Snow still pecked at the glass. If he didn't subdue his attraction to Justine soon, he'd have to pack one of his own body parts in snow. "Heath says they're not dangerous to adult humans."

"What's his story?" Her playful tone was gone. Thank God.

Meade dropped the curtain and turned to face her. "I don't know him well. Darby told me he had a rough time in Afghanistan. She mentioned PTSD."

"Oh." Justine hesitated. "You don't like him."

"I didn't think bouncing around on the back of a snow-mobile would be good for your brain," Meade corrected, surprised that she'd picked up on his irritation with Heath.

"If I have a concussion, it's mild." Justine echoed the diagnosis as she dug a fistful of snow from the trash bag and pressed it against the lump on her forehead.

"Do you need another ibuprofen?"

"No. What I need is sleep." Her snippiness was back. "You're not going to let me, though, are you? Except two hours at a time."

Meade considered claiming most women didn't complain when he kept them up all night, a quip one of the heroes in his books might make. The statement had no bearing on the truth—unless the woman happened to be reading one of his novels and couldn't put it down.

"That's right," he agreed. "Hey Siri, set a timer for two hours."

Justine shook her head as if she couldn't believe he'd set an alarm to wake her.

"I'll see you in a few," Meade said. "Call me if you need anything. I'll be upstairs."

It had been a long time since he'd wakened a woman in the middle of the night, he mused as he climbed to the loft. Years, actually. He and Elaine had stopped making love all night short-ly after their marriage. The desire for constant sex tapered off as he'd poured his passion into his burgeoning career. She'd...

done whatever. Whomever. Meade had lost all interest when he learned about the whomevers.

Even so, he'd remained a faithful husband. The divorce hadn't changed that.

Oh, he still wrote spicy sex scenes. Steamy was one of his strengths. *You write porn, not real books,* Elaine had accused. Yet in the beginning, she'd happily acted out the passages he created. And those 'not real' books continued to keep her in designer clothes and overpriced shoes; they paid for her luxury vehicles and extravagant vacations.

No matter how financially successful Andromeda Zeus was, Elaine longed for more. Glitz. Fame. The lavish book signings and parties they'd sporadically attended for other authors in his publisher's stable—authors like Moss Crockett, the twenty-first century's answer to Ernest Hemingway.

In the end, Elaine had brazenly demanded fifty percent of Andromeda's royalties as part of the divorce settlement. She'd settled for forty, the price he paid to buy her silence. As soon as Andromeda penned her final contracted romance, he was throwing her—Andromeda, not Elaine—a retirement party.

A new pen name to fuck with his ex was only part of his motivation. He no longer believed in love, let alone romance. The world lacked both heroes and the women who deserved one. No, he planned to write about life. Real life. The gritty streets beneath glittery existences. Squalor juxtaposed with splendor. Greedy, grasping women and the men who used them.

He'd already picked out his new pen name: Andre Jove. He would discuss everything when he met with his agent, who was at The Write Place for the week. "Weeding out my slush pile," India Snodgrass had told Meade. "We should meet."

Ha. If she had an inkling of what he planned to hit her with, she wouldn't be so amenable. He—Andromeda Zeus—was responsible for a huge chunk of India's income.

He stared at his laptop. All he had to do was press the power button and open his document. *You've been in plotting mode ever since you rescued Justine,* he chastised himself. Except he didn't want to write the story playing in his head over the past several hours. He was afraid that whatever actually happened would destroy his creative magic.

He'd been imagining Justine, Heath, and himself in terms of a love triangle, a perfectly ridiculous scenario, and one more reason for him to write in another genre. Meade Godwin wasn't any woman's hero.

The very idea of being a sex fantasy made him queasy. Add in the heat from the woodstove and no wonder he was a sopping mess.

He pulled off his sweater, then tossed it to the floor. After using his t-shirt to swipe at the beads of sweat trickling down the side of his face, it joined the sweater. He debated shedding his jeans. He usually wore only his boxers when he worked in the loft, due to the way the heat collected in the rafters, but he wasn't alone tonight.

He did not want to hand Justine any excuse to grab a knife.

CHAPTER 7

JUSTINE JERKED AWAKE. SHE took a moment to orient herself. She tried to sit up. Pain chomped into her leg. Agony filled every cavity in her skull. She was hot, sticky, and damp. Dry heat from the woodstove followed by the cool water from the melted snow packed around her leg equaled being braised like a brisket. *Terrific.*

To top it all off, she needed to pee. Badly.

There was no sign of her host. So much for keeping an eye on her all night.

She slowly eased into a sitting position. The contents of the trash bag sloshed. Her fingers were tacky with perspiration and stuck to the plastic as she clumsily tied off the top of the bag. No point risking spilling the water.

She set the bag on the coffee table before gripping the arm of the sofa and swinging her feet to the floor. Her right knee protested. She clenched her teeth, as she waited for the pain to subside. The bathroom wasn't far. She refused to embarrass herself by asking for help.

The floorboards overhead creaked. "Justine?"

She flinched and knocked against the coffee table, where her chef's knife perforated the plastic bag. Cold water cascaded onto the floor and her sweatpants. Her breath whistled between her teeth before she cursed. "Fuck!" Braised, then blanched. Her lucky night.

"What the hell?" Footsteps thudded on the stairs. "It hasn't been two hours yet."

"I spilled the melted snow." Justine gripped the sofa arm tighter.

Meade came into view, and she swallowed another oath.

He had shed half his clothes. A wedge of brown curls in the middle of his chest tapered to a thin line trailing into the waistband of his jeans. She bit her lower lip to keep from asking if he'd ever modeled for romance novel covers.

Meade focused on her instead of the mess on the floor. "Why didn't you call me?"

Justine ignored his question. "I need the bathroom. Now."

Meade invoked gods of whom she'd never heard as he trod in the icy puddle in his sock feet. He lifted her into his arms and carried her to the bathroom.

Once she was alone, she peeled the wet sweatpants from her legs as carefully as she would peel a tomato. After completing her business, she studied her knee. The skin had gone from pale and gray to the color of overripe watermelon. She decided icing the joint was to blame. It certainly didn't do anything to reduce the swelling. And now, thanks to the melted snow, the sweatpants Meade had loaned her were soaked.

She stood and studied herself in the full-length mirror mounted on the back of the door. The tails of Meade's flannel shirt were long enough to protect her modesty. The woodstove kept the cabin toasty, so she'd be okay bare legged.

After hanging the sweatpants over the shower door to dry, she eyed the open shelving stocked with linens in various shades of orange.

A sharp rap on the door startled her. "Are you okay in there?"

"I'm fine," she replied as she pulled towels from the shelves. "Just getting something to mop the water from the floor."

The door opened. She turned, off balance because of the terrycloth filling her arms, and twisted her knee. Pain vacuumed the air from her lungs. She dropped to the floor.

Meade muttered more curses as he swooped in for the rescue. Again. There was no escaping the hot brush of his bare forearms against her naked thighs as he lifted her. She couldn't even think about relaxing against that chest and letting him coddle her because she wasn't a delicate, fragile egg. She was the one who took care of people by feeding them, which in turn nurtured her.

WHEN MEADE HAD FERRIED Justine from her car to his, then from his vehicle to the cabin, he'd tossed her over his shoulder. Now, transporting her from the bathroom, he cradled her as if she were his bride and they were crossing a threshold. Her naked thighs against his forearms made him glad he'd kept his jeans on instead of exchanging them for sweats or pajama pants. It was bad enough that he'd shed his sweater and undershirt.

He knew part of his reaction was due to working on the opening chapters of Andromeda's final book. Justine had been on his mind with every keystroke. Every pen scratch on an index card. She would be Andromeda's final heroine.

No, he was *basing* his character on Justine. A female chef. He could pick Justine's brain for details to make the book more realistic.

Except spending more time with her might not be advisable. He hadn't lusted after one of his characters in years, but damned if the rightness of his actions, including heading for the bedroom, struck him as an option he should explore. Wasn't insta-lust a popular trope?

But he wasn't one of his heroes, and he wasn't that kind of man.

Justine tensed as he'd skirted the couch.

"Relax," he said through the gravel suddenly filling his throat. "You'll be more comfortable here. I'll sleep on the futon in the loft."

"Right." Her breath warmed his bare skin. "You only rape and pillage when the temperature is higher than sixty-eight degrees and the sun shines."

It took him a beat to recall his sarcastic reaction to her caution at their initial meeting. What had seemed funny at the time now made him uncomfortable. Lust? Sure. He admitted it. Rape? He suppressed a shudder. "About that. Let's reframe my dark side."

"Plunder and loot?" she suggested.

Better than rape and pillage, but not by much.

"Seduce and debauch," he offered as he placed her on the bed. Cold, snowy nights invited seduction.

She looked up at him. "I don't think so."

Right. No seduction. She was a retreat employee. He was a guest. Tossing sex into the mix would make the future extremely awkward.

At least he wasn't thinking with his dick.

His dick begged to differ.

Meade backed away from the queen-sized bed as far as the room's cramped confines allowed. "I think I'm supposed to quiz you about things like who's the president, governor of New York, and monarch of the United Kingdom to make sure you're cognizant."

"A better test might be using the names of famous chefs," she suggested. "Wolfgang Puck, Gordon Ramsey, Julia Child."

"Right." He scrubbed his face with his palms. Justine needed to be elsewhere, out of temptation's reach. "If the snow hasn't stopped by morning, I'll head to the lodge to see if Sal has an outfit you can wear."

"Thanks, Rumpelstiltskin, I appreciate it."

CHAPTER 8

The next morning, Justine rewound her audio book as she stared out the window. Snow continued to sift from the sky like confectioners' sugar in search of a jelly donut. She was alone, her head hurt, and her knee complained about the abuse it had suffered while she cooked breakfast for Meade.

He'd fled to the main lodge immediately after eating, as if escaping a demon. Justine didn't blame him. He was at The Write Place to work, not babysit an injured chef.

She had nothing to do but listen to her book.

Araminta slapped his hands. "Lazlo, please. You mustn't touch me like that."

"I only want a chance with you," Lazlo declared.

Yeah, that was about where Meade had dropped his f-bomb when he realized she was listening to a romance novel. She remembered thinking, *Hello? That's what Lazlo is trying to do.*

Andromeda Zeus proceeded to have Lazlo think of Araminta as a fruit salad: peaches and cream complexion; lips like strawberries; the bumpy pucker of her nipples against her satin gown reminiscent of summer raspberries. Justine choked when Lazlo's inventory included longing for the sweet cherry of Araminta's innocence.

Justine had always believed in food's sensuousness, but really? Then again, who was she to judge? Ingredients excited her more than sex ever had.

Food obsessed her. Even now, she only half listened to her book while she wondered what supplies she would find once she made it to her new kitchen. The weather begged for soup. She could concoct an apology to the guests for missing last night's dinner and this morning's breakfast. A hearty, comforting repayment.

She looked forward to overseeing a kitchen where she didn't own the bottom line and could feed people instead of the egos of influencers and critics; without Lenny undermining everything she did or sabotaging her business plan with his own ambition.

Justine retained her self-respect despite everything that had happened. No one could steal her sense of worth. It was all she had left.

WHY HAVEN'T I EVER written a chef character before? Meade wondered as he climbed the freshly shoveled steps to the lodge.

Darby had hired a genius. Justine had conjured a magical breakfast from leftover pasta, which inspired ideas for the character starring in Andromeda's final book.

Once in the lobby, warmth embraced him from a fireplace large enough for a SEAL chopper to land. He pulled off his hat and gloves. He eyed the picked-over breakfast buffet that had been set up and pitied the guests stuck with such mundane offerings while he hoarded the chef.

He found Salome Stone standing by a card table in the library, while Moss Crockett, an asshole action-adventure author, pontificated in his usual arrogant manner.

Meade and Crockett had crossed paths at literary functions and frequently vied for the orange cabin at The Write Place.

Finn Upshaw, a legendary editor with whom Meade would love to work, hovered nearby. He'd have to mention Upshaw's presence to his agent. Upshaw would be the perfect editor for Meade's new pen name.

A younger man sat in a wingback chair with a book on his lap and an expression of disgust on his vaguely familiar face.

Meade approached Sal. "Can I talk to you for a minute? Privately?"

"Sure." She beamed at him. Her hair resembled a fountain of shiny new pennies sprouting from the top of her head and spilling down her back.

"What's up?" she asked, as she positioned herself behind the registration desk in the lobby.

"Did Darby tell you what happened to the new chef?"

Sal's smile morphed into concern. "Heath told me she might have sprained her right knee. Sprains take a long time to heal. Does she need a reiki session? Herbal teas might—"

"All she needs right now is clothes until Heath can get to her luggage," Meade interrupted in a low voice. Meade knew Sal's compassion was genuine, but she did tend to go on. "She had to cut off her jeans, and Heath suggested you could help."

"Of course I'll lend her an outfit. Let me grab a few things." Sal headed toward the employees-only section of the lodge.

"Excuse me." The man who'd been reading in the library interrupted.

Sal turned, professional face in place. "Yes?"

The man rounded the seating group, holding up a lipstick-sized tube. "This belongs to Vivid. Vivienne Rowan. I don't know what room she's in."

Vivid? Really? And Elaine had accused him of having a weird pen name.

"Vivienne Rowan?" Meade's agent clattered down the stairs.

Shit. India Snodgrass was the next-to-the-last person Meade wanted to talk to this morning.

"She's across the hall from me," India explained. "I can return it to her."

"That would be great," Sal said.

The young man handed the tube to India. "Thank you." He glanced toward the library before dropping onto a couch in front of the fire. He opened his book.

"I'll be right back," Sal said. She scurried away before another interruption waylaid her.

Meade unzipped his jacket, then leaned against the registration desk and brainstormed possible titles. *Josephine's Cuisine* barely masked his model's name. *Carlene's Cuisine.* Or Christine. Kathleen. He wanted the hard "c" or "k" sound.

"Meade." India interrupted. "What time did you want to get together?"

Double shit. He'd forgotten their plans. He straightened. "I've got a conflict today. Tomorrow morning should be good. Where should we meet?"

India sniffed at the enormous berry-studded scone she'd plucked from the breakfast buffet. "You seem more weather-proof than I am, so let's meet in my rooms—Crown Suite, second floor. Ten o'clock." She waved her scone at him and headed toward the stairs.

The front door opened, admitting Heath, a uniformed man, and a gust of frigid air.

Heath stomped the snow from his feet as he spoke. "Meade Godwin is leaning on the desk. His Hummer is stuck at the back driveway and Route 73. The new cook ditched—literally—her car on 73, between here and I-87. Meade has a better idea of the spot. And Paxton Benedict, on the couch, abandoned his Honda Accord in a field on the Keene Valley side of 73. No reported injuries, except for the cook, who sprained her knee and bumped her head. Guys, this is Deputy Dylan King, Essex County Sheriff's Department."

"Does the cook need an ambulance?" King pulled a small notebook from his pocket.

Heath exchanged a look with Meade before replying. "She could use a trip to Urgent Care, but no need for an ambulance."

Paxton Benedict—the name wasn't familiar to Meade—slammed his book shut and shot to his feet. "May I have a moment?"

"Have we met before? You look familiar." King eyed Benedict suspiciously.

"I get that a lot." Benedict's tone rivaled the weather.

Meade tuned them out. He spied India, lurking on the stairs and eating her scone, but forgot her odd behavior when Sal returned with a bulging plastic bag.

"Hi, Dyl," Sal greeted the deputy.

"Sal." King nodded at her. "Hey, did Laurel make it to work today?"

"Darby told her to stay home. I have a favor to ask. Would you be able to give the new chef a ride to the lodge? She's injured and can't walk here from Sacral Cabin and probably shouldn't be on the back of a snowmobile."

"Sure."

Sal turned to Meade and extended the bag. "Here are the clothes for Chef Justine."

"Thanks." Meade took the clothes from Sal before asking King, "Can I hitch a ride with you to my cabin? I'll fill you in on where the cook's mini city car left the highway."

"Didn't Heath say your Hummer is stuck, too? I ought to issue tickets to all of you for driving during a state of emergency. That means no unnecessary travel."

Meade zipped his jacket. "I wasn't aware of the state of emergency until I called to tell Darby I'd found her new cook in a ditch. Once I knew, I tried to take shelter." *I carried the woman a mile during the storm. Are you going to ticket me for helping a stranded motorist?*

He pulled on his hat and gloves, then opened the door and stepped onto the porch. Icy wind slapped a reality check on his face: once Justine returned to the lodge, Meade would lose her. He had no excuse to interact with the retreat chef. But he needed her to flesh out his character. He couldn't give life to Colleen without Justine's help.

CHAPTER 9

Justine plucked at the scratchy metallic gold sweater that Sal, whoever she was, had lent her. The turquoise leggings printed with glittering golden suns, shimmering silver moons, and sparkly lavender stars irritated her sensibilities in addition to her skin.

Her socks and leather boots were dry but the swelling in her right knee extended up her thigh and down her calf and ankle. Attempting to force her boot onto her foot launched daggers of agony.

The cute Deputy King who'd accompanied Meade back to the cabin offered to carry her to his cruiser, but Meade seemed to think he had a claim on her. "Let me find an extra pair of socks for you to wear to protect your feet."

Heat rose in Justine's face.

"Are you sure you don't want medical attention?" King asked once Meade departed. "Sprains can be worse than breaks."

"I'm fine." People with decent health insurance never stopped to consider those who weren't as lucky. Her lack was another detail she blamed on Lenny. If he ever showed his face again, she would gut him with her chef's knife.

Meade reappeared. He knelt in front of her to dress her unshod foot, mimicking Prince Charming claiming Cinderella, except he wasn't charming, and no fairy godmother hovered on the horizon to rescue Justine. Then, much to her exasperation, he scooped her into his arms. She wasn't a custard in need of a *bain-marie* to keep from cracking. Even worse, she hated how quickly being comfortable in his arms had become.

King opened the rear passenger door of his official SUV. "She can keep her leg elevated back here," he said as Meade gently transferred her to the seat.

Then Meade climbed in next to the deputy.

"I've got her, Meade," King said. "Don't you have a book to write?"

"I need to talk to Darby."

Meade's alleged mission did not reassure Justine. What if he planned to tell her new boss false tales about their evening together? Justine didn't know what kinds of books he wrote, but the odds were good that he was skilled at embellishing the truth.

Lenny had destroyed her trust in men.

Besides, Meade was a guest at the retreat. Justine knew not to get involved with customers. The authors would come and go.

Her job was to feed them. No matter how attractive she found Meade, he remained off limits.

A minute later, King pulled up in front of the porch of the main building. Meade carried her inside, past a lobby fireplace large enough to house the Vulcan 10-burner restaurant range of her dreams, around the registration desk, and into the employees-only portion of the lodge.

"Darby, I have your cook!" he called out.

"Chef," Justine muttered.

"Uh-huh." Meade's eyes were the same shade of blue as the forget-me-nots that had grown in Gran's garden.

Two women emerged from one of the doorways opening at irregular intervals from the hall. "Can't she walk?" the plumper woman asked.

"I can manage," Justine replied.

"She couldn't get her boot on because of the swelling," Meade said at the same time.

"Thanks for the lift, Meade." Justine hoped he'd take the hint and put her down.

"Justine, this is Darby Winehouse, your employer, and Salome Stone, the assistant manager and head of other services. Sal provided the clothes you're wearing."

"Nice to finally meet you in person," Justine greeted her new boss and coworker before addressing Meade. "I'm good from here."

"Where do you want her?" Meade asked.

"The kitchen." Darby and Justine spoke simultaneously.

"I'm sorry I'm late for work." Justine peered over Meade's shoulder at her new boss.

"The storm isn't your fault," Darby said.

Her words were kind enough, and her cocoa-colored eyes gave away nothing.

"Darby, as soon as I get Justine settled can I have a word with you?" Meade asked.

The rusticity of the lobby gave way to a twenty-first century kitchen.

Justine didn't hear Darby's reply. Her first sight of her new domain demanded her attention. The photos Darby had e-mailed didn't do the room justice.

Darby had explained the retreat didn't require a restaurant-sized kitchen. There were never more than fourteen guests at one time, although seven tended to be the average. Each cabin and suite included stocked kitchenettes should the resident opt to fix their own meals. The small live-in staff fended for themselves.

Stainless steel appliances gleamed in the unfiltered daylight streaming through a bank of windows, whose generous sills could easily accommodate pots of herbs. The walls sported white ceramic tiles. A mix of gray granite and white marble topped the counters. Gray restaurant-grade vinyl covered the floor. A cordless phone sat in a charger on the counter.

Justine fell in love.

MEADE FOLLOWED DARBY INTO her cluttered office. He closed the door.

Darby's gaze flicked from the door to Meade. "What's up?" She took her time settling behind her desk.

He sank onto the guest chair. "I want to buy the orange cabin. Sacral. Whatever you want to call the place."

Darby's full lips thinned. "As I've told you every time you've asked, Sacral is not for sale. None of the cabins are. If you seriously want to buy in the Adirondacks, one of my cousins is a realtor."

"How about a lifetime rental if I can't buy the cabin? Actually, leasing would work better for me." He preferred the convenience of having his meals prepared and delivered, of scheduling housekeeping and laundry around his needs.

Darby opened an old-fashioned ledger. "You have Sacral until the end of March. April is unavailable. I have other bookings for the rest of the year. I can work you in around those if you'd like."

He didn't see what the problem was. "Move everyone else to different cabins."

"No can do. The April guest specifically requested the most isolation we offer. That would be Sacral. Besides, the other cabins are reserved, too."

"Doesn't my loyalty count for anything?"

"I appreciate all my guests' loyalty." Darby steepled her fingers and rested her chin on them. "But I am running a retreat, not a residential hotel."

"Oh, all right." Meade made a show of being disgruntled. He and Darby had this conversation a couple times a year, usually when he and Moss Crockett wrangled over the orange cabin. Today, however, the discussion was a prelude to another matter, one he doubted Darby would agree to without some fast talking on his part.

"I want to job-shadow your cook." He stated his request in as impersonal language as he could manage.

Darby blinked and straightened in her chair. "I'm sorry. I don't think I heard you right."

"For my work-in-progress. I'm writing a female chef, but I don't have a sense of how one operates. If I job-shadow yours, my story would be more realistic."

Darby looked skeptical. "What happened at your cabin last night?"

Meade didn't hesitate. "She cooked me an amazing meal from the stuff in the cupboards."

"That's not what I meant." Darby's dry tone cued him.

"She slept downstairs while I worked in the loft. Heath suggested I wake her a couple times and pack her knee in snow to help with the swelling. I behaved myself."

"Heath told me she'd sprained her knee." Darby's tone remained cautious. "I'm not questioning your behavior. Otherwise, I wouldn't have assured her you're safe. The motivation behind your request is... out of the ordinary. For you. If I didn't know you better, I might worry about an ulterior motive."

Explaining his motivation was going to be tricky. "I watched her do stuff in the cabin kitchen that never would have occurred to me. I always research my characters' careers. Observing your cook is the most expedient way for me to do that while I'm here."

Darby studied him, her mud-colored eyes giving away nothing.

Meade's chair creaked as he leaned back. He summoned his laziest smile.

"Don't try to charm me." She sounded irritated, but her tone softened as she continued. "You're not responsible for Chef's injury, and I'm not going to fire the girl because she hurt herself trying to report for work during a storm. I'm not heartless."

Meade managed to keep his smile in place. "You have me confused with someone else. I'm not charming, and I'm useless in the kitchen, which is why I need to observe a cook at work. She's here, I'm here—no brainer."

Darby's expression revealed nothing. "Only if Chef Justine agrees. I won't have her being upset."

CHAPTER 10

No!

Instead of shrieking her refusal to have Meade shadow her, Justine swallowed the protest and smiled at Darby.

"I told him you had to agree," Darby explained. "I don't want you uncomfortable, and his request is unusual. My chef normally doesn't interact with the guests."

That isolation played a major role in why Justine wanted this job. She was hiding from her past, for Puck's sake. She did not belong in anybody's book unless she wrote her own cookbook. And publishing a collection of her recipes had been a Lenny dream, not hers.

Meade jumped into the fray. "The protagonist in my current work in progress is a celebrity chef—"

"I am *not* a celebrity chef," Justine interrupted. She didn't bother to hide her gritted teeth. Of all the mushrooms in the field, Meade had chosen the poisonous one.

"You should be. Last night's dinner—"

"Cooking 101."

"In your world. Basic cooking for me is opening a jar of pre-made spaghetti sauce—"

"All right." She practically shouted her agreement. She'd agree to anything to get the awkward moment past her. Meade Godwin hadn't known her twenty-four hours, yet he knew exactly how to scramble her composure.

Why couldn't he leave her alone? She wanted to acquaint herself with her new domain: familiarize herself with the pantry; study the binder Salome had handed her; embrace her new life, not dodge yet another person trying to mold her into something she wasn't.

"Great." Meade zipped his jacket "Let me run back to my cabin to get my laptop."

His smile was evil. One might call it devilish. Justine knew better. Too late she recalled the real Rumpelstiltskin demanded a heavy price for his assistance.

"You didn't have to say yes," Salome said once Darby and Meade departed.

"He helped me last night. I owe him." Justine eased herself onto a stool at the center island and perused the binder's plastic-enclosed pages.

"You don't owe anyone anything." Salome crossed her arms under her breasts. "Besides, getting involved with the guests is not a good idea. I'm sure Meade's sexual prowess is reflected in his writing, but—"

"If you're asking me if Meade and I were intimate last night, the answer is no. Not on my agenda. I'm here to feed the guests amazing meals. Nothing else." Justine did not want to gossip about Meade's reputation, especially if his reputation focused on sex. She tapped a binder page. "What's this?"

Salome dropped her arms. "Your new bible."

The binder impressed Justine. Each guest filled out a questionnaire itemizing their dietary requirements—allergies, restrictions, and special considerations. Another section listed foods the guests wanted stocked in their kitchenettes.

"Are these internet forms?" Darby had told her there was no internet at the retreat, yet she'd hired Justine using the web and had emailed photos of the kitchen.

"They are," Salome confirmed. "The only web access on the property is at Darby and Cam's house, further along the lakeshore. Cam requires cloud access for his job, their sons need it for schoolwork, and Darby uses a website to advertise, book rooms, and have guests fill out various forms. The lodge has a landline with several cordless handsets, including one in the kitchen and the one I have on me at all times."

Salome further explained that Justine's job included grocery shopping and delivering the meals, in addition to restocking food supplies for long-term guests and before new guests arrived. Meals were served in color coded bento box-like containers. Hot soups couldn't spill into cold salads. The system impressed Justine.

"Given your injury and your car's location, I'll drive you to the supermarket at the end of the week. Heath or I will deliver the meals for now. You'll have to be patient with us. Laurel, the housekeeper, couldn't make it in today, and I'm picking up the slack."

The aches in Justine's knee and head were grateful. "I wish my accident hadn't added more to your plate. I really appreciate your help."

"No worries. We offer breakfast, light lunches, and hearty, but not heavy suppers," Salome continued. "Every writer has a unique circadian rhythm, and we try to respect their body clocks. Many rise with the sun to work. Others emerge with the moon. We accommodate their schedules. Heavy meals make people sleepy. We want to avoid causing any excuses not to write."

"Absolutely." Justine flipped through the binder. Yes, Meade had filled out the questionnaire: jarred pasta sauce, spaghetti, fake cheese, etc. No food allergies or constraints.

She turned the page. Moss Crockett, Solar Plexus Cabin.

"Hmm. Meade's pen name isn't Moss Crockett. Glad I didn't guess that."

Justine didn't realize she'd spoken aloud until Salome responded.

"In case you've forgotten, you signed a non-disclosure agreement as part of your contract. We protect our guests' privacy. Pen names are confidential."

"Oh. I didn't mean anything," Justine hastened to assure Salome. "Meade and I were…"

Were what? Teasing each other? Their banter had been a way to pass the time.

"Any other kitchen questions before we finish your tour?" Salome asked.

"I'm good."

Justine accepted Salome's assistance dismounting the stool. She limped, but she managed, despite the slick soles of her socks on the tile floor.

Salome opened one of the doors leading off the kitchen. "You might find this handy."

Justine's jaw dropped. She could mark potting herbs to set on the kitchen windowsills off her mental list; the plants were already in place. Here. In a warm, humid, and fragrant space. The compact greenhouse contained thyme, sage, several types of basil, two kinds of parsley, and cilantro. A variety of leafy salad greens and a rainbow of cherry and grape tomatoes occupied one short aisle.

"I use herbs for cleansing, teas, healing, and such." Salome brushed her fingers against a rosemary plant, releasing a burst of aroma. "I smudge each suite and cabin with sage to clear out residual energy before each guest checks in. You have a salad garden."

"I never expected such bounty." Oh, what Justine couldn't do with fresh produce at her fingertips.

"Heath built it a couple years ago. He can be handy to have around."

Salome's tone hinted she had more than a working relationship with the retreat groundskeeper.

"You and I share quarters," she continued. "I'd take you to our cabin now, but you don't have boots. We're about a quarter mile from here. The lane is well-marked year-round, but don't wander off the trail. People have vanished in the Adirondacks. Six million acres, mostly wilderness, means getting lost could be deadly.

"Our place is bigger than the ones used by retreat guests—two ground floor bedrooms instead of one. I use the loft to dry the herbs. We can access the laundry facilities in the lodge after hours. We share the kitchen in our cabin, where I blend teas, tinctures, tisanes, and tonics, in addition to cooking for myself. I hope you're neat. Housekeeping doesn't come to our quarters, and I dislike messes."

"Not a problem," Justine lied. Restaurants hired underlings to handle non-cooking chores, so she'd gotten out of the habit of cleaning up after herself in the kitchen. She could adjust. "As long as you do the same and don't poison me, we should be good."

Salome beamed. "You're right, I think we will be. Let's check the cards to make sure."

Snowflakes frolicked in the air instead of slashing at Meade's exposed skin as he trudged back to the lodge. The wind off the lake had taken a timeout. Heath had plowed the lane. The Write Place had returned to February normal.

He nodded an acknowledgment to Paxton Benedict, who hiked in the opposite direction.

Meade kicked the snow from his boots before he traipsed across the lobby and into the bowels of the lodge. He found Justine and Sal in the kitchen. Justine wore a black bib apron and had pulled her hair back into a low ponytail. Sal's tarot cards covered the island counter.

Meade muttered an oath. Write Place regulars often joked that Sal was the assistant manager and head of woo-woo. Her metaphysical offerings made Meade uncomfortable. He'd once considered booking a massage with her but worried she would tinker with his chakras or whatever. He definitely didn't approve of Sal reading Justine's fortune.

"That's... interesting," Justine murmured.

Her tone gave away nothing, yet he wondered if pain, Sal, or a combination of both was behind the pallor emphasizing the vibrant color of the bruise on Justine's forehead.

"You're meant to be a part of The Write Place," Sal intoned.

Time to interrupt. "Hi. I'm here to shadow you."

He interpreted Justine's reaction as relieved he'd arrived—a seismic shift in attitude from half an hour ago. She must not buy into Sal's psychic utterings any more than he did.

Sal touched random cards as she continued her hocus pocus. "The Three of Cups represents what surrounds you. Friendship. Community. The World card in this position contains your hopes and fears—wholeness, abundance, success."

Justine grimaced as she squatted to rummage through a lower cupboard. "Is there a Dutch oven or other *abundantly* large, heavy pot?"

Meade grinned.

Sal ignored Justine's sarcasm. "The Ten of Cups is all about happy endings coming to you. Wholeness again. Divine connections."

Justine clanged through another cupboard. "Yeah, ten cups would be a good size. Bigger would be better, though."

"After the betrayal revealed by the Three of Swords, you've earned your happiness." Sal acted as if she expected Justine to take her mumbo-jumbo ramblings seriously.

"I'm trying to earn a paycheck." The heavy black pot that Justine set on the stove resembled a cauldron Salome might use to brew potions. "Found one. Light lunch. Soup."

As if cued by Sal's mention of swords, Justine pulled a gigantic knife—the one with which she'd initially threatened him—from her tote.

His stomach muscles clenched. *Someone is in trouble.*

Nope. She went after the onions sitting on the counter.

Thwack. "Meade, make yourself useful and check the refrigerator for butter," Justine instructed. "Not margarine, not spread, but real butter."

Justine's unwillingness to go into woe-is-me mode piqued Meade's curiosity.

"How much butter?" he asked.

"Two sticks, unsalted." She punctuated her response with several quick *thwacks.* The pungent aroma of freshly cut onion filled the kitchen.

Sal droned on. "The Ten of Swords indicates you've hit rock bottom. Your future can only get better."

Meade rifled through the refrigerator. "I only see salted butter."

"My future lunch would be better with unsalted butter." Another *thwack.* "How much do I have?"

"Four sticks."

"I'll need all of them if I make grilled cheese sandwiches," Justine muttered. "Bring me two, then add unsalted butter to the shopping list."

What list? The whiteboard near the refrigerator?

He suppressed his irritation. He'd volunteered to help her because her sprained knee hobbled her. Book research simply provided a convenient excuse. He wasn't accustomed to being ordered around.

But story creation, when it clicked, overshadowed everything. *Colleen's Cuisine* was now as real to him as The Write Place kitchen. He wanted to immerse himself in the sounds, scents, and sights of a chef's world. He longed to type his initial reactions.

Sal stopped trying to impress Justine with her psychic ability and gathered her cards.

"Where should I set up my laptop and not be in your way?" Meade asked as he used a faded black marker to scrawl "butter" on the whiteboard.

Justine clamped a can of tomatoes onto the electric opener. "Your cabin would be best." The blade slowly ground through the metal.

Her sweet smile might fool others, but he knew better. Antifreeze was allegedly sweet, too. Sipping it, though, could kill you.

"Meade, when are you going to let me do a reading for you?" Sal shuffled her cards.

"Not in this lifetime." He searched for an available outlet as far from the sink and Sal as he could get. "Woo-woo isn't my thing."

Justine opened a second can of tomatoes.

Sal laid down a card, frowned, then picked it up again. "Yet you always insist on booking Sacral Cabin, which represents the chakra of creativity and sexuality. Must be a reason you're determined to write there."

"I like orange," Meade replied through clenched teeth.

An empty can clattered to the floor. Tomato juice spattered like blood on the gray tile, as if Sal had opened his veins and revealed his secret.

"Let me clean that up," Meade offered, thinking there was no way would Justine be able to. Justine proved him wrong by tossing a paper towel on the mess, then using her good leg to blot the spill.

"I've got it." Sal swooped down and retrieved the paper towel. "You know, Justine, as you get familiar with the cabins and suites, you'll appreciate how they assign themselves to the appropriate guest. Take Meade for example."

Meade had enough of Sal's mystical musings. "Are you trying to scare off the new cook before tasting her food?"

"Not at all. I'm alerting her to the possibilities the Universe has for her." Sal switched to an unbelievable innocence. "She may believe she left her personal woes behind, that she traded anxious Brooklyn for the blissful Adirondacks, but life has more in store for her than work. She's in the right place at the right time."

CHAPTER 11

JUSTINE HANDLED SALOME'S NONSENSE by ignoring her. The strategy might not work in the future, but for the time being, Justine embraced the tasks before her. Learning her way around a new kitchen, prepping lunch, and creating workarounds for her knee were great distractions from both the things she had come here to be distracted from and her new anxieties about getting along with Salome. If they were going to be roommates, Justine was going to have to tolerate the other woman's quirks. She just had to figure out how. Tomorrow.

One thing was certain, though: she would not tolerate the prying into her past or her reasons for being at The Write Place. Salome hadn't fooled Justine with her alleged "tarot reading."

Justine had shared the truth with Darby during her phone interview. After all, an internet search for Justine's name or the name of her defunct restaurant were out there. The facts—sensationalized by many sources—were available for anyone to read. But Justine's heartache remained private. She wasn't about to open up to a nosy roommate she'd just met.

Fortunately, a call on her cordless phone lured Salome away.

Justine peeked at Meade, whose thick fingers poked at his laptop keyboard. What if this alleged celebrity chef book research was just a ruse? Could he be writing about her, Lenny, and the demise of Just Food?

No. The scandal didn't contain enough drama to sustain a short story, much less a full-length book. Maybe an article for an internet gossip sheet, if there were any left who'd missed the first go-round. Meade probably didn't realize her notoriety.

She twitched her shoulders, trying to shrug off the thoughts. The past had no standing in her new life. The Write Place provided the perfect job for her. Isolated. No internet. Surrounded by people whose sole purpose was to pursue their own agendas. As long as they were comfortable and fed, nothing outside their muses mattered.

Or so Darby had claimed during their phone interview.

Until Meade thickened the plot with this thing about writing a female chef. When had that particular character wandered onto his screen? Funny how he'd never mentioned her until he'd arranged with Darby to job-shadow Justine. He could have kept her awake last night by asking questions about her work instead of heads of state.

She rubbed at the knot still marring her forehead.

She'd already learned Meade preferred secrecy. Otherwise, he'd admit to what category of books he wrote. Rumpelstiltskin indeed. An evil little fairy-tale man. Except Meade was real. And not little. At least not visibly. She refused to ponder body parts not on public view. Not her business, the same as her past was her business and no one else's.

She was finished with men. The only worthy ones were confined between the covers of romance novels. She'd joked with Meade about trashy books, but love stories offered a promise of hope. Justine existed for hope, especially after the fiasco with Lenny.

Right now, all she wanted to do was lick her wounds and reclaim her roots. That was her first goal. Her first love: feeding people. Nurturing others nurtured her.

She needed to reclaim her identity. Her love of cooking. If Meade insisted on being underfoot, he had to work. For all his bluster claiming to job-shadow her, he'd balked at loading the dishwasher and washing the utensils she'd used to prepare lunch. She'd explained how, in a professional kitchen, the various chefs prepared the meals and the underlings handled everything else as assigned—such as cleaning up. Since she prepped the food, all the other chores belonged to him. His job-shadowing was going to be hands on. If working bothered him, he could return to his cabin.

While Meade cleaned, Justine inventoried her supplies. Until she could get to the supermarket, she had to work with the ingredients on hand. The well-stocked freezer made planning the next few meals easy, and Justine's mind began to wander.

Salome had explained the retreat had gotten by with help from the culinary management department at Paul Smiths, a nearby college, after the last chef fled in the middle of the night. "Cabin fever, I guess," she'd replied when Justine asked why her predecessor resigned.

Justine pulled her thoughts back to her work as she took chicken from the freezer to thaw. Chicken cobbler would be the perfect dish for a frigid winter night. The ingredients were on hand, and nothing in her recipe violated anyone's food issues. Her lighter version of a pot pie would fit in with the circadian rhythm standards, whatever the Puck those were.

Heath stomped into the kitchen via a back door. "Here's your suitcase." He dropped the bag to the floor.

"Does this mean my Hummer is unstuck?" Meade asked before Justine could speak.

"Nope. It means I grabbed the cook's suitcase, along with your Knob Creek." Heath pulled a bottle from inside his jacket.

"I'm a chef," Justine corrected. "Classically trained."

Meade grasped the bottle. "I owe you a drink."

"I don't drink," Heath said. "Not whiskey, anyway."

"Thank you for my suitcase." She wanted to crouch next to her bag and rifle through its contents, but if she did, she wouldn't be able to stand again. Besides, Heath had tracked in snow. Only socks protected her feet from the floor.

She hated being indebted to Heath. He'd given off creepy vibes while he'd examined her. When he'd touched her bare knee, her flesh cringed. But since they'd be working together, she needed to reset her impression of him. She could have misread him last night due to bumping her head and the other stresses. Heath's day probably hadn't been much better, given his job and the weather.

Everyone deserved a second chance. He'd earned his by retrieving her bag while the weather tried to overwhelm him.

She focused on her suitcase. She hoped her clogs were in this bag. If not, well, Heath wasn't at fault. Or Meade. He'd been kind enough to go back for a bag when he'd rescued her. She never specified which one.

"Need help?" Meade asked. "Your underling is finished washing the dishes you wouldn't let him put in the dishwasher."

She didn't want Meade—or Heath—leering at her belongings.

"Where do you want your bag?" Heath lifted the suitcase. "Your cabin? The counter?"

"You're getting snow all over the floor, creating a hazard for everyone, not only the cook," Meade pointed out. "And she can't very well get to her cabin without boots."

The two men glared at each other.

Oh, Puck. An *oeuf*ing antler war. In her kitchen. Her domain.

She squared her shoulders. "Heath, I appreciate everything you've done for me. I owe you. What's your favorite meal?"

Heath smirked and returned the suitcase to the floor. "I'll get back to you on that." He dipped his head in Meade's direction before departing.

Meade retrieved the suitcase and swung it onto the counter. "He gets his favorite meal?" he growled.

Someone was in a snit again.

"You get to job-shadow me." She unzipped her suitcase. Yes! Her chef's clothes and clogs. She'd feel much better in uniform instead of Salome's weird castoffs. Yeah. She was gonna get her mojo back. The where didn't matter. She'd never been in the business for name fame. Celebrity status had been Lenny's doing. She merely wanted to feed people. Here, at The Write Place, her "customers" weren't A-listers trying to be seen at the newest dining hot spot. They simply wanted to eat. The Write Place and Justine Macko—the real Justine Macko—were a perfect match.

"I carried you to safety in a blizzard," Meade reminded her. He rolled his shoulders as if they ached. "I let you sleep in my bed. You're wearing my damn socks."

He made good points, but her point consisted of not allowing him to weaken her resolve. He was too attractive for her peace of mind.

"And I cooked dinner for you last night, and breakfast this morning, Rumpelstiltskin. What more could you want besides my firstborn?"

MEADE REFUSED TO TOUCH Justine's question. Okay, the phrase was a joke, but coming from Justine, the words sent chills prancing along his spine. Sure, she'd roused his libido, which had lain dormant since before his divorce. Being horny after so many years didn't mean he planned to act on his lust. Especially not with her. Her firstborn had nothing to do with him.

He could not believe how pissed he was at Justine for being nice to Heath. But Meade deserved accolades, too. If not for him, she'd be a frozen stiff in a ditch out on Route 73.

"Let's not forget your negative review of my choice in grated cheese," he reminded her, making sure he used his most sarcastic tone. "I think I deserve a banquet."

"I'm letting you job-shadow me," she repeated. She pulled a pair of ugly shoes from the suitcase and dropped them to the floor. "You saved me. I'm saving your book in return."

What happened to the distrust of Heath that Meade could swear he'd seen the previous evening?

"My book doesn't need saving," he grumbled. A man couldn't save what hadn't existed before meeting Justine.

Nor would he divulge the truth to India during their meeting tomorrow. His agent should trust Andromeda's work by now. The future—Andre Jove, gritty fiction, and possibly Finn Upshaw's editorial magic—headlined Meade's agenda.

Justine draped several articles of clothing over her arm. "Is there a place where I can change?"

"How would I know?"

"Don't pout," Justine advised. She hobbled to her stool, wincing the entire way.

She had to be in pain.

Meade cursed himself. He was in the kitchen to help her. Yeah, he'd given her grief about cleaning, but only to see how she handled being a boss. She'd spent hours on the leg she was supposed to keep elevated. He was the one falling down on the job.

"Why don't I take you to your cabin?" he offered. "You can change, unpack, rest a bit before cooking dinner."

"I don't need to rest."

"You're supposed to keep your leg elevated," he reminded her. "Do you want me to get Heath back here to reexamine you?"

Her face lost all color and animation. The livid bruise on her forehead blemished her pale skin.

Yeah. He'd thought so. "Why are you being nice to him if he makes you uneasy?"

"He's my co-worker. Darby said the staff is like family because it's small and we're isolated." Justine wouldn't look at Meade.

"That's why you haven't pulled a knife on him like you did on me?" Her action still rankled. "If he's being inappropriate, tell Darby. She won't put up with any shit from him, ninth cousin, twelve times removed or not."

"He hasn't done anything. He touched me to check my leg."

Meade crossed his arms and glared at her. "I was keeping an eye on him."

"I noticed. Did I say thank you?"

Her apology blindsided him, and he wasn't sure how to respond. He dropped his arms.

"And yes, you're right," she continued, her voice cracking. "I would like to get off my leg for a while, except I don't know where my cabin is. Are you sure you don't mind helping me?"

She tossed her clothes and shoes into her suitcase and zipped it shut as she spoke.

"Let me find Darby or Sal," Meade offered. He headed toward Darby's office.

"I hate being so *oeuf*ing needy," Justine muttered.

Meade paused in the doorway. "Did you just say hoofing?"

Justine's cheeks turned pink. "*Oeuf*," she corrected. "It's French for egg."

"Instead of saying effing like anyone else, you oof? You verbally egg people?"

She nodded, her face the color of the tomato soup she'd served at lunch.

He snickered. "I may have to borrow your favorite curses for my book."

Borrow? He was definitely stealing the phrase for his work-in-progress.

Her revelation so delighted him, he wanted to pick her up, swing her around, and plant a nice big kiss on her. But touching her without a valid reason would put him on the same level as Heath, a subbasement he did not want to visit.

Justine rubbed her forehead, as if trying to erase a headache.

"I'll be right back," Meade said.

He found Darby in her office. "Justine needs a break, but she doesn't know where her quarters are."

"Didn't Sal show her their cabin?" Darby sounded surprised.

"Justine doesn't have boots. Or shoes. Her foot is too swollen from her knee injury for her fancy leather boot to go on. I'll carry her."

Darby tapped a pen against the surface of her desk. "You're a paying guest. Job-shadowing doesn't mean you're responsible for the running of the retreat. I appreciate your offer, but you've lost enough writing time helping Chef Justine. I'm not going to ask you to do anything more."

Meade had his reasoning ready. Besides, carrying Justine worked as a substitute for cuddling her. He would take what he could get. "I'm not proposing to elope with her. Heath is the only other person around who's capable of carrying Justine, and the weather is keeping him busy. I'm available and willing right now."

Darby studied him for a moment. "My staff is not your problem. Chef Justine might fit into an old pair of Ozzie's boots. I swear that child grows so fast, he wears a different size every month. Better yet, I can unearth one of the boys' sleds, and Sal or I can drag her to her cabin. Chef Justine wouldn't risk twisting her knee again if she rode a sled."

Darby's forthright manner explained why she ran a successful business. She cut past the bullshit with barely a twitch. Meade hated the way she found not only one work-around, but two. He much preferred his solution, because carrying Justine meant touching her, cradling her against his body the way a man cradled his woman after making love.

"Ever suspect the universe is conspiring against you?" Darby asked, as if she'd forgotten to whom she spoke.

What would she do if he replied, "yes, like right now"?

"I found a chef I'm comfortable with, and everything about getting her here and cooking is a challenge. The way things are going, I half-expect her to run off in the middle of the night like her predecessor. I should order Heath to leave her car in the ditch."

Sal stuck her head into Darby's office. Used bento boxes filled her arms. "I've collected the lunch dishes from the suites. Heath said he'd deal with the cabins. Do you need anything else right now?"

"Yes. Meade offered to help Chef Justine to your cabin, and neither of them know the way." Darby kept her tone cool.

"Yeah. About that." Sal's expression struck Meade as sly. "While studying my tea leaves after lunch, I realized Justine should use the housekeeper's rooms since Laurel didn't come in today. Laurel stashes Nilla there when she can't find childcare. I've already changed the sheets on the bed."

"That," Darby slowly said, "is a good idea. Then boots won't matter."

"I try to earn the big bucks you pay me," Sal replied. "Also, I didn't mean to eavesdrop, but I overheard you wondering if Chef Justine is going to stay. She is."

Sal's bright turquoise gaze shifted to Meade. "She's going to marry another transplant, and they'll make their home conveniently close by. She'll keep working here because The Write Place is her destiny."

When Meade tried to exchange a what-the-fuck look with Darby, he found her staring at him with wide eyes and mouth hanging open.

"See you in a few!" Sal saluted them with the bento boxes and left.

"What's she talking about?" he asked.

Darby blinked. "Sal has a knack for... knowing things. Her..." Darby waved her fingers in the air. "... is random."

"Don't tell me you believe her hocus-pocus crap." Meade had always considered Darby a sensible woman.

"Within ten minutes of seeing us together, Sal told Cam and me we would get married and have two sons. That was the morning after our first date."

"Really?" Meade suppressed a shudder. "Predicting your marriage was specific, as opposed to the vague statement she made about your chef."

"She told me everything I need to know." Darby's firm tone warned him not to argue.

He couldn't fathom Sal's suggestion that Justine would marry and remain at The Write Place. He hadn't experienced anything other than rage toward a female in so long, he didn't know what to do with the overwhelming sense of loss Sal's words unleashed in him.

Well, yes, he did. Put his distress on the pages of Andromeda's final romance novel.

Chapter 12

JUSTINE LEANED AGAINST THE closed door of the housekeeper's suite and squeezed her eyes shut, listening for anything the Winehouses might say about her as they walked away. . Darby had brought her forest ranger husband, trained in first-aid, to check Justine's knee. While Justine was grateful her boss cared, she felt like everything that had happened kept testing the limits of how much humiliation one woman could bear.

She'd already borne so much, and she'd been on the verge of seizing control of her life and reclaiming her dignity until the Adirondack weather said, "Hold my beer."

Before the Winehouses left, they'd tried to extract her promise to visit Urgent Care in Lake Placid.

She hated lying to them, even by omission. She could not afford professional medical care. Lawsuits, fines, and bankruptcy had claimed Just Food, forcing Justine to sell the restaurant equipment and furnishings at a loss. All she retained were her knives, her professional wardrobe, and her tarnished reputation.

She'd slashed personal expenses by not replacing the tires on her car when her mechanic warned her the treads weren't legal and not finding new health and car insurance after Lenny let her coverage lapse. Room, board, and getting paid for feeding people at The Write Place resolved a lot of issues, if the Universe would just stop throwing curveballs.

Tonight, she desperately wanted time to reset in solitude. Search for balance.

Justine opened her eyes and resumed settling in. She dragged her solitary bag to the bedroom. The sparsely furnished room contained no closet, only a few hooks on the wall, currently occupied by doll-sized clothing. A package of disposable diapers, wipes, and a changing pad covered the bureau top. More clothing packed the drawers.

She tried to settle her mind. A faint scent of urine tainted the air, as if the ghosts of wet diapers lingered in the empty garbage pail next to the bureau.

She pulled her phone from her pocket and tapped on her audio book. Not jamming earbuds into her ears while her head ached so badly helped her mood. Hopefully Lazlo and Araminta's doomed affair would distract her from her own woes.

The first being Meade. He was far too attractive for her peace of mind. His intrusion into her workspace was bad enough, but every cell in her body longed to latch on to him.

Temporary infatuation.

At least Lazlo was still trying to boink Araminta. All remained constant in their world.

"You're so cold to me," Lazlo complained to Araminta.

"Want to talk about cold?" Justine muttered. She needed an icepack. The last thing she wanted to do on a blowy winter night was apply ice to her bare skin. Instead, she opened the solitaire app on her phone, telling herself as soon as she won a game, she'd hobble to the kitchen.

A knock on the door interrupted Lazlo and Araminta's incessant bickering.

"It's me. Salome. I come bearing gifts."

Justine prayed the gifts didn't include another tarot card session. She turned off the book, but not before Lazlo stifled Araminta's constant whiny protests with a passionate kiss. "Come on in," she called.

"I swear I just heard *Desire's Revenge.*" Salome sauntered into the room. A fragrant aroma clung to her. "You listen to romance novels?"

Justine lifted her chin. "Usually while I work. I spotted the author's name—Andromeda Zeus—on the retreat website. She's one of my favorites, so I downloaded a couple of her books to listen to on the trip here. Is everyone at the retreat familiar with her writing? Darby and her husband stopped by a little while ago, and they both recognized the story immediately."

Salome set two ceramic cups on the low table in front of the sofa, then slipped a square cooler bag off her shoulder. "The author is a regular guest."

"I didn't see a page for her in the binder—but don't worry. When she does book time, I won't go fangirl on her."

"Embarrassed because you read romance novels?" Salome settled into a chair.

"No. I'm not easily impressed by so-called celebrity." Justine had fed plenty of alleged stars and influencers in Just Food's brief existence.

"There's a shelf of Andromeda's paperbacks in the library. A lot of authors donate copies of the books they write here. Feel free to borrow them."

Justine shrugged. "I don't have time to sit and read. Audio books let me multitask."

"Well, they're available if you're interested." Salome unzipped the cooler and took out a plastic bag filled with ice. "I fixed a couple cold packs for your knee. Heath mentioned you should apply one for ten minutes every few hours."

"Oh. Thanks." Justine summoned her professional mask. "I've been dreading dragging myself back to the kitchen to make one."

"No problem. And I brought you a cup of ginger and turmeric tea. It's good for inflammation. I brought chamomile for me. I figured we could both use a dose of girl time."

"Thank you." Justine had no quarrels with herbal teas. Girl time, however...

"Keep your leg elevated," Salome reminded Justine. "By the way, Darby is going to leave a pair of her son's outgrown boots for you by the back door."

The furnace kicked on, ruffling the curtains hanging above the register. Outside, coyotes yipped at the sky.

"So, do you have any questions after your first day?" Salome lifted her mug to her nose and daintily sniffed before she sipped.

"A couple." Justine slapped the ice pack right onto her pant leg. "You mentioned going to the supermarket for supplies. Doesn't the retreat order from a wholesaler?"

Salome peered at Justine over the rim of her mug. "We're not big enough to justify the delivery costs we'd be charged."

"Oh." Justine tasted her tea, leaned back, and closed her eyes. How different tonight was from last night when Meade plied her with coffee. When she'd been afraid of him. Not that she was altogether comfortable with Salome, especially her metaphysical drivel, but Justine wasn't as tense as she had been. She'd survived her first day on the new job.

"Nothing else?" Salome asked. "Aren't you curious about Heath? Darby and Cam? Me? Laurel, the housekeeper whose rooms you're using? The staff of misfits who've found a home at The Write Place?"

Justine resented being labeled a misfit. She was suffering a temporary slump. "I'd rather get to know you and the others without preconceived notions. I met Cam earlier, when he and Darby stopped by. He seems nice enough."

Salome stared into the depths of her mug. "Cam and Darby are great. Heath and I, on the other hand—we were together for all of high school. After graduation, he enlisted in the Army. Two tours in Afghanistan. I told him I'd wait for him. But when he came home, he didn't want me." Her voice broke. "He's available. If you're interested."

Justine chose her words carefully. "As far as I'm concerned, co-workers, like the guests, are off-limits." Not a mention of Heath's creepiness or her new policy of not connecting romantically with a co-worker, no matter how attractive.

Her policy included Meade Godwin.

Besides, she needed time to recover from past mistakes before she trusted anyone again. Intellectually, she realized not all men were lying, cheating manipulators; for now, wallowing in her anger comforted her the most.

She didn't want to rehash her history with Salome. Eventually she might be comfortable enough to swap stories with her new co-worker, but not on her first official night at the retreat. Gossiping about the guests or staff had to wait until she'd earned her place.

"Explain the cabin and suite names to me," Justine invited. "You mentioned how Meade always books Sacral. The binder doesn't list numbers for the rooms, only weird words. I could understand if names like Hemmingway, King, or Roberts were used to identify the rooms and cabins, but Sacral? Crown?"

Salome's demeanor turned dreamy. "Years ago, when Darby first inherited the property, she and Cam came into the diner where my mother worked for breakfast the morning after their first date. Darby worked as a waitress there, too."

She sipped her tea. Swallowed. "For Cam, it was love at first sight. Convincing Darby to marry him took a month. She was all a-dither about converting the Great Camp into a writing retreat, as stipulated by the author who'd left the property to her. She considered naming the cabins and suites after the days of the week. Cam persuaded her otherwise. I suggested using the chakras."

"Chakras?"

"We all have seven chakras—spiritual centers deep within the human body. Darby loved the idea. She decorated each space with the namesake's color."

"I still don't get it," Justine confessed.

Salome flipped a silver chain hidden beneath her high-necked eggplant-colored sweater into view, then unclasped the necklace and handed it to Justine. "See the line of smaller gems?"

The long, smooth purple pendant was warm from Salome's body. Justine studied the strip of peppercorn-sized stones set in silver marching along the length of the larger piece. "Yeah. So?"

"The bottom one is the root or foundation chakra, which is red and promotes survival, security, safety. One of the suites is decorated in shades of red. Next would be Sacral. Orange. For creativity. Or sex. Meade and Moss Crockett both prefer working there." Salome laughed. "I still haven't figured out which aspect attracts them. In Meade's case, I'm guessing creative sex. He keeps offering to buy the cabin from Darby."

The mystery of the pumpkin-spicey décor of Meade's cabin now solved.

Salome continued. "The Solar Plexus Cabin is furnished in yellow for power and energy."

"Moss Crockett is there this week." Justine remembered his name from the binder because of Crockett's fame.

"Right." Salome's sunny expression clouded for a moment. She quickly recovered. "Solar Plexus suits him better than Sacral, although you'll never get him to admit he's wrong. The green suite represents the heart or love. Heart is popular with romance authors. Throat Cabin is turquoise for communication and truth. The current guest writes true crime novels, so I suggested he reserve that cabin when he called. The last two are suites. Indigo, which is the brow or third eye and focuses on wisdom and intuition, and violet, for the crown chakra or spiritual connection."

And Justine had a bridge in Brooklyn for sale. "Roy G Biv." Justine invoked the mnemonic she'd learned to name the colors of the rainbow as she returned the pendant to Salome.

"Busted." Salome grinned. "Colors were assigned to the chakras in the 1970s by a spiritual leader who wrote a book and assigned rainbow hues—or energy vibrations we can see—to them. Ancient Tantric texts link the chakras to the five elements and their colors, but the modern interpretation is the rainbow.

"Sounds like cheating to me." Justine sipped her tea and waited for Salome to get angry because she'd called the color system a fraud.

"I like you," Salome said. "I'm glad you'll be around for a while. Now, let's read your tea leaves."

MEADE BLESSED THE ICY air as he trudged the mile between the main lodge and his cabin. He hated being cold, but the temperature helped cool his ardor.

He snorted. Old Andromeda would have written that phrase. Current Andromeda might say, "deflate his erection," or "lose interest."

Carrying Justine from the lodge kitchen to the housekeeper's suite had definitely interested his dick. Four years had passed since he'd learned of Elaine's infidelity, and his dick had sulked ever since.

Meade couldn't help himself. He believed in commitment and faithfulness.

No, Andromeda Zeus, New York Times Best Selling Romance Author, believed in commitment and faithfulness. Andre Jove planned to fuck his way around the glitterati. Metaphorically speaking.

Meade's reawakening lust could inspire Andre. But if Justine was Andre's muse, why was Meade's romance pen name writing the celebrity chef?

The frigid air burned in Meade's nostrils. The coyotes yipping in the distance sounded as lonesome as his nights.

Didn't it figure that the first woman to catch Meade's amorous attention in years was off-limits to him. The guests came to the retreat to write. The Write Place promised no distractions. Darby could never know how diverting he found the new chef.

His foot slipped on a patch of ice, but he caught himself before he fell. He needed to pay more attention to where he stepped. Otherwise, he'd be hobbled like Justine or damage his laptop.

Today had focused on research, not words. When he wasn't busy with the drudgery Justine assigned to him, he'd taken notes. Observations. Snippets of imagery. Mostly he'd studied Justine. Analyzed her movements, her facial expressions, and her body language. Her body.

Sal's clothes clung to Justine in interesting configurations. Once Heath delivered Justine's suitcase, the enticement ended. She'd shed the magically delicious ensemble provided by Sal for loose, pajama-like pants printed with colorful peppers and a heavy, double-breasted black jacket. Her hideous clogs barely contained her swollen foot.

When he'd commented, Justine explained that a chef's uniform was for safety, not style. She demonstrated a few scenarios for him. Loose pants allowed flexibility, and the wild pattern helped camouflage stains. The clogs, too, were for easy removal. The double-breasted jacket protected the chef from hot liquids splashing on her. She'd even tucked her hair into the tall white chef's hat she called a toque, which, she explained, kept perspiration from dripping into food and helped keep the wearer's head cool.

Thank God he'd remembered to type his observations because Justine's lively persona captivated him. Her face muscles relaxed. Her voice gained authority. She lit the room as she limped around, familiarizing herself with her new domain. If he'd found her fascinating when she'd pulled a knife on him the previous evening, that attraction paled compared to his current state of mind.

He should have taken photos of her with his phone to copy into his story bible.

He'd never met, much less interacted, with any of the previous chefs in the years he'd been coming to The Write Place. He knew Sal only in her role as assistant manager and had rarely spoken with Heath. And of course, Darby. He might have met Darby's husband once or twice but, compared to the amount of time he spent at the retreat, he seldom mingled with the help. Darby's invisible staff handled everything as if by magic—precisely the way a writer in the throes of creativity needed.

Without the staff to see to such things, one of the opening scenes of an old Michael Douglas and Kathleen Turner movie, *Romancing the Stone,* came too close to the truth: typing "the end" only to discover no essentials such as food or toilet paper in the house.

He reached his cabin and punched his divorce-date code into the keyless entry pad. The place was chilly. He should have asked

Heath to stop in and toss a log on the fire in the woodstove, a bonus chore to keep Heath occupied and away from Justine.

The cabin heated quickly once the logs in the firebox caught. Meade changed out of his jeans into the only clean sweatpants he found. Until he pulled them on, he'd forgotten they were the ones he'd lent Justine. Her scent clung to the fleece, teasing him and reviving the hard-on he thought the walk in the cold had taken care of. But he didn't change, convinced the smell would keep his head in the story.

He paced the confines of the main room, pausing to study the explanation of the sacral chakra posted on the back of the door along with evacuation instructions. Sacral was the energy center of sex and creative expression. Emotions. Based on the brief description, he was definitely blocked in every area the chakra supposedly controlled. He'd be damned if he'd schedule an adjustment with Sal, as offered at the end of the paragraph.

He yawned. His eyes watered and burned. He needed to sleep. Yet if he slept, he might dream, and given his state of mind, dreams weren't a good idea. His imagination—and body—refused to accept Justine was off limits.

She's the heroine of your book. He splashed a couple fingers of Knob Creek into a glass.

No, The Write Place chef *inspired* Colleen-Christine-Carleen-Kathleen. They weren't the same woman at all. Colleen would be soft, yielding. A gentle spirit braving a man's world. Gentle wasn't in Justine's DNA.

Meade plopped on the couch and took out his laptop. He sipped his bourbon while he waited for the machine to boot. If he couldn't sleep, he should write. The sooner he put Andromeda's final book to bed, the sooner Andre could start writing. The sooner Meade could exorcise his obsession with Justine.

He made a note to check the statistics—or ask Justine—but he assumed most professional chefs were male. They could compare experiences about being outliers in gender-dominated professions.

Except Justine didn't know Meade wrote romance, and he'd prefer to keep her ignorant. She didn't need to be in on his secret. She might be one of those readers who harbored odd ideas about romance authors. No one ever asked a sci-fi author how many space battles they'd fought. Too many people considered a romance author's sex life fair game. Andromeda's books were steamy. Everyone assumed if a romance author wrote even a bit kinky, the author must have first-hand experience. He'd done his share of blog tours and faceless social media events in the past and had never gotten used to the too-personal questions thrown his way.

Meade squirmed. He'd forgotten how warm his computer could get. He should have used the retreat-provided lap desk. The heat seeped into the fabric of his sweatpants, mimicking the pressure of a woman's bottom on his thighs, and intensifying the lingering scent of Justine permeating the fleece. His dick stirred.

What did he have to do to get her out of his head?

Write. Purge his thoughts to his hard drive. Weren't relationships always easier on the page?

If he were going to get any sleep, he'd have to type out his fantasy of making love to Justine, then finish the first draft, so to speak, by hand.

CHAPTER 13

Augustus, Duke of Ravenshire, burst into the room. "What is the meaning of this?" His outrage at finding his sister alone with the likes of Lazlo Gordon filled the salon.

"Excuse me?"

Justine jumped. She'd been so intent on listening to her book while she prepared lunch, she hadn't heard the tall woman arrive. *Now what?* So far this morning she'd talked to Salome (who'd offered to read her coffee grounds), Heath (who'd muttered negative comments concerning her car), and Darby (who'd dropped off a pair of her son's outgrown boots).

Justine muted her book and forced her mouth into a smile. "Can I help you?"

The statuesque stranger lifted her chin. "I was told I'd find Meade Godwin in the kitchen."

"He's not here this morning." As the woman could see for herself.

"Do you have any idea where he might be?"

"I'm sorry, I don't." Meade hadn't shown for his shadowing shift. If he were an intern or employee, Justine would have composted him.

She resumed rubbing seasoning into the raw chicken she was prepping for lunch.

The woman inched closer and gestured toward Justine's phone, which sat on the counter. "You listen to romance novels?"

Why did everyone at the retreat question her reading preference? Weirder yet was how everyone claimed familiarity with this particular book. She considered trying the earbuds again, if only to avoid the perpetual conversation. "You recognize the story?"

"Lazlo and Araminta are... memorable." The woman extended her hand. "I'm India Snodgrass, a literary agent. I represent Meade Godwin."

Full make-up. Annoyingly floral perfume. Represent or something more? Not Justine's concern, but the woman dressed as if she were attending a meeting in midtown Manhattan. Or going on a date. Justine wasn't style-savvy enough to figure out the difference. Thank Child, Puck, and Ramsey that chef whites took care of wardrobe decisions.

Justine held up her vinyl-glove-covered hands to indicate she couldn't shake. "Justine Macko, chef for The Write Place."

"You made the delightful tomato soup yesterday," India acknowledged.

"I'm glad you enjoyed your lunch."

India peered at the raw chicken breasts. "Today's lunch?"

"Chicken salad wrapped in lettuce." Justine waved toward the leaves she'd harvested from the greenhouse and were currently drying on paper towels strewn across the counter.

"Sounds yummy. Do you listen to many romance novels?"

Justine braced herself to be mocked. "I like them. They're easy to digest while I'm working. It's uplifting to be assured happy endings do exist, even if they're only fiction."

She inwardly winced. She hadn't meant to confess the last part, especially to a stranger.

India's smile became genuine. "I don't mean to pry. Market research is an occupational hazard. Romance has a negative rep, so I enjoy talking to a person who'll admit to reading love stories."

Something loosened in Justine's chest. "Lots of people hating pineapple on their pizza doesn't make pineapple bad. Pineapple simply isn't their choice. Even when romance stories turn depressing, you know everything will end up okay. They give a person hope. A reason to hang on. We all need reasons to hang on."

"True enough. I wish more people understood that. Well, I'd better let you get back to work. If you should see Meade, please tell him he's late. He never showed up for our ten o'clock meeting. I'm in the Crown Suite on the second floor."

Ten minutes later, the seasoned chicken sizzled on the stove's pre-heated grill. The aroma slowly replaced the lingering ghost of India's perfume. Lazlo had managed to defuse the duke's ire and resumed his verbal sparring with Araminta.

"Let me protect you," Lazlo pleaded with Araminta. "You don't deserve what Cain Dago has planned for you."

Lazlo was an idiot, but Cain Dago personified pure evil.

Meade slammed through the back door. "Sorry I'm late. I overslept." He stomped the snow off his boots. He hadn't shaved. Justine usually didn't care for scruffily bearded faces, but it worked for her. That is, the style worked on Meade. He looked as if he'd just rolled out of bed. Well, what she assumed how he looked after rolling out of bed. Not that she imagined Meade or beds. Much.

Araminta adjusted the shoulder of her gown. "He plans to take me to the continent for our wedding trip if I marry him. I've never been to the continent."

"Do you know what happened to the last wife he took to the continent?"

Justine clicked off the book. "India Snodgrass dropped by. She left a message for you."

Meade swore. "I forgot about my meeting with her."

"She's waiting for you in the Crown Suite." Justine plucked the chicken breasts from the grill and dropped them onto a plastic cutting board. Better to take her foul mood out on the meat than on Meade. "Why don't you wait a few more minutes and deliver all the meals to the second floor and save Salome the work. I'll include yours so you can eat with your... agent."

Meade narrowed his eyes. "India *is* my agent. What else would she be?"

India Snodgrass was beautiful. Tall. Curvy. Even worse, she was gracious. Everything Justine was not and never could be. India and Meade would look good together. They fit. Her geniality balanced out Meade's surly tendencies. "Your relationships are none of my business."

Justine's sweet tone could cause a diabetic coma, but Meade focused on her big-ass knife. The Demon Chef of the High Peaks. A spoof on *Sweeney Todd* would make a great bonus for Andromeda's newsletter subscribers. Meade would have to remember to tell his assistant next time he had email access.

A minute later Justine scraped bite-sized chunks of chicken into a bowl. Her movements were as graceful as a ballet.

"You won't accomplish anything by job-shadowing me if you're not here to witness the process." She ladled the mixed contents of the bowl into large lettuce leaves.

Ooh, he was being scolded. Her tone had changed. She sounded stuffy and offended.

"Are you saying you missed me?"

"Not at all. I relished the peace and quiet to work without being distracted by questions that don't matter to whatever you're writing." She folded the lettuce leaves to resemble wraps. "And I got to listen to my book."

"How do you know what I'm writing?"

"I don't," she admitted as she placed the wraps in the bento boxes. "Nor do I care unless you involve me personally. I'm a woman who values her privacy. Remember that."

She stacked five boxes and handed them to him. "Two for you and your agent, and three for the other suites. I'll get Heath to deliver to the cabins."

Heath. Doing favors for her. Meade clamped his jaw shut. As Justine had pointed out, they were co-workers. Nothing more. Her dealings with Heath shouldn't matter to Meade.

He ought to concentrate on his upcoming meeting with India, although his plans had changed since he'd made the appointment. His career's distant future no longer took priority. His current work-in-progress consumed his brain. Passion for his writing hadn't surfaced in a long time, and he didn't want to jinx his momentum by outlining the next project.

Fortunately, he'd brought his laptop. He'd have access to his notes.

"Anything else, boss?" he asked.

"No."

A window at the end of the upstairs hall provided sufficient light for Meade to decipher the suite names. India's door was the closest to the stairs on the left, so he started on the right, rapping lightly on each door and announcing, "Lunch," then leaving the meals on the tables outside each suite.

India opened her door almost immediately. "You're late. I was starting to get worried because you're never late. You're my most deadline-focused author." She stood aside and let him enter.

He'd never been in a retreat suite before, always requesting the orange cabin, or, if Sacral wasn't available, the yellow one. He wasn't prepared for the purple. Yes, the hues varied, as they did in his cabin, but India had drawn the deeply colored drapes, blocking out the sunlight, bruising everything in the room.

He dropped the bento boxes on the table. "Working lunch?"

"It'll have to be." She sounded annoyed.

Time to remind her who worked for whom.

No, not yet. Later, after she'd recovered from Andromeda Zeus's demise.

They sat and opened the boxes. "I will say, the meals have improved since the new chef arrived," India said.

"She was hurt in a car accident," Meade muttered.

"Oh, your heroics are the talk of the retreat. She's lucky you came along when you did. I was more surprised to learn you weren't in your cabin writing during the worst of the storm. Bad weather is usually your most productive time."

"I met with my lawyer in the city."

India arched her eyebrow.

"Which is the main reason I wanted to talk to you while you're here." Meade picked up his wrap and bit into the crisp lettuce. Sweet mango filled his mouth, along with garlicky chicken. Pineapple. A zing of hot pepper. Cilantro—he knew the flavor because Elaine loathed the herb.

India picked up her wrap. "All right."

"Actually," Meade said, after he'd swallowed, "I want to discuss a couple things."

"I hope Andromeda's next book is on your agenda."

Meade cleared his throat before launching into a disjointed synopsis of *Carlene's Cuisine*, the tale of a female chef, an emotionally wounded soldier, and some other guy doing some other thing. "Only in my story, the soldier doesn't get the girl," Meade concluded.

India didn't speak. She didn't even bite into her wrap.

"Well?" he prompted.

"We have a situation," she said. "Your last two books didn't do well. If the third book of your contract doesn't measure up to Andromeda's usual standard, the publisher is threatening to drop you."

"Those books made money," Meade protested. Okay, his royalties were down, but he'd gloated because lower earnings meant paying less to his evil ex-wife. "But you're right. My heart wasn't in them."

"I know the divorce hurt you." India's caring tone rang false with Meade.

Hurt? He'd never been so glad to get rid of anything as he'd been to see the back of Elaine.

"Um, no. If anything, I resent that the bitch gets forty percent of Andromeda's royalties."

"Even on books you wrote after the divorce was final? You're kidding." India compressed her lips. "Sorry. Not my business."

She tried to backtrack. "That may explain why the publisher believes you've lost your edge."

"You didn't find anything wrong with them," Meade pointed out. India supposedly read every manuscript before forwarding to his editor. "Never mind. Those books don't matter. Andromeda is retiring after *Kathleen's Cuisine*."

"Isn't the title *Carlene's Cuisine*?"

"I haven't settled on the heroine's name yet, but again, not important. Once I turn in the chef book, Andromeda is done." He braced himself for an argument.

Instead, India became thoughtful. "Retiring the name might not be a bad career move. We can work with your publicist and craft a story—"

"You don't get what I'm telling you. I have other plans. Ideas. My new pen name is Andre Jove. And he's gonna write man books. No more ripped bodices."

"You've never written a ripped bodice. You came closest with your first book. The chef was listening to *Desire's Revenge* when I went to the kitchen to find you, by the way."

Meade resumed eating. He'd assumed India would be more resistant. "Yeah, I know. She listens while she works."

"I take it you haven't confessed your secret identity."

"No, and I have no plans to do so."

"Your ex-wife—"

"Will be in a shitload of trouble if she ever reveals my Andromeda Zeus identity. Not only will she lose her alimony, but I will sue her ass into the next millennium." He'd made sure those provisions were iron clad in the divorce agreement.

"All right. Define 'man book.'"

Meade outlined his ideas. He concluded with: "And the best part? Finn Upshaw is here this weekend. You can pitch my idea to him—without revealing the Andromeda connection."

"Yes, Finn and I have run into each other. Except, I don't represent the kind of book you described. You'll need another agent if you choose to write what you've proposed to me."

"What?" What the hell was she talking about? She was a literary agent, for fuck's sake. He wanted to write more mainstream. What was the problem?

"I represent romance. Toxic masculinity redeemed, not revealed or revered. I've also branched out into women's fiction and LGBTQ authors. Marginalized populations."

"Heaving bosoms and throbbing monster cocks," he muttered.

"Will you stop disparaging your work? You've never written anything even close to that, and I wouldn't represent you if you did." India finally picked up her wrap and sniffed it.

Was she checking for arsenic? Might be a problem since Justine included slivered almonds in the filling.

"Okay." He laid his wrap on the table. "Except life isn't all making love with a soul mate."

"You're right. And there is more to the world than white male privilege, too, which is what you just pitched me. I won't peddle stories that contribute to the problem. Give me another solid romance or women's fiction, and I'll continue to play on your team."

"There is nothing wrong with what Andre Jove wants to write," he growled.

"Really?" she asked in a gentle, condescending voice.

India Snodgrass, cutthroat agent, talking to him as if he were a toddler who'd ridden his tricycle into traffic.

"I understand why you want to change pen names," she continued. "Your personal problems have poisoned you, and it's showing in your writing. Wanting a fresh start is healthy. I will support you in recovery in any way I can, just not with your *man* book."

He would get another agent. A man. A partner who appreciated the anxiety of having one's balls threatened on a regular basis and who would fight back.

"Andromeda's final book has to be the best one you've ever written. You can take the sales numbers to your new agent and let him see you can deliver profitable fiction. Remember the romance genre is about hope and change, not the mechanics of sex, and you'll be fine."

"All my readers want are the mechanics." He tried to keep the sneer out of his tone.

"Do you read your fan mail, or do you pass the chore off to your assistant, along with your newsletter and social media?" She studied the exposed end of her wrap. "You should try touching base with your core readers again. Read what they tell you and try to remember why you wrote your first romance."

"I wrote the story as a joke. In college. I was as shocked as anyone when you took me on as a client and sold *Desire's Revenge* to a mainstream publisher."

"You wrote *Desire's Revenge* as a love letter to Elaine, vowing to become the man she deserved. To take care of her. You ought to tap into those emotions again."

"Go back to my roots?" He didn't hide his sarcasm. India was getting as flaky as Sal.

"If that's the way you want to frame it. You have a faithful following. All kinds of people—including the chef here at a writers' retreat—buy your books."

"The chef bumped her head driving her car into a ditch." He didn't mention Justine had been listening to the book when she'd slid off the road.

"You and I both know she didn't download the files here, so she either owns a copy or borrowed one from a library before she headed north."

India crunched into her wrap. She moaned. Over a chicken wrap. The world was skewing sideways.

"And your point is?"

India swallowed before replying. "The chef is your ideal reader, Meade. The reader you're trying to reach with your version of hope."

He couldn't contain his snort. "The only hope I have is that she doesn't go after me with one of the knives she carries in her bag. She pulled one the other night."

"Then she is clearly a woman in need of hope. In need of your books. Your damn ideal reader. Talk to her."

Chapter 14

"You deserve better than Cain Dago," Lazlo protested. "I am that man. Let me take care of you."

"Do I HAVE TO listen to this?" Meade dropped two used bento boxes next to the already-full kitchen sink. "Can't you use earbuds like a normal person?"

"No." Justine gritted her teeth as she continued to stir the rice toasting in a skillet. She shouldn't have to defend her reading material. The kitchen belonged to her. She didn't complain about whatever he listened to while he worked. Of course, she'd only witnessed him writing once in his own space, the night she'd arrived. Didn't matter. Her workspace, her choice.

"The story is tiresome," Meade whined.

Okay, not whined, but he was definitely in a testy mood. His meeting with his alleged agent must not have gone well.

"Slight concussion, remember? Earbuds make the headache worse. Besides, you might find the book educational." Although she'd rewound the audio after India's interruption, she now let the narration continue. The story was heating up. "You might learn a thing or two."

"What is that supposed to mean?" He scowled at the dirty dishes crowding the sink.

"What have I ever done to make you mistrust me?" Lazlo asked Araminta.

Justine splashed a cup of water into the rice. "I only know what I see. Your charming personality isn't exactly getting you... romance."

Meade opened the dishwasher, cursing when he found it full. "I'm not here for romance, I'm here to write. Your problem is you still believe in fairy tales."

"You mean the house-elves or woodland creatures who deal with the dishwasher? News flash, Rumpelstiltskin. Loading, running, and emptying the dishwasher is your responsibility."

"Funny." He started piling the clean dishes into a precarious pyramid on the counter. "I meant the living-happily-ever-after part."

"What's wrong with having goals?" she goaded him, even though she'd learned the hard way that Prince Charming didn't exist and that romance novels were modern-day fairy tales in disguise.

"Goals?" Meade snorted. "That explains why a cook with your skill level is hiding in the High Peaks preparing meals for a bunch of neurotic authors. You can't handle reality."

"You're boring," Araminta sniveled. "Safe."

"Did you ever stop to consider I'm living my dream?" Justine used her most sarcastic tone to hide how close to the truth he'd come. "You don't get to judge or define."

"You know what your problem is?" He opened a lower cupboard door, as if searching for something.

His meeting definitely hadn't gone well.

Didn't matter. Justine was not in the mood for his snit. "I have another problem? Oh! Wait! You're going to give me a list, filtered through your toxic masculine lens."

"Toxic?" He snorted again as he shoved a clean pot into the cupboard. "Another part of your problem right there."

"Oh, so my multiple problems have parts. Ingredients, like a recipe for being female?" She wished she hadn't finished slicing the onions for the koshary because she desperately needed to chop something.

Meade glowered at her. "Perfect analogy."

Justine glared back. "Says someone who eats sauce from a jar and sawdust cheese."

"And what is that supposed to mean?"

"It means you don't know what you're talking about."

"Oh, and I suppose you're an expert." He plucked another pan from the counter and tossed it into the cupboard. Metals clashed.

"On recipes? You'd better believe it." *Men thinking they know what's best for me? Still recuperating from that one.* "Romance novels? Probably more than you. I mean, have you ever even read one?"

Meade made another one of his animal sounds.

Maybe he wrote children's books featuring barnyard creatures or woodland beasts. He certainly had the dialogue down pat.

No matter. She continued to defend herself. "I already know the answer, so don't bother using your big boy words. You think romance novels are trashy. Remember?"

"Wait a minute." Meade sounded offended. "You were the one who said the book you were listening to belonged in the trash. Twisting reality is a perfect example of a female indulging in too much fantasy."

She tapped her foot but managed not to cross her arms or reach for a weapon. "Maybe we need fantasy because reality is such a disappointment."

If she didn't know better, she'd swear Meade flinched.

"Are you insinuating you're disappointed I didn't try to jump you the other night?" he finally asked. "If it's that important to you, I can try to work up some enthusiasm for seduction, despite how nervous your knives make me. If that's what you really want."

"Be quiet and listen to the book. Consider it an instruction manual or inspiration."

"What? You want me to come on to you?" Meade's tone turned incredulous. "I suppose accusing me of sexual harassment is one way to stop me from job-shadowing you."

"What a great idea!" Except he did help her in the kitchen. Once in a while. With tasks her injured knee prevented her from doing. She would never tell him she appreciated his assistance. Feeding him should be enough.

"My brother keeps me wrapped in cotton wool. I want to live," Araminta declared. "I want adventure."

"I don't need an instruction manual," Meade continued in a rough tone. "Maybe I wrote the book on seduction. Ever consider that?"

"Nope. I don't know what genre books you write, and I don't care. We have work to do in this kitchen today. That's all that matters to me."

Meade's good looks didn't blind her to his flaws. And his charm didn't take his... kindness into account. He hid his compassion behind gruff behavior; his actions spoke louder.

She hated how much he appealed to her.

She ought to ease up on him. Her insane attraction to him was her problem, not his.

He flexed his fingers before tackling the dishes in the sink. Justine couldn't tell if the banging and clanging as he loaded the dishwasher was natural or an outlet for his crankiness after his meeting. She debated increasing the volume on her book, but figured jabbing at him would be akin to igniting the brandy on a flambé dessert.

He closed the dishwasher and hit the start button before crossing the kitchen and plugging in his laptop.

Watching him tap away on the keyboard mesmerized her. His thick fingers looked too big for the keys, but he managed to type. Fast.

If he hadn't taken his computer to his meeting, she would have snooped. Only to protect herself. She'd believed Lenny, and all her trust left her was broke and living inside a snow globe in an alien landscape. At least she'd found work cooking. Still a chef. Still in charge of her own kitchen. Where, if she wanted, she could listen to romance novels to her heart's content.

She stopped the audio on the book. Because at that moment, her heart wasn't content.

THE KITCHEN SMELLED OF garlic and other aromas Meade couldn't identify. The scents reminded him of Justine—sharp and tangy.

India had suggested he talk to Justine. What a joke. He didn't want to talk to her. He could think of better uses for his mouth besides words when contemplating the retreat's chef. Such as kissing her. All over. Tearing off her clothes with his teeth, licking every inch of her body before—Oh, hell. Writing the chef book played havoc with his resurrected libido. Except revived lust meant he could channel his horniness onto the page. India had told him Andromeda's swan-song book must be the best he'd ever written. Why not go for extra spicy steam?

Meade focused on getting the words onto the screen. The strategy promised a dual outcome: a finished book and ridding his brain of fantasies where he nailed Justine in the flesh.

Justine refused to cooperate.

"Salome offered to drive me to the supermarket. I have to replace the supplies I've used and shop for the ingredients I'll need for my menus. She said another storm front is predicted for the weekend."

Why did he give a rat's ass about grocery shopping? He tried to tune Justine out.

"As soon as I finish the prep work here, I'm going to plan out a month's worth of meals. Your chef might do the same, depending on where she's working."

Meade swallowed his irritation. She was honestly trying to help him, not bait him.

At least she hadn't turned on the damn book again. *Desire's Revenge* represented his past; he fixed his focus on the future. *Christine's Cuisine* was his ticket forward.

India was wrong. Manliness mattered. If he found an opportunity, he'd speak to Finn Upshaw himself. He wouldn't seek him out—that would be bad business. But social schmoozing so Upshaw would recognize his face wasn't out of bounds.

Don't be pissed at Justine, be pissed at India. One tried to help him, the other tried to trap him in the slot she considered his. How dare his agent—the woman who worked for him, damn it—not want him to grow? Mature as an author.

Despite the two bad books, he generated a lot of income for India. She had no reason to want him to expand his horizons. He was, to borrow a cliché, the goose who'd laid her thousands of golden eggs.

India had no business blaming the quality of his last two novels on Elaine and their divorce. The marriage spent a couple years dying before they'd buried the corpse. He'd written best sellers during the death-watch period. They'd been his most successful books ever. In an era where few publishers offered long-term contracts, India had negotiated the three-book deal for him based on those pre-divorce stories.

"You aren't paying attention," Justine said. "Have you heard anything I've told you?"

Meade glanced at his screen. His notes resembled a rant instead of segments he could use for his book. No, wait, yes, he could use bits of the tirade as part of the hero's stream of consciousness—the hero being the male character vying with the wounded soldier for the heroine's affections. Meade could pluck from the bluster.

"Sure, I'm listening," Meade grumbled. "You're planning menus because another storm is due this coming weekend."

"What did I say about stocking the cabins and suites with basic ingredients and easy recipes for better eating?"

"It's a blur," he admitted after spending several seconds listening to her toe tap on the floor.

"That's what I thought." She sounded disgusted. "I didn't mention the cabins or suites at all. You're a fraud at job-shadowing."

Meade clenched his jaw to keep from exploding. First his agent, now the damn chef, accusing him of not being real. A real man. Of living a pretense. Why didn't they recognize—especially India—that he was finally coming into himself by throwing off the shackles of his shitty marriage?

"I'm trying to work," he bit out.

The back door opened, and Heath stomped into the kitchen. "Smells good in here."

Meade did not need the wounded soldier distracting the heroine, whose attention ought to be on the hero.

"Thanks," Justine muttered. A timer dinged, and she checked one of the pots and pans on the stove, then adjusted the heat of the burner.

"I pulled your car out of the ditch and towed it to your cabin. Saves having your insurance company getting involved," Heath said.

"Thank you." Justine sounded sincere. Nicer to Heath than to Meade.

"What about my Hummer?" Meade asked.

Heath continued speaking to Justine, as if Meade weren't even there. "You're lucky I towed you, and not the authorities. Your inspection has expired, and your tires are bald."

Meade could not believe his ears. "Bad enough you didn't listen to the weather report before you headed out, but you drove into a snowstorm on bald tires?"

"I'm here, aren't I?" Justine lifted the cover off a pot, releasing fragrant steam, and gave the contents a quick stir with a wooden spoon.

"Thanks to me," he reminded her.

"And I cooked for you so you wouldn't have to eat sauce from a jar. We all have our strengths and weaknesses."

Heath snickered before answering Meade's question. "I worked on the snow around your Hummer. You should be able to rock it free now. Do it soon. Another storm front is moving in at the end of the week."

"Are we expecting more guests?" Justine asked.

"One incoming, one outgoing, although the outgoing isn't really leaving." Heath smirked. "The author in Heart Suite is moving to Solar Plexus Cabin with Moss Crockett."

"Good to know. Thanks. By the way, you should eat here during the storm. You won't have time or energy to fend for yourself."

"Great." Dimples framed Heath's predatory white teeth.

Why the hell was Meade noticing Heath's facial deformities?

"Get Sal to take you food shopping soon," Heath advised. "Like tonight."

"She already offered," Justine said.

"I'll drive her." Meade interjected. He hated how Justine sucked up to Heath. Pulling her car out of a ditch and towing it to The Write Place didn't make the man a hero. Meade understood heroes. He created them. Brought them to life.

"You're a guest," Justine reminded Meade.

"I'm job-shadowing you."

"Are you going to job-shadow me when I'm up before the sun rises to hit the produce market for the freshest ingredients I can find?"

Meade scoffed. "Given that February in the Adirondacks limits the number of farm stands, I doubt you're going to find any produce other than at the local supermarkets."

"I can drive myself, now that Heath rescued my car."

She smiled at Heath, who shook his head.

"Not a good idea. Inspection expired, bald tires, sprained knee. Besides, you don't know where the grocery stores are yet. I'll tell Sal you're good to go tonight after dinner."

Heath exited more quietly than he'd arrived.

Then the only sounds were the clatter of a loose cover on one of the pans on the stove and the faint burble of something boiling. Justine fiddled with the knobs again, lifted a lid or two, sniffed, and stirred.

Meade focused on his screen, fuming at the way she'd dismissed his offer.

"Why are you so nasty to Heath?" Red sauce dripped from her wooden spoon to the floor. "You could have thanked him for digging out your man-mobile."

"Why were you flirting with him?"

She reacted as if he'd struck her. "Even if I were, which I was not, my behavior is not your business."

Meade didn't have a response. The idea of Justine with Heath irritated him. "He and Sal are an item. I don't want to see you getting hurt."

Sounded good to him.

"Salome explained their relationship to me," Justine said. "It doesn't matter. I don't get involved with co-workers. Been there, done that, don't even have a t-shirt to show for my trouble, much less treads on my tires."

Her voice broke, and she busied herself with a mundane task. "I don't flirt. With anyone. I offered to feed a coworker while he's overwhelmed. To say otherwise insults me, and I don't deserve to be demeaned."

"You know what?" Meade reined in his irritation. He figured his unsuccessful meeting with India had triggered his reaction. He needed to blow off steam. "I'm going to finish digging out my car." Burn calories along with his anger. He never should have returned to the kitchen.

"Good idea." Justine's chilly tone rivaled the frigid air Heath had dragged inside with him.

Meade shut down his laptop. "I'll pick you up for grocery shopping at seven."

"No. You are here to write. You need to focus on your job, not mine."

"Job-shadow," he reminded her. He fumbled for a reason. "How does a chef choose her meat? Learn how a tomato is perfectly ripe?"

"Instinct and training. Nothing you can put in a book."

He opened his mouth to argue, but she cut him off.

"Don't make me go to Darby."

Chapter 15

"You and Meade are feuding?" Salome asked as she steered her Jeep into a curve too fast for Justine's comfort.

The road twisted worse than a clump of saffron threads. Thank Child, Puck, and Ramsey that Salome drove them. Meade had been right: Justine would never have found her way in the darkness as dense as black bean soup.

"Not feuding." Justine knew better than to complain about a paying customer. She aimed for tact. "There's not much more he can learn from job-shadowing."

"His was an unusual request," Salome said. "I'm surprised Darby agreed. Are you sure you want to cut him off? He helps with a lot of physical tasks."

"I'll manage." She'd have to. The distraction of having him around outweighed any pain in her knee. "I'm sorry, because losing him means more work for you."

"Oh, I'll be fine. I always am. I mean, we survived before Darby hired you, and that was worse because we were the ones cooking." Salome waggled her eyebrows. "Darby tried to hire a student from Paul Smiths College to come in and help, except they were between sessions. Meals got embarrassingly basic around the retreat."

"They're not going to get fancy," Justine said. "I figured I'd develop a ten-day meal plan for each of the three meals we serve. A different plan for each season. And flexible, too. I don't know what inspiration I'll find when I shop."

"You do get days off," Salome interjected.

As if Justine's life required time away from the kitchen. She loved cooking. Correction. She'd loved cooking until Lenny twisted her dream for the warped wreck of his ambition that she didn't see until she'd lost everything. One beauty of The Write Place job was her lack of responsibility, unlike with the restaurant. Yes, she needed to work within the budget Darby set, but Darby set the budget. Someone else's business meant someone else's headaches. Justine could focus on cooking and reading. What more did a woman need?

"I have time off built into the plan," she assured Salome. "Freezer meals repurposed from earlier entrees. I've already stockpiled a few. The bento box system is sheer brilliance."

"A professor at Paul Smiths assigned the creation of a meal delivery system as a class project. We chose the bento boxes. A student suggested the online form we have guests fill out before they arrive. Our current guests are an easy bunch to feed, but many authors have food foibles—"

"Special dietary requirements," Justine gently corrected.

"See, you just confirmed why you're the perfect chef for The Write Place." Salome dimmed her headlights as another vehicle approached from the opposite direction. "You're sensitive to how people relate to food. You instinctively grasp how our guests eat."

Great. Now Salome wanted to imbue her with nonexistent psychic qualities.

"I only want to serve simple, healthy meals to busy people. Easy-to-eat meals."

"Tomato soup? I wouldn't call soup easy to eat."

"I have other soups planned, too," Justine confessed. "Don't writers need their spirits fed as well as their bodies? What is more perfect on a cold, snowy day than a hearty soup?"

"You are so much the right person for this job."

"Any chef would do the same."

"Nope. The problem with the college interns is how they were out to make a mark in the world. Be creative. Fussy. Esoteric."

"Oh boy," Justine muttered. "I rely on the basics. I plan to lean on the street foods of various cultures."

"Street food?"

"Most cultures have the equivalent of hotdog carts on every city corner. Street food. The koshary we ate tonight is an Egyptian favorite."

"You're kidding. That was pretty elaborate."

"Basic," Justine insisted. "Rice, lentils, chickpeas, pasta, fried onions. The two sauces are the key. The time is in the preparation. Once the elements are cooked, they're easy to assemble and simple for the customer to eat."

The headlights caught the eyes of a nocturnal animal perched at the side of the road. The reflection reminded Justine of why she'd gone into the ditch in the first place. "How often do you see moose?"

Salome cast a sideways glance at her. "Moose? They're around. They mostly leave us alone if we leave them alone. The worst time is in the fall, during mating season. They get dangerous because, well, they protect their privacy. And the bulls are extremely territorial."

"I saw one. Right before I spun into the ditch. Scared the stuffing out of me."

"You're lucky you hit the ditch, because if you'd broadsided the moose with your car, you'd have more than a sprained knee and a bump on your head. And you wouldn't have been rescued by Meade. The volunteer ambulance squad would have used the jaws of life to extract you."

"Meade rescued me. I thanked him. His heroism doesn't give him the right to harass me in the kitchen."

Salome's tone became gentle. "He's keeping an eye on you because you were hurt. He's worried about you. Don't take his sliver of humanity away from him."

Sliver of humanity?

"You know him fairly well?" As soon as the question left her mouth, Justine wished she could take back the words. She didn't want Salome to think she was pumping her for information on Meade... although the temptation lingered.

"He's here a lot. He jokes with Darby about wanting to buy Sacral."

Deflection time. "Do many writers spend a lot of time here?"

"Moss Crockett. Lacey Dover, the famous poet. And authors aren't the only ones who retreat here. Finn Upshaw, who's an editor for one of the big publishing houses, comes a couple of times a year, as does India Snodgrass, who's a literary agent."

"Meade's agent." Guilt twinged for doubting him. Only a twinge. There could be more to their relationship than whatever a literary agent did for his books.

"Yup. Dublin Kennedy, the mystery author. A translator is due tomorrow for a few days. Oh, and this might interest you. A cookbook author is checking in at the end of the week, weather permitting. The two of you can exchange recipes."

"Not happening," Justine muttered. A cookbook had been one of Lenny's plans for her celebrity-chef future, one she'd resisted.

The wilderness around them thinned. Signs of civilization gradually increased, starting with piles of snow marking driveways. Streetlamps provided regularly spaced puddles of light. A fast-food franchise logo glowed yellow in the night. Then a tourist town blasted into being. Souvenir shops, restaurants, outlet stores, various lodgings. The road curved sharply up a hill, leaving the hospitality businesses behind. They passed a synagogue, a car dealer, and a pharmacy. A few moments later, Salome pulled into the dimly lit supermarket parking lot. "I'll grab a motorized shopping cart for you once we get inside."

"Thanks." Justine eagerly anticipated buying her own supplies instead of creating meals from another person's ingredients. She hadn't had the luxury of autonomy in a long time.

MEADE PARKED HIS HUMMER in the plowed-out space next to his cabin. Rescuing his vehicle meant he could come and go as he pleased. He yawned as he punched in the code to unlock his front door. An insulated bag on the shelf used for meal deliveries told him he'd missed dinner with Justine at the lodge. She and Sal were on their way into town.

Disappointment displaced his exhaustion.

Except distancing himself from her was good. Space would give him perspective. He needed to create a complicated character. A flawed woman. All humans were imperfect. Some were deeper and more complex than others. Justine's temper defined her.

God, she'd been cute when she'd pulled her big-ass knife on him.

No, not a big-ass knife. A chef's knife. She'd explained the names and purposes of all the blades in her custom tote.

The delivery bag included reheating instructions for his meal, but the insulated bento box had kept everything warm enough.

Meade splashed a shot of bourbon into a glass before sitting at the kitchen table to eat the weirdest looking meal he'd seen in a long time. He usually avoided garbanzo beans, but whatever she'd done to them made them palatable. Maybe because they were mixed in with lentils, rice, elbow macaroni, and a tangy sauce. The contents of a smaller container labeled "frizzled onions to top the koshary" added more flavor.

Justine had been on the job only two days and had already put her mark on The Write Place kitchen. If she kept working her way inside him via his taste buds, he wouldn't be able to evict her from his head.

He'd rather have her in his bed.

There. He'd admitted his weakness. He lusted after the chef. The more time he spent with her, the more he wanted her. Sexual impulses had been absent from his life for far too long. Writing steamy sex scenes for his books had lost their appeal. Words on the screen meant nothing. Shifting to another subgenre of Romance wouldn't help. He would simply be bed hopping.

But one bit of India's advice worked for him. His current contract's final book needed to be the best story he'd ever written. Not as a last hurrah for Andromeda, but for himself. To prove he'd banished Elaine to the past.

Although... to whom did he have to prove anything?

Himself. Meade Godwin. Not Andromeda Zeus. A new pen name wouldn't change anything. Elaine had eroded his sense of self.

He resented that she still collected royalties on the books she'd denigrated. Why should she continue to benefit from something she mocked? Time to stop the hypocrisy. His new identity would fix her good.

He poured another finger of Knob Creek into his glass. He normally didn't drink much, although he did appreciate a good bourbon. After his disastrous meeting with India, he deserved a shot or two.

Justine's eyes were the color of whiskey in a glass held to the light, as if they'd been infused with a trace of maple syrup. If he kissed her, would she taste of vanilla and cinnamon?

Probably not. Nothing so mellow. Pure horseradish or a hot chili pepper. Justine wasn't a laid-back woman. Her profession required strength and independence.

He checked the microwave clock. Still early, and now that he had his Hummer back, he could drive to the all-night diner in Keene. Not to eat, although he would order coffee, but to use their free Wi-Fi. He had a sneaking suspicion Darby's ban on the internet here helped underwrite the cost of the diner's connectivity. She understood that authors periodically required the internet for research or correspondence, but she wanted to make accessing social media and other time wasters as difficult as possible. The ten-mile drive inconvenienced the guests and therefore limited spur-of-the-moment side trips to the world-wide web. Genius.

Moments like this, when he wanted to delve into Justine's past or needed to log onto the net to conduct research for his work-in-progress, knowing he didn't have to drive all the way to Lake Placid made the diner very appealing. Another yawn watered his eyes. He considered taking a nap. He felt as if a year had passed since he'd last slept. His brain might be less muddled if he let his process work.

CHAPTER 16

"WE'RE GOING TO HAVE a change today." Salome entered the kitchen from the public area of the lodge. She swapped the cordless phone she carried for the one in the charging base on the counter.

"Let me guess." After a week, Justine had adjusted to the rhythms of The Write Place and Salome. "Talia Quinlan is moving back to the Heart Suite now that it's vacant again because she's sick and tired of Moss Crockett."

"Not quite," Salome said after she snickered. "The translator in Heart left early this morning. The cookbook author I mentioned is due later today."

Only the Heart Suite had changed occupants since Justine's arrival. The author booked for the Presidents' Day weekend had moved in with Moss Crockett in the Solar Plexus cabin in order to extend her stay. The sex lives of the guests weren't Justine's business. Nor did she care. Salome hadn't been gossiping by sharing the change in number and locations for lunch delivery. Those details mattered to the chef.

Everyone except Meade had a departure date on their meal sheet. Embarrassment kept Justine from asking Salome if she knew Meade's plans. For all Justine's bickering with Meade, she enjoyed his company. And worried because she did.

"Plus, you get to meet Laurel, the housekeeper," Salome continued.

Justine laid her knife on the counter. Salome had been doing double duty in the mysterious Laurel's absence, so the housekeeper reporting for work would relieve Sal, except Justine depended on the convenience of using Laurel's suite.

"Her daughter has been sick," Salome explained. "Can't send a sick kid to daycare. Nilla is well enough now to accompany Laurel here."

"I guess I'll be moving into our cabin." Justine purposely kept her tone light.

"I'm sorry." Sincerity oozed from Salome. "I'm not a bad roommate."

"Sharing a cabin isn't the problem." Justine refocused on chopping vegetables. Both the beef and barley soup she'd planned for dinner and the japchae scheduled for lunch required a wide variety of ingredients. The yeasty scent of the rolls she'd put to rise battled with the fragrance of the browning chunks of beef for kitchen supremacy.

"Right. Your leg."

"Yeah. Not having to walk in the snow has helped." Meade carrying her around posed more danger than the risk of slipping on ice.

"We'll come up with a solution," Salome assured her. "You ought to have your knee looked at. Heath and Cam are great for first aid, but you need professional attention. You're not getting any better."

"As soon as I get a chance." *Chance,* using Justine's definition, meant *never.*

Salome narrowed her eyes and studied Justine, who worried Salome's woo-woo extended to mind reading. The moment passed, and Salome beamed her usual sunshine.

"The new guest didn't fill out the meal sheet for the binder," Salome said. "He was probably in a hurry—he didn't book until last week. I'll get one from him at check-in."

"No worries. I can manage, as long as he doesn't have allergies or sensitivities. Soup and rolls tonight. Japchae—a Korean noodle and veggie dish—for lunch. Lots of flexibility in both."

Plus, she'd stocked the freezer. Justine had spent the week working ahead. Generous batches of entrees allowed for leftovers. After Salome warned her about the expected storm, Justine devised a plan where she would send extra meals to the cabins once the snow started, complete with reheating instructions so the guests wouldn't be dependent on their own cooking.

Like Meade and his jarred pasta sauce.

"Good to know. The cookbook guy won't be here until after lunch, so you have one less mouth to feed."

"Good to know," Justine echoed. "Thanks."

"Are you going to try to impress him?"

"Meade? I impressed him the first night."

Salome looked at her strangely. "No, the cookbook guy."

Justine's cheeks heated. "Nope. There are more bad cookbooks on the market than the number of bad cooks. I'm not threatened by him, and he shouldn't be threatened by me."

"Want me to keep him out of the kitchen?"

"The only guest who should have access is Meade, and I want to revoke his privileges."

"Why?"

"I don't have anything else to explain to him, short of teaching him to cook, and he doesn't approve of my reading material." Perfectly sound reasons, even if not the entire truth. She needed distance from him.

Salome bubbled with laughter. She wiped tears from her eyes as she pulled a tarot deck from her pocket and said, "For what it's worth, he doesn't approve of my reading material, either."

Justine swallowed her urge to join Salome's mirth. She'd gone as far as she dared in discussing a guest. Her comments intentionally weren't personal, because personal would only lead to trouble.

"I wanted to give you a heads up about Laurel, Nilla, and the new guest," Salome said. "Oh, and the key code to get into our cabin is one two eleven eighteen twenty. And don't wander off the trail. I'll catch you later."

Once she was alone again, Justine tried to wrap her head around why she found Meade disturbingly attractive. She'd taken a hiatus from relationships. Lenny's betrayal had done a number on her. She'd assumed a job in the middle of nowhere, cooking for a half-dozen or so reclusive writers, would protect her from things like... sex.

Not that she was highly sexual. The spicy scenes in romance novels were enough for her. The sensuality she found on the pages paired well with the sensuality of food preparation. Textures, tastes, aromas, visual appeal, the whispers of sounds such as the snap of a fresh green bean or the hitch of breath—Lenny often accused her of being non-sexual. Justine figured her priorities were different.

Until Meade upended her and carried her out of the snowy ditch.

Oh, Meade's behavior that afternoon had in no way been sensual, but did smack of an old-time bodice ripper romance, the ones with half-naked couples clinching on the covers. Way too alpha male for her taste.

Fortunately, he'd stifled his inner beast once they'd arrived at his cabin. She didn't for a moment believe clutching her chef's knife induced his more civilized behavior. He wasn't a mountain man with few social graces. He had to be a successful author. Hummers, even old ones, and the gas to drive them didn't come cheap. Nor did time at The Write Place. Meade seemed quite settled in his cabin, meaning he paid more than a guest staying for only a weekend. Yeah, he was successful.

Justine pulled her phone from her pocket and tapped on the audio book. She wanted to finish listening before the library reclaimed the file.

When she and Salome had gone grocery shopping, Justine had used the store's free Wi-Fi to check her phone. Messages from Lenny filled her voicemail inbox, which she'd emptied without listening to them. He'd also spammed her email inbox. Again, she deleted everything he'd sent without opening a single one. The few friends Lenny hadn't driven off, and one former employee he hadn't alienated, admonished her to keep in touch. Other than those people, Justine had no one. The grandmother who'd raised her after her drug-soaked parents abandoned her had died five years ago. Gran's money, Justine's inheritance, had seeded Just Food.

Her solitude probably explained why Justine had easily fallen prey to Lenny's silver tongue. She had listened to his big dreams instead of following her own bliss. At the time, she'd believed their ambitions fit. She'd imagined she and Lenny fit, physically speaking.

The way Meade and his agent fit.

Well, Justine had concocted many disastrous dishes in her career. Wasted time and ingredients creating the inedible. Lenny proved to be merely another miscalculation on her part. She would endure. She'd carried on after the Just Food fiasco. Her grandmother had often told her she'd been born resilient.

She was a survivor.

MEADE ENTERED THROUGH THE back door as Lazlo dictated a list of why Araminta should spurn Cain Dago. Except Lazlo hesitated to tell Araminta the truth about the depth of Dago's depravity. She was too pure, in Lazlo's head-up-his ass opinion, to grasp the dark, evil side of man.

What a stuffy, pompous blowhard. Thank God Andromeda had learned how to construct better characters since Meade's long-ago college days. Several of the more villainous threads needed updating. Evil maharajas and Asian brothels specializing in British virgins were old, cringeworthy plot devices. Meade didn't care enough to make the changes. The romance book communities could stone him for all he gave a damn.

Still, the story was good enough to land India as his agent.

Meade stomped the snow from his feet. Bad weather threatened the area, just as Heath and Salome predicted.

Justine stood over a wok, stirring its contents. Bento boxes lined the counter, ready to be filled. Yeah. He was late.

He automatically glanced at her right ankle, which remained twice the size of her left one. In his non-medical opinion, the swelling confirmed she wasn't staying off her injured knee as much as she should. His fault.

Many aromas mingled in the kitchen. Meade couldn't separate the scents. A pan draped with a red-checkered cloth sat near the stove. Two slow cookers occupied the space he usually used for his laptop.

"You're late," Justine said. "I'm nearly done with meal prep for the day. If you still want to help, you can deliver lunches in a few minutes."

Meade made a non-committal sound and lifted the cover on one of the slow cookers to see what she'd prepared for dinner.

"Leave that alone." Justine's sharp tone sliced through his exhaustion. "You'll release the heat, making the food take longer to cook."

"I only wanted to see what's for dinner."

"Then you should have been here for prep." She wouldn't look at him. "Your job-shadowing isn't working out."

He'd written four thousand words overnight, which is why he'd overslept. "Sure it is. I get to experience a nasty-tempered chef up close and personal."

Justine kept her attention on the contents of the wok. "I'm going to speak to Darby."

Why did he feel as if she'd stuck one of her blades in his gut? He only wanted to help her.

She did have a point, though. He couldn't do much to assist in the kitchen. She relied on finely honed instinct, a culinary skill he would never master.

He decided to ignore her threat and distract her with talk of food. "In the meantime, what's on today's menu?"

"Japchae—Korean vegetables and noodles—for lunch. Beef and barley soup with fresh yeast rolls for dinner."

No wonder the kitchen smelled good. "You made enough soup for an army."

Justine extinguished the burner under the wok. "I made a double batch. I'll freeze half for later, when I have a day off. In the meantime—" She gestured toward the windows with the wooden paddle she'd been using in the wok. "Another storm is on the way. A nice hearty soup will comfort people, to make up for me not being here for the last blizzard."

"At least we're both safe and warm this time, and I'll bet your knee agrees."

"Thank you for your concern, but my leg is fine. I'm fine. You should return to your cabin with your lunch and your laptop and write your book."

"My main character is a cook," he reminded her. "I'm job-shadowing so I will have a sense of what she does."

"Chefs are prompt." She began spooning the contents of the wok into the insulated containers. "Do you have any idea how cranky restaurant patrons get if their meals are late? Even pizza delivery has to be on time. Private chefs cater to the whims of their employers. A chef who is habitually late won't last long in anyone's kitchen."

She lifted her chin. "You are done in my kitchen."

Her haughty tone echoed Elaine's when she'd told him their marriage was dead.

He swallowed the unexpected pain. Justine booting him from her presence shouldn't bother him. Totally not the same as his wife emasculating him. "A writer keeps his own hours."

"You're lucky. Whoever pays the chef sets her schedule, so your research with me has to happen while I'm working, not on authorial whim time."

"My ex called it WST—Writer's Standard Time. Your job here is to cook meals, not judge the guests' lifestyles. The main reason I'm here all the time is because I like having my every whim catered to. That's your job."

"I'm not judging you. And yes, my job is cooking for the guests, which means catering to their food whims, like fake Parmesan cheese, even though the genuine stuff is better. You're disrupting my ability to do my best work. I can't count on you to be prompt, much less present. When you are here, you're more distracting than useful. I've tried to help you create your character by letting you shadow me, but continuing no longer benefits either of us."

Oh, that was interesting. "I distract you?" Probably not as much as she distracted him.

"You ask questions about meaningless things." She sealed the thermal compartments and placed them in the bento boxes. "Take the food upstairs, then come back for the cabin deliveries."

"We're not done here," he said, as he gathered four of the boxes.

"Yes, we are. You need only three lunches. Heart Suite is empty."

He stalked from the kitchen, his mind racing in a dozen different directions, gathering arguments to get Justine to change her mind. Darby would back her employee. She'd been clear from the start that Meade's presence in the kitchen depended on Justine's approval.

As he passed through the lobby, he overheard Sal talking to a stranger at the registration desk. A valise rested at the man's feet.

"We weren't expecting you until after lunch," Sal told the newcomer.

"I got an early jump due to the weather report, hoping to beat the storm."

The man's smarmy smile conjured crooked politicians.

"Your room isn't ready yet," Sal explained in an apologetic tone Meade had rarely heard from her. "Check in isn't until after three, but I'll have housekeeping get on your room right away. We have a library through the door on the other side of the fireplace if you'd like to read or simply relax in there."

The man scanned the lobby. "I can wait here. The fire's nice after that drive. The last twenty miles or so were crazy. I wouldn't say no to a cup of coffee." The man rubbed his palm over the top of his head, as if to make sure the weather hadn't dislodged his slicked-back hair. "And a bite to eat along with the coffee would be great."

"Let me check with the chef, Mr. Palmerton," Salome said.

Again, he flashed a phony smile, nearly as oily as his hair.

"I'll check," Meade volunteered. "I know you're busy, Sal."

"Thanks." Her sincere reply contrasted with the guest's phoniness. "I'll deliver the lunches, since I'm going upstairs anyway."

"Great." Meade handed off the bento boxes, then told Palmerton, "I'll be right back."

"I'll come with you. I'm sure my bag will be okay here."

If another guest accompanied Meade, Justine might not be so quick to evict them. "Sure. Follow me."

"Meade, I'm not sure that's a good idea." Sal's genuine smile faded into one as false as Palmerton's. "Insurance. The insurance doesn't cover having guests in the kitchen."

Funny how insurance suddenly became an issue. Meade narrowed his eyes at Salome.

She slowly tilted her head to one side, wearing her woo-woo face as if she were channeling vibes or auras or whatever the hell.

Well, Meade wasn't in a cooperative mood. He'd rather disrupt the chef for threatening to cut him off. He shrugged before heading toward the kitchen.

"Don't you care about your sister at all?" Lazlo raged at the Duke of Ravenshire. "Cain Dago traffics in British virgins."

Justine's audio book grew louder as he approached her domain.

"What do you write?" Meade had never heard of Palmerton. Either he used a pen name or wrote in a genre Meade didn't follow.

"I'm working on a cookbook," Palmerton replied. "I can't wait to meet the chef."

CHAPTER 17

"SMELLS GOOD IN HERE."

Justine recognized that voice. She grabbed the closest knife and whirled toward the door, ignoring the jolt of pain in her knee as she pivoted. Her worst nightmare stood with Meade on the threshold of the kitchen. "What the Puck are you doing here?"

"We didn't finish our conversation," Meade replied.

"Not you." She used her knife to point. "Him."

"He's checking into the Heart Suite, arrived a little early, and is hoping for a cup of coffee, maybe lunch," Meade explained.

"Is this your idea of a joke?" She couldn't believe Meade would be as cruel as to bring Lenny to The Write Place.

A beat later she admitted Meade wasn't paying her back for ending his apprenticeship. He didn't know about Lenny and what he'd done to her self-esteem. To her.

Lenny sneaking up on her was simply Lenny being Lenny.

"Hey." Lenny sauntered into the kitchen as if he owned the place. "You left town on me. I had a hell of a time tracking you down. I managed to salvage the TV deal, with a few concessions. The cookbook deal is still pending, but I figure we can—"

"Get out." Justine tightened her grip on her knife.

"Babe, you gotta let your anger go. We're finally on our way."

"I'm not going anywhere with you."

Lenny, as usual, ignored her. "I've scheduled a meeting for us in the city on Thursday. That'll give you time to tie up any loose ends here, and—"

"How did you find me?" Her voice vibrated with rage, but she'd stopped shouting.

"Your phone."

"There's no cell service here."

"Doesn't matter. GPS is built into all mobile phones, and we're on the same plan."

Great. She'd stayed on Lenny's account to save money. He'd certainly used her assets. No reason for her not to return the favor. Except she wished she'd known her decision would let him trace her. Time to make a change as soon as she could afford to.

"Go away." She tried to growl. Failed. "I'm done with you."

"Smells like you've got dinner under control." He acted as if she hadn't spoken. "Go pack your stuff. If you hurry, we can get out of here today and avoid the risk of being snowed in."

If she could have stomped her foot without inflicting more pain on her knee, she would have. "Get out of my kitchen."

"Perhaps you'd better leave," Meade suggested to Lenny.

Justine had forgotten Meade's presence.

"Mind your own business," Lenny snapped.

"She doesn't want the TV deal," Meade replied.

"Justine doesn't know what she wants. She still a little miffed at me about the health department thing, but—"

"I am not a little miffed," Justine corrected, clenching her teeth to keep from screaming. "I'm *oeuf*ing furious."

"She's gonna be the next big celebrity chef. I have plans—"

"I don't want to be a celebrity chef."

"See?" Lenny said to Meade. "She doesn't know what she wants."

"Sure she does. The chef wants you out of her kitchen," Meade said. "Do you need help finding your way back to the lobby?"

"Hey." Lenny crossed the room and grabbed Justine's left hand. "Where is your engagement ring?"

She wrenched free of his grasp. "Gone. The diamond went toward settling the debts."

His reaction was almost worth seeing him again.

"That was a family heirloom!"

"You bought the ring from the diamond guy in the plaid suit who advertises on the local cable station," she reminded him.

"It would have been our family heirloom."

"The stone turned out to be a big, flawed joke, Lenny. Like you. Now leave."

"What's going on in here?" Darby pushed past Meade. "Why is everyone yelling?"

Lenny pasted on his most cunning smile, preparing to charm Darby.

"My fault." Meade lifted his chin. "I thought Mr. Palmerton wanted a bite to eat since he missed lunch."

"Palmerton?" Darby asked, turning to look at Justine. "Lenny Palmerton?"

Justine swallowed hard and nodded. "Mrs. Winehouse, may I have a private word?" She'd already told Darby most of the truth, including Lenny's identity, but hadn't related their plans to marry. She never thought Lenny would chase her down and act as though nothing had changed between them.

Everything was different.

Each hour in The Write Place kitchen reconfirmed how much she'd hated being a restauranteur. At Just Food, she didn't get to cook, only develop menus and oversee the running of the establishment. No way would she allow Lenny to drag her back to that version of hell. She'd only been at the retreat a week, but she hadn't been as happy in years.

"A private word isn't necessary," Darby said. "Mr. Palmerton, perhaps you'd be happier at an establishment closer to Lake Placid. The village offers plenty of fine dining. Perhaps one of those chefs would be happy to contribute to your cookbook."

Lenny twinkled his most ingratiating grin—the one he used to deflect the reality of what he said when he was negotiating his deals. It seldom worked, and today was no exception. "I just drove several hours through a storm, which is getting worse, and I am not going to drive elsewhere when I have a reservation here—unless it's to head back to the city with Justine."

"I won't have Chef Justine upset. The kitchen is off limits to guests."

"I'm not checked in yet," Lenny reminded her.

"Then you're trespassing."

"I'm Justine's fiancé and business partner."

His fantasy needed immediate correction. "No, he's not. I broke off the engagement when I found out—" She stole a peek at Meade. "When I found out what he'd done. And the business is no more."

Meade stood as tall and solid as a brick oven, his arms crossed over his chest. No reaction flickered across his features. His blue eyes were as icy as the inside of a sub-zero freezer. "You hocked your engagement ring," he murmured, as if to himself.

Her heart constricted. How dare Meade judge her without having all the facts?

The raspiness in his voice when he spoke again chilled her. "Mrs. Winehouse and Chef Justine have both asked you to leave the kitchen. Do you need help?"

Her heart hitched. She'd misread Meade's reaction.

Lenny eyed Meade's bulk, then held up his hands. "No worries. The receptionist mentioned a library?"

"I'll show you the way," Meade offered.

As soon as the men left, Justine dropped her knife to the counter. She wanted to bury her face in her hands but should apologize to Darby first.

"I'm sorry. I had no idea he would follow me." Tears clumped in her throat, choking her words.

"His behavior is not your responsibility."

"I've gotten off to a poor start with you," Justine confessed. She prayed her sobs wouldn't leak. "First with the car accident and not being able to report to work, then being injured so I can't competently do my job, and now my past stalking me."

"He's the man who lied to you about how he sourced your venison and rabbit?"

"Yes." Justine choked on the word. "I'll resign if you want me to. I've stockpiled a week's worth of repeat meals in the freezer, so you'll be good for a few days."

Darby leaned against a counter. "I don't want you to re-sign. I know you've been on the job only a short while, but you've brought a new and fresh aspect to the meal offerings. Sal shared a few of your ideas with me, and I approved of what I heard. So no more talk of leaving, okay? As far as Mr. Palmerton, who booked his room under false pretenses, while I can't evict him in this weather, I can make sure he doesn't bother you again."

Justine glanced out the window, which was like trying to peer through spun sugar. No, Darby couldn't turn Lenny away. "Thank you." Justine could barely squeeze out the words.

"You wouldn't happen to have a restraining order against him, would you?" Darby asked. "If you do, I'd have legal grounds to not rent him a room."

"I didn't need a restraining order. He vanished quickly enough when the health inspectors showed up. I thought he was gone for good."

She hadn't been rational those first weeks. Numb, yes, but never rational. Yet she'd handled the fallout. Coping is what she did. She'd sold the equipment, pawned her engagement ring, and declared bankruptcy. If Lenny had shown his face during that period, she'd have drained his blood and sold the plasma.

"I'll alert the rest of the staff as to what's going on," Darby promised. "If he gets out of line, I'll have Cam arrest him."

The tears traveled from Justine's throat to prickle in her eyes. *The rest of the staff.* Heath, Salome, and the housekeeper. Her coworkers were going to find out just what a fool she'd been. It was bound to happen sooner or later. On the other hand, she wasn't alone. Not anymore.

"You work here?" Lenny Palmerton asked Meade.

They were the only occupants of the James Coolidge Astin Memorial Library, which meant no witnesses should Meade lose his temper.

Even if Meade hadn't seen Palmerton's treatment of Justine firsthand, he would have disliked the man on sight. Palmerton was a puny punk. The dark blond, slicked-back, and overly-gelled hair; stereotypically beady eyes so small Meade couldn't determine their color; a scraggly excuse of a goatee—if the guy didn't already resemble the villain in one of Meade's SEAL books, he should.

What had drawn Justine to such a disgusting specimen?

"I'm an author, so yes." Meade put aside his revulsion and settled into one of the wingback chairs. This man offered a primer on Justine Macko, skewed as it was. Book research was the only reason Meade wanted to engage with Palmerton. Wanting to know more about Justine had nothing to do with his interactions with her ex.

"An author?" Palmerton paused in his perusal of the titles on the bookshelves. Derision colored his tone. "Based on the movies I've seen, literary types smoke pipes and wear cardigans with leather patches on the elbows."

Meade bit back the urge to brag he preferred the feather boa and sparkly tiara stereotype, but figured the cliché would go over Palmerton's head. Instead, he said: "In the movies, villains wear black hats."

Tiny eyes narrowed into slits. "I don't know what she told you, but Justine isn't real good with details."

"She hasn't mentioned you at all." That ought to deflate the asshole's ego.

Palmerton returned to scanning the bookshelves. "Well, the scandal turned nasty when the board of health shut us down."

"Us?" The single syllable unleashed a torrent of emotions in Meade, mostly anger, but also, other foreign feelings he didn't have time to define. Like jealousy. There had to be a reason Justine had once thought to shackle herself to Palmerton in marriage.

"Just Food. A restaurant in Brooklyn. You might have heard of the place if you're familiar with New York City. It was the place to be in its heyday." Palmerton plucked a book from a shelf, scowled at the cover, then shoved it back in place.

Meade had heard of the restaurant. In fact, he'd dined there, although the trip from Manhattan to Brooklyn wasn't a journey he undertook unless forced, no matter how excellent the food. The memory of his last meal at Just Food with Elaine still rankled.

"See, Justine is a genius. A food genius. Stunted in other areas, though, if you know what I mean." Palmerton pulled out another paperback. "Hmm. Moss Crockett."

Meade was tempted to snatch the book from Palmerton's hand. But he also wanted to hear Palmerton's version of why Justine ended up at The Write Place. "Tell me more about Justine."

Palmerton ruffled the pages of the book as if he was searching for hidden money or a lie to tell Meade. "She focused on developing recipes and presentation, leaving the day-to-day details to me. We're a great team. She just needs to get over her tantrum."

As much as he was on Justine's side, Meade conceded she was capable of holding a grudge if she was pissed off enough. And he could see where Palmerton could piss her off.

"Maybe the Just Food cookbook will be on this shelf one day." Palmerton gestured to the Andromeda Zeus collection with Crockett's book. "Add class to the romance garbage she listens to."

Meade wadded his fingers into his palms and clenched his teeth. Palmerton and his glibness irked the hell out of him. No wonder Justine ran away.

"Except she won't be here long enough to count, I guess." The sound coming from Palmerton might have been a laugh if Meade used his imagination.

Even his creativity couldn't stretch that far.

Palmerton replaced the book on the shelf. "Although I'm starting to appreciate her brilliance in coming here. There's so much untapped potential for promoting her TV show. Maybe I should let her stay a while longer. 'Moss Crockett loves my venison tartare.' That sort of endorsement. What do you think?"

"Your plan is a gross invasion of privacy." Every cell in Meade's body shuddered to imagine his food choices being made public. He wasn't a rock star or teen idol, for God's sake.

"No time right now, anyway." Palmerton jammed his hand into his coat pocket and jingled his keys. "Hey, why don't you help me convince her to leave here as soon as the snow stops? I have a bunch of meetings scheduled for us in the city—"

Was the man out of his teeny tiny little mind? "No."

"What? Why? Her talent is wasted here. I don't care who's eating her food. A bunch of nobodies."

Precisely how Meade preferred his identity to be considered, but that didn't stop him from needling Palmerton. "What don't you understand? 'No' is a complete sentence."

"She's bigger than this!" Palmerton's keys fell to the floor as he waved both hands in a circle like a magician trying to shrink the retreat library. "Even bigger than Moss Crockett. Or she could be, if she'd stop being difficult."

"She doesn't want to be a celebrity chef," Meade reminded him.

"She doesn't know what she wants," Palmerton insisted. "First, she agreed to opening the restaurant, then she fought me about how we should operate. She's fickle."

Déjà vu threatened to swamp Meade. Palmerton's rant echoed Elaine's whining.

Meade forced himself to relax, uncurling his fists and flexing his fingers in his lap. Palmerton was wound up enough for both of them.

"She's naïve," Palmerton blithely continued as he paced between bookcases. "Can't function outside a kitchen. The real world intimidates her."

Meade used every ounce of his willpower not to laugh. He didn't believe anything intimidated Justine. How long had Palmerton known her?

"You know how she's always grabbing a knife?" Palmerton resumed playing his version of literary Jenga with the books on another shelf. "No, I suppose you haven't been around her enough to get on the wrong side of her temper, but you saw it just now, in the kitchen. She tries to play bad ass, but she lets people trample all over her."

"Including you?"

"Me?" Palmerton slammed a book into its slot. "I have plans for her. For us. Big plans. I made one trivial mistake, and she stomps off to Nowheresville to pout."

Now they were getting to the heart of the matter. "What exactly did you do?"

Palmerton turned to face Meade. He fiddled with his zipper tab, another nervous tic. If the guy was this twitchy all the time it was no wonder Justine sought refuge in her audio books.

"I was trying to save money. Game—wild animal meat—is a big seller. Rabbit and venison—that's deer meat, in case you don't know—is hideously expensive to buy from licensed farms. The state health code has a bug up their ass that any game served in restaurants has to be farm raised. Well, I met a guy in the Catskills, a hunter, who offered to supply rabbit and venison at a discount. A substantial discount. Who knew the health department would spring a surprise inspection?"

"Shocker. What happened?"

"The inspector found the meat in the freezer, in the wrong packaging, and without the rights stamps, or some such bull-shit. Nobody died or even got sick from eating at the restau-rant. Justine is a real stickler for following health department guidelines. Fired one person for farting in the kitchen or something. But boy oh boy, the health department went batshit crazy when they found the meat. Temporarily shut her down until the premises were sanitized. Imposed fines—outrageously hefty ones. Media circus. Negative social media posts from snotty influencers, the whole shebang."

Meade must have been either under a rock, on deadline, or working here in the Adirondacks if the scandal had been as big as Palmerton claimed. Palmerton, Meade decided, loved to exaggerate.

"She lost her shirt when a couple people sued." Palmerton rolled his eyes. "And she blames me. She's the one who didn't repackage the meat to look farm raised."

Meade thought his head would explode. "And where were you during all this?"

Palmerton dropped the zipper tab and jammed his hands into his pockets. "I had some, er, business. Very important business. Out of town."

"In other words, you deserted her to save yourself."

"I'm not the one who left town without a forwarding address," Palmerton snapped.

Meade's fingers wadded into his palms again. "You just left town."

"Business trip," Palmerton insisted. "Very important. Justine's future and all that."

No wonder Justine fiercely guarded her kitchen, stayed adamant about not accepting help, and maintaining control. "A future she doesn't want."

"She doesn't know what she wants," Palmerton repeated. "She needs a strong partner to point her in the right direction. Guide her. Otherwise, well, look around you."

Chapter 18

Looking back, maybe losing Just Food was a blessing.

Justine surveyed the kitchen she'd come to love in a very short time. She belonged at The Write Place, not in a television studio with cameras in her face. If Meade's job-shadowing presence made her uncomfortable, working in front of a production crew would be torture.

She stuck the pans of rolls in the unlit oven, where the dough could finish rising while she sanitized the counters.

Lenny's arrival brought back all the stress, all the tension of how he'd twisted her ideas to bolster his ambition. No way would she let him return her to Nightmare on Flatbush Avenue. Not only would she never trust him again, obviously, but she was so much clearer now about what she wanted for herself and her career.

She loved cooking. Planning and executing meals. All she'd ever wanted was to cater intimate events or work as a personal chef for a wealthy, reclusive billionaire like the ones in the books she listened to. Even being a chef at some corporate headquarters, preparing their business meals, would have suited her.

The restaurant had been Lenny's... Justine didn't want to qualify his plan as a dream. A dream implied magic, and Lenny Palmerton's body didn't contain a single microgram of magic. She'd mistaken his machinations for charm instead of the bamboozlement they turned out to be.

She put away the clean wok and utensils she'd used to make lunch before disinfecting the sink area. The smell of bleach temporarily displaced the yeasty aroma of the rising rolls.

At least she hadn't burst into tears when Lenny ambushed her today. That ordeal had been humiliating enough, thank you. She was all cried out over him, his lies, and his underhanded dealings. She compared herself to Snow White waking from an evil spell, except no Prince Charming waited to kiss her wounds and make them better.

Unless she counted Meade Godwin rescuing her from a ditch. Hah!

Once the sink was germ free, she searched for another task. The rolls needed a few more hours before she preheated the oven. The soup burbled in the slow cookers. She couldn't prep the oatmeal for tomorrow's breakfast until she served the soup and scoured the slow cookers, but she could start the dough for the stromboli she'd planned for the next day's lunch. The cheddar and gruyere for Saturday's baked mac-and-cheese needed shredding. There was always more to do.

Exhaustion slammed into her. As much as she wanted to keep busy, she knew her best option would be to rest for a couple hours. Except the housekeeper and her daughter had reclaimed their suite. No room in the lodge for the chef.

Salome had told her the housing they were to share lay a quarter mile to the north of the lodge. A quarter mile didn't sound bad. She had the key code. She could locate the cabin on her own. And the cold weather ought to numb the knee, right?

Bonus: Lenny wouldn't be able to corner her again.

Justine limped toward the back door where Darby had left her son's outgrown boots. Justine grabbed one.

"Hey there," Meade greeted her as he walked into the kitchen. "Hot date?"

He didn't miss a trick.

Justine dropped the boot. "I want to find my cabin. The housekeeper is back with her daughter, and they're using their suite. I need to elevate my leg. Ice my knee."

"Hallelujah. It's about time you got off your feet. Let me help." Meade lifted her as easily as she'd picked up the boot.

"Thanks." Protesting wouldn't stop him, so she saved her energy. Besides, she trusted Meade more than she trusted Lenny. Meade had taken care of her from the moment he'd rescued her from the ditch.

And he smelled nice. He always did, but she hadn't appreciated his provocative natural scent until she'd encountered Lenny again. Lenny's body odor had never appealed to her.

Maybe the clean mountain air had cleansed her palate. Meade didn't have the same repellant effect on her.

He set her on the stool at the center island before kneeling at her feet. His hands were gentle as he removed her clogs.

Justine winced.

"What happened?" Meade used his thumbs to massage the tender flesh. "Your ankle wasn't swollen this badly earlier."

"I tweaked my knee when Lenny showed," she admitted.

"Have you been—"

"Taking my ibuprofen, drinking herbal teas from Salome, and staying off it as much as I can, ice whenever circumstances allow," she interrupted. Meade didn't need to lecture her, and she didn't want another man hovering and questioning everything she did or didn't do. She only wanted to lie down and close her eyes.

"The boot won't go on your foot. You should go to Urgent Care." Meade peered at her, the expression in his blue eyes unreadable. He released her foot and stood.

She immediately missed his touch. "I'm good. I just need to put my leg up for a bit and ice it."

"You've had a week, Justine," he said as he grabbed her coat from a hook by the back door.

"And I'm getting better," she insisted.

He gave her a look suggesting he recognized nonsense when he heard it.

He helped her put on her coat, then pulled on his own jacket. "I'll carry you, unless Darby found a sled."

"Sled?"

"To pull you. Even if you could have gotten the boots on, you shouldn't walk on snow and ice."

"Good point," she admitted as he swept her into his arms.

She resisted the urge to bury her nose in the side of his neck. Worse yet, she wanted to lick him, learn how he tasted.

No sled waited by the back door.

"Do you know where we're going?" Meade asked.

"Salome said roughly a quarter mile in the opposite direction of the guest cabins. She also warned me not to wander off the lane because I might get lost in the woods."

Ankle-deep snow clogged the path. Instead of large and fluffy, Christmas-card-worthy flakes, a barrage of hard, mean pellets assaulted them. The wind blowing off the lake only increased the attack's velocity. Meade lowered his head as he battled the elements. Justine struggled to breathe.

An eternity passed before they reached the snug-looking cabin. Smoke spritzed from the chimney, perfuming the air. The cold numbed the tips of Justine's ears.

"Hurry up and punch in your key code." Meade's teeth chattered. He bent his knees so she could access the number pad.

She was afraid to let go of him. If she loosened her arms from around his neck, she'd end up in the snow.

"You don't know the code?" Meade sounded peeved.

"Give me a second." She squirmed, trying to get closer to the pad without releasing her hold on him. A blast of frigid air convinced her to free one arm.

Meade shifted his weight again. "Come on already."

Gloves made her fingers clumsy. She bumbled the first try.

Meade cursed, the wind blowing away the words.

Second time was the charm, and they practically fell through the door together.

The woodstove heated the cabin well. The mingling scents of the unlit candles lurking on every flat surface warred with the aroma from logs burning in the stove. Crystals hung in the windows. A spindly bamboo bookcase held tarot and oracle cards in addition to incense.

Isolation might not be the only reason the previous chef had fled in the night.

Meade stomped as much snow off his feet as he could before he carried Justine across the room to the sofa. "You doing okay?"

"Yes." Lenny asked personal questions only after sex. After merely a week, she had better history with Meade than the years she'd wasted with Lenny.

She swallowed. Hard. She had no business comparing the two men. One polluted her past, the other helped her manage the day-to-day of her present from the moment they'd met. Neither represented her future. However gruff or sarcastic Meade could be, there was something solid about him. Not just his physicality, but something in his character felt immovable and safe, like a concrete storm shelter. A place to hide and survive. Lenny, by contrast, preferred life on the edge. He was slick, a slippery shark who'd conned her into opening a restaurant with the money Gran left to her—the inheritance Gran had intended to be a safety net, not a risky investment.

Maybe the universe hadn't kicked her to knock her down, but to knock some sense into her. And to knock her out of an untenable situation with both the man and the restaurant; destroying her world in order to rescue her.

Salome's woo-woo must be rubbing off on her.

Meade interrupted her musings. "Any idea which bedroom is yours?"

"Heath said he brought in my suitcases. Wherever he put them." She yawned.

Meade pointed his forefinger at her and winked. "I'll get back to you."

He wandered the perimeter of the room before returning to the sofa and lifting her into his arms. "Found your room."

The bedroom was decent sized, although sparsely furnished. What more did a person need besides a double bed, a chest of drawers, and a night table with a reading lamp? Sure, a closet would have been nice, but the four hooks lining one wall would suffice. Brightly colored woven curtains hung at the solitary window. A dreamcatcher dangling overhead cast a shadow on the crazy quilt covering the bed.

Justine had rented worse places. She'd shared horrific apartments with cockroaches, rats, and people stranger than Salome. She could do this.

"I'll be back with an ice pack in a minute," Meade said after depositing her on the bed.

"You're being awfully nice to me."

"Believe it or not, I'm a nice guy."

"Or you want something." She couldn't help herself. Lenny's treachery left her raw and doubting her instincts.

"Yeah. I want to get ice for your knee. I want you to keep your leg elevated. Then I want to sit on the couch and write until it's time to take you back to the lodge so you can finish cooking dinner, which I want to eat."

While he collected an icepack, she rolled the leg of her chef pants as high as possible and pondered Meade's words. His list of wants differed from anything Lenny ever demanded. When Meade returned with a freezer bag filled with snow and a colorful hand towel, she told him: "You know, hauling me around is not part of job-shadowing."

He gently draped the towel across her knee before adding the makeshift icepack. "What kind of man would I be if I let you try to return to the lodge on your own?"

The more she learned, the more she appreciated him and his code of honor—not that the knowledge would do her any good. A paying guest remained temporary and off limits. "What's your favorite meal?"

Meade's lips quirked. "I finally rate my own special dinner?"

Justine shrugged. "Cooking is what I do. I don't know how else to thank you. You've been a big help to me."

"You don't need to repay me."

"But—"

"No buts. After meeting your ex, I understand why you try to do everything yourself, why you believe you can't trust anyone."

She wanted to ignore Lenny. Lenny was ptomaine lurking in potato salad left out in the sun too long. And Meade was the last person she wanted involved in her personal drama. She didn't want anyone at The Write Place to know what an idiot she'd been, especially not a guest. She'd been hired to feed them, not provide fodder for overblown plots.

"Try to nap. I'll be in the living room working."

Meade's lips brushed her forehead, and she nearly levitated from the mattress.

"Meade, what the Puck?" She jackknifed up. Her heart pounded as if it were tenderizing itself. She *knew* spending too much time with him would lead to trouble.

"Instinct," he muttered, his eyes not meeting hers.

"You're out of line. I said I would cook your favorite meal for you."

He silenced her with a kiss. Hard. Quick. On her astounded mouth.

Heat flashed through her body like a grease fire. She clutched the quilt to keep from grabbing him and demanding more.

Yeah. Trouble.

"Now you have something to dream about besides Palmerton."

MEADE PLOPPED ONTO SAL'S couch and smacked his forehead with the heel of his hand. What had he been thinking, kissing Justine? He'd been out of line, like she'd said. Way out of line. But he refused to apologize. He only regretted that the kiss was a generic gesture, void of anything important. His emotions were anything but.

He opened his laptop and waited impatiently for the machine to cycle on. He most certainly did not want to dissect his action. Jotting down notes on everything he'd learned from his discussion with Palmerton would be a lot easier than examining his jumbled feelings right now. Besides, Meade wanted to recapture his revulsion with the other man while the memory was fresh.

As far as his disgust with himself, he'd revisit the kiss later. Analyze how the astonishment in Justine's eyes matched the shock in his heart. He'd think about it tonight. In his bed. Alone.

Okay, now he was channeling Andromeda Zeus, and that—actually, he welcomed Andromeda. Hadn't India told him Andromeda's final contracted book had to be the best one he'd ever written? Well, Andromeda finally showed up for her swan song. He clicked on the icon for his writing app and started typing the details Palmerton had provided.

Meade wanted to hear Justine's version.

Every bit he learned about Justine helped him create a stronger character. He didn't plan to use Justine's background for anything other than a jumping off point for Colleen's goal, motivation, and conflict. He could brainstorm with Justine, dig deeper into her psyche—

No. Just… no. He refused to use another woman as his muse. Fantasy colliding with reality made for a disaster. Witness his contentious divorce from Elaine.

Still, elements of the situation were available for him to use. Perhaps one last time for Andromeda's final book…

He opened a new scene file and entered his reactions, including his shame for having taken advantage of Justine's vulnerability. Maybe he could find an excuse within his plotting to justify being an asshole. He'd been swept up in playing the role of the big, strong man, hero in his own mind, and reacted to her vulnerability. But a physically injured woman, one also emotionally depleted by her ex, did not deserve to be sexually harassed by the man who claimed to only want to help her.

He was a hot mess. His French-toast-and-sausage breakfast churned and flipped in the coffee he'd guzzled in an effort to stay alert enough to help Justine in the kitchen. Plus, he was exhausted, despite the gallons of caffeine in his system. He'd written a lot of words the previous evening. Most of them needed tweaking into a semblance of order if not outright deleted, given the new insights provided by Palmerton.

Carlene/Colleen/Christine/: "Why did you kiss me?"

Basil: "You're irresistible and cute as hell when you're irked with me.

Basil? He'd named the hero Basil? Or was Basil the wounded soldier who wouldn't end up with the girl?

Meade must have been asleep when he'd typed those words. Nor could an irritated Justine be described as cute as hell. She glowed with an inner fire that mesmerized and would singe a man's skin like a brand.

He didn't blame Palmerton for pursuing her.

How could a man who wanted to marry her not listen to her? Justine was upfront about her goals. She wanted to cook. Nothing else. Meade clearly remembered her reaction when he'd first broached the topic of shadowing her: *I am not a celebrity chef.* Couldn't get more open or specific.

Meade could relate. He wanted to write. Nothing more. Put the finished product out into the world and start again with a new story. No hoopla. No parties or grand gestures. Only the work.

But not the work in the way Palmerton had presented his plans to Justine. Palmerton's demands from Justine resembled what Elaine had aspired to for him: not promoting the end product, but the personality—not person—behind the successes. Justine had as much interest in accolades as Meade did: none. They both craved a quiet life.

Meade's mind drifted into scenarios it had no business creating. He imagined himself and Justine together in a cabin, not unlike their current situation, but free from the baggage of their pasts. He'd be writing, making good progress on his story, when he'd decide to call it quits for the night. He would slip into their shared bed and gently kiss her awake. She would welcome him with the same passion she put into her cooking, and he would finally learn firsthand the spectrum of emotions Andromeda Zeus wrote. He would discover love.

Palmerton had never said he loved Justine. Never claimed any kind of affection for her. Had, in fact, shown more contempt than anything else toward her. He didn't respect her, and Justine deserved respect.

Which made Meade's kiss all the more odious.

He still wasn't sorry. Did not regret anything except she hadn't kissed him back.

CHAPTER 19

Justine stopped trying to nap once she heard Sal arrive.

"Meade? What are you doing here?" Her housemate's voice penetrated the kiss-induced stupor into which Justine had plunged. Meade's mouth on hers had sucked out all her brain cells.

"I brought Justine over. She needed a break, and Nilla is playing in Laurel's rooms," Meade replied. "I'm hanging around to carry her back to finish dinner prep."

Yeah. Staying in the other room, keeping distance between them. After he'd unleashed her fantasies and her libido by pretending to kiss her.

""What's the deal with the new guest? The cookbook author. Palmerton." Salome's voice barely carried above the racket she made while stoking the woodstove in the other room. *Thump. Clang.* "I'm supposed to keep him away from Justine. Darby's orders. Is he here to steal recipes?" *Slam.*

Must have missed that when you read the tarot cards, Justine thought.

Meade didn't answer right away, as if he were weighing his words or formulating a believable lie.

Justine refused to let him sugarcoat the truth. Salome ought to know the facts. Justine left the bed and limped to the doorway. "Lenny Palmerton is here for me."

Meade set his computer on the coffee table and stood. Took a step toward her. "Weren't you going to nap?"

"I'm not as tired as I thought. Too much on my mind." *Like a fake kiss I wanted to be real.*

Meade's cheeks darkened beneath their scruff, but his gaze didn't falter.

Salome peered at her, then at Meade, her eyes wide.

"I can rest after tonight's dinner and prep work for tomorrow's meals." Justine continued. "I'd like to go back now. The sooner I can finish, the sooner I can stay off the leg for a decent amount of time."

"Wait for me, and I'll go with you," Salome said. "The snow is getting worse, so I'm packing a bag in case I have to spend the night in the lodge. You'd think I'd have learned to keep at least a change of clothes in the dorm."

"There's a place we can stay in the lodge, besides the housekeeper's suite?" Justine wondered why Salome hadn't mentioned a dorm earlier.

"Third floor. Former servants' quarters." Salome had the grace to appear guilty. "I use the space to hold yoga classes, reiki sessions, tarot readings—the metaphysical services the retreat offers. The dorm has a couple beds where staff can stay if the weather turns bad. You'll never be able to manage two flights of stairs."

"Would Laurel be willing to stay in the dorm for the night so Justine can use the first-floor rooms?" Meade beat Justine to the question.

"Probably not. No baby gates, and Nilla sleepwalks. Besides, I've stocked the rooms with stuff that isn't child friendly. And while Darby doesn't mind Laurel bringing Nilla to work on occasion, she wants her contained so she won't disturb the guests. But I can ask."

"I don't expect special treatment." Justine spoke firmly.

"Why not?" Meade sounded irritated. "You're injured."

"Because I not only need this job, I want it. If I act privileged or in any way above my co-workers, Darby would—and should—fire me. I've gotten off to a rough start, and it seems like every day another *oeuf*ing thing happens to add to the column of 'I made a mistake hiring Justine Macko.'"

"You don't know Darby," Salome interjected. "If she knew you felt this way, she would be hurt. You're part of The Write Place now."

"Yeah. If Darby boots anyone, it's going to be me," Meade muttered.

Salome's eyes widened. "What did you do?"

"Nothing," Justine quickly defended him, but couldn't resist a dig. "Nothing worth mentioning. Nothing at all."

"I KISSED YOUR COOK." Meade didn't bother knocking on Darby's office door. He would be damned if he would ask forgiveness, but he could confess his sin. Darby needed to know the incident was all his fault.

She looked up from perusing an oversized ledger. "I beg your pardon?"

"I kissed Justine without her consent," he clarified. "I would apologize, except I'm not sorry. Well, not sorry I kissed her. I should have gotten her permission first, though."

Darby's jaw dropped, a phrase he'd often used in his prose but wasn't sure he'd ever actually seen before.

"I know you told her I'm safe," Meade continued, working to keep his tone flat and emotionless. "I guess I should apologize for making a liar out of you."

"What were you thinking?" Darby demanded. She did not invite him to sit.

Not me. My dick. But no way would he admit that to Darby, the woman who could banish him for life from his favorite place to write.

He shrugged, hoping to look appropriately contrite. "I was plotting my book and holding a desirable woman in my arms. I got carried away."

His faux confession sounded as bad as if he'd disclosed he'd been obsessed with thoughts of naked Justine. Not only naked. Other thoughts. Gentle, tender scenarios. Or moments when he defended her against Palmerton's machinations, only to be rewarded with steamy, spicy sex. Of course he wouldn't require payback for being supportive of her. He wasn't a complete jackass. Justine needed an advocate. Why not him?

No one had needed him for a long time.

And he was an idiot. A raving lunatic. He'd known the woman a week. She was a fantasy he'd concocted for his work-in-progress. He had no business dreaming about a future with her.

Time to man up. "I wanted you to hear it from me first. It wasn't her fault. She wasn't flirting or teasing or leading me on in any way. It's all on me."

"I don't need this today." The strain in Darby's voice added to his guilt. "And neither did she. On top of her ex ambushing her, the impending storm, and her injuries, now you hitting on her, she must be ready to quit. What did she do?"

"She told me I was out of line," he admitted.

"You think? If I lose my chef because of you, you will never book a cabin, a suite, or a patch of moss under a tree at The Write Place again." Darby slammed the ledger in front of her shut. "How could you be so stupid?"

Meade shuffled his feet. "Don't worry. She'll stay. She wants this job and is worried you're going to fire her."

Besides, according to Heath, Justine wouldn't be going anywhere anytime soon. Bald tires and snowstorms weren't a good mix, but Meade decided to keep that tidbit to himself.

"You'd better hope she stays," Darby threatened.

"If you'd sell me Sacral Cabin I could marry her. That way you won't lose her."

Marry Justine? He scrubbed his face with his hands. He'd finally found a way to break free of Elaine. Why would he shackle himself again? Okay, he definitely needed more sleep. Sex. More time spent with Justine to learn how she would irritate him with multiple annoying habits. A prenuptial agreement.

Darby's gaze flickered at something behind him before she fixed a glare on him. "Close the door," she ordered in a tight voice. She waited until he'd complied before she continued. "This isn't one of your books, and my property is not one of your castles in the air."

He tried to inject his voice with humor. "I was just kidding. But seriously, I don't want you to lose another chef because I messed up. If you want, I can up her salary—hazard pay—while I'm here."

"Messed up? Try sexual assault. I will not tolerate anyone harassing my employees. I knew letting you carry her around was a mistake. You're not shadowing her for your book. You're stalking her. Well, your job shadowing stint just ended."

Whoa. Time to draw a line. "I am not a stalker," he said between clenched teeth. "And yes, I *am* job-shadowing her for my book. Helping her doesn't make me a bad guy. She's worried she can't function, and I'm doing whatever I can so she can keep her leg elevated and keep working." He'd nearly convinced himself that his motive was all about protecting his muse.

So there.

He didn't mention a word about getting to know Justine better, or about how he loved watching her move in the kitchen as if performing a culinary ballet; how talking to her sharpened all his senses.

Darby studied him as he barely managed to keep the expression on his face bland and noncommittal. "I'm going to talk to Justine," she finally said. She pushed away from her desk.

A cry from the kitchen had Meade running, without waiting for Darby.

Chapter 20

Justine sat on the stool at the kitchen island and wondered where everyone disappeared to. Meade had vanished as soon as he'd settled her. Salome had removed the rising dough from the oven, then set the appliance to pre-heat before she, too, found another place to be.

At least Meade wasn't distracting her. Better to focus on her work, the situation she could control, instead of on Lenny and his deals. Or Meade and what he'd done.

Justine tapped on her audio book.

The timer pinged, signaling the oven was preheated. She slipped from the stool and limped across the kitchen.

In the background, the *Desire's Revenge* narrator droned on. Araminta beseeched her brother, the Duke, to allow her to wed Cain Dago instead of Lazlo Gordon. Justine decided Araminta personified every whiny brat who ought to be locked in her room until she matured. And Cain Dago? Anyone who promised the moon if they couldn't fly was suspect.

Justine opened the oven door, and the escaping hot air ruffled the short wisps of hair surrounding her face. She slid the pans of rolls inside.

"I thought I'd find you still here."

Justine slammed the door and whirled to face Lenny.

"I love the way you're always working," he said as he turned off the audio book.

"You don't love me." Justine crossed to the counter, weighing every word so Lenny wouldn't get the wrong idea. "You never loved me. You loved the *idea* of a celebrity chef. A franchise. A woman you could exploit to line your own pocket."

"You're not being fair," he pouted.

Her grief over Gran's death had blinded her to his ambition. She should have paid more attention, especially when he put her name, but not his, on anything containing the possibility of liability. *We're in this together,* he'd assured her. She shouldn't have given her trust so easily. Done more gut checks, instead of brushing aside her doubts.

"You're right," she admitted, as she shuffled to her stool. "What happened is not fair. I will never forgive myself for allowing you to use me. Now get out of my kitchen."

"I just overheard your author pal tell the owner he kissed you. Is he offering you a better deal than mine?" Lenny sniggered. "Or should I wonder what you're offering him?"

Fresh pain surged in her already aching head. *How dare he insinuate—*

A few deep inhales returned her blood pressure to normal as she reminded herself that Lenny was only trying to goad her into doing what he wanted. His sneaking around and eavesdropping on other people's conversations was nothing new. If not for the fact that Meade *had* kissed her, she wouldn't believe a word coming out of Lenny's lying mouth.

But why would Meade tell Darby what he'd done unless he planned to discredit her for ending his alleged job-shadowing? Which made no sense, because she'd done nothing wrong. Darby had insisted from the first that Meade's presence in the kitchen was up to Justine. She'd agreed to his ridiculous plan because she didn't want to appear difficult her first day on the job. Meade had bolstered his masculine ego by insisting on lugging her around like a side of beef. He was the one who'd kissed her.

No matter. She refused to dignify Lenny's statement with a response. The dishwasher, humming through its cycles, emphasized her silence.

"We have to talk," Lenny persisted.

"I have nothing to say to you and no patience for your schemes and lies. Your disregard for rules, guidelines, and boundaries." She reached for her phone to resume listening to her book.

Lenny slapped his hand on the phone and slid it away from her. His pale brown eyes bulged. A vein pulsed in the side of his neck. "You can't dismiss me so easily. You owe me for the time and energy I've put into this TV deal."

"I don't owe you an *oeuf*ing thing. You left me holding the bag for *your* illegal cost-cutting methods. I've paid all I'm going to pay."

"Too late. I signed the contract."

Something stilled deep inside her, the place she'd discovered while recovering from the body blow of Lenny's initial treachery. "You forged my name?"

Lenny rolled his eyes. "I wouldn't say forged."

"Signing my name without my consent is forgery."

"I'm your business partner."

"What part of 'the business is gone' don't you get? I filed for bankruptcy and sold everything, including the engagement ring, to satisfy the creditors. And I'm still liable because someone let the business insurance lapse."

"You declared bankruptcy?" His voice squealed on the last syllable. "If you'd done what I told you and repackaged the meat—"

"Stop!" She curled her fingers into her palms. "No more blame game. There's nothing to salvage. Not in business, not in our questionable personal lives. All I have left is my name, and you tarnished that. You shouldn't have come here. You need to leave as soon as the weather permits."

"Not without you." His thin lips formed a grim line.

"I am not your path to success. I am not your dream. You've never understood me, Lenny." She should have paid more attention when he asked her to invest her entire inheritance in the restaurant. Grief over Gran's passing had numbed her. She'd been too eager to grasp any connection. "I want people to eat for love, not because the menu is 'in' or 'fashionable'. Influencers, critics, and accolades are distractions. Headlines and top ten lists don't matter to me. Please leave me alone."

"Aw, Babe—"

"Stop sniveling and get out of my kitchen. I distinctly recall you being told by the owner that the kitchen is off limits to you, yet here you are."

His brain must have had gas because he kept belching out the same excuses. "I'm not leaving without you. We have a meeting on Thursday about the TV deal—"

"I am not doing a TV show!" Justine's temper steamed. Any minute, she'd start whistling like a tea kettle. "No cookbook. I am not a brand for you to exploit. Now get out before I do something drastic."

Lenny pointed at her and clicked his tongue. "Perfect. Your temper will be great in front of the camera. You'll be better than Gordon Ramsay."

Justine searched for an object to throw at him. She didn't see the puddle of melted snow leftover from people tramping through the kitchen in their boots.

Meade found Justine on the floor, curled into a ball, holding her bent leg close to her breasts. Her chef's toque rested next to her, and her face mirrored the color of the gray tiles. He knelt next to her and glared at Palmerton. "What happened?"

"I didn't touch her!" Palmerton protested, holding up both hands as if to ward off Meade's ire.

"Are you alright?" Darby asked.

"I slipped," Justine admitted in a hoarse voice. "I'm okay. Just startled."

Meade studied Justine's face and wondered if she'd lie to protect Palmerton. The douchebag had a history of manipulating her, and Meade couldn't help but suspect his behavior included physical abuse. Meade had done enough book research to know women often hid violence against them, even when it wasn't in their best interests.

"There's melted snow on the floor," Justine pointed out, as if reading Meade's mind. "They need to be wiped up."

Yeah. His knee rested in one. She was telling the truth.

"What are you doing here?" Darby's frigid tone echoed the wind battering the lodge. "You were told the kitchen is off limits to guests."

"Answer Mrs. Winehouse's question," Meade growled as he lifted Justine from the floor. He cradled her against his chest, the end of her ponytail brushing his forearm in a gentle caress.

Palmerton took a step back. "You're another guest, and you're here."

"He's job-shadowing me for the book he's writing." Justine winced as Meade settled her on her stool at the island. She gripped the edge of the counter as if to steady herself.

"What?" Palmerton's mouth gaped. "You can't do that!"

"Sure, I can," Meade stretched his grin and made sure he bared a lot of teeth. He stood behind Justine, next to Darby, providing a united front against Palmerton with the island creating a barrier. If Darby hadn't been there, Meade might have slipped his arm around Justine's waist, not only to mess with Palmerton, but to let her know he was on her side. He settled for resting a hand on the small of her back.

"I have exclusive rights to Justine!"

"What?" Outrage reverberated in Justine's tone. "You have no rights to me. At all."

"No, no." Palmerton slapped his palms on the counter. "The contract I signed gives exclusive rights to the cable network to market you."

Justine's fingers curled into fists. "You have no business doing anything involving me."

"Everybody knows I'm your manager."

"News to me," she spat back.

"Can you prove you are?" Meade stepped into his self-appointed role of her champion.

Palmerton sputtered before snapping, "Precedence."

"There is no precedence," Justine bit out. "You weren't around for the aftermath of your actions. You know, when you managed to lose Just Food. In the meantime, Mr. Godwin is job-shadowing me to learn how a professional chef operates for one of his books."

"You don't understand what you've done," Palmerton insisted. "No one can know. No one can ever find out that you gave him access to you."

"Too late," Meade nearly gloated. "The resort staff knows. My agent, who happens to be here, knows. And oh yeah. Justine's name is going into the book acknowledgements. That's standard. In fact, I may dedicate the book to her just to fuck with you."

Palmerton tugged at the neck of his sweater. "This is bad. A fucking disaster."

"For you. Not for me," Justine assured him. "You have no right to represent yourself as my manager or my agent or anything else. I am not a commodity, a brand, or a franchise."

"Nope," Meade agreed. "You're a romance heroine."

"What?" Justine's voice squeaked.

Oh, I shouldn't have said that.

"You read romance novels?" Justine twisted on the stool to look at him, and Meade gripped her hips to keep her from falling. "Or do you write them?"

At the same time, Palmerton guffawed. "Justine Macko? Romance? You have her confused with another woman."

Justine stiffened beneath Meade's hands.

"The situation sounds like the stuff she's been listening to on her phone." *Good save,* Meade thought.

"Not hardly," Justine said.

"He's not trying to sell you into bondage?" Meade kept his tone firm.

Justine blinked several times before slowly turning to study Palmerton. "You think he's a modern-day version of Cain Dago?"

"He sure as hell isn't your hero."

"Now wait just a minute," Palmerton blustered.

"No," Darby interjected. "You wait."

Meade had forgotten Darby's presence. "Do you want me to deal with the situation?" He jerked his head toward Palmerton.

"No," Darby said.

"Then why don't we find Cam or Heath, since you won't let me do the honors?" Those two men had more legal right to pound the living shit out of Palmerton than Meade did. They also had the muscle and skills, especially Heath, to inflict serious damage.

"That won't be necessary." Darby sounded far too calm. "In case I didn't make myself clear, I will not tolerate anyone—" Darby quickly glared at Meade, her gaze flicking toward his hands on Justine's hips "—harassing my staff in any manner.

Mr. Palmerton, do you need help finding your way back to your suite?"

Palmerton glowered at Justine. "We are not finished with this conversation." He stalked from the kitchen.

Meade released Justine and started to follow him to make sure Palmerton did as he was told.

Darby stopped him. "Meade, we're not done here."

CHAPTER 21

IF JUSTINE HATED ONE thing in romance novels, she would say the preponderance of weepy heroines drove her crazy. Yet here she sat, on the verge of personifying what Meade accused her of being. The throbbing in her newly twisted knee threatened to wring tears from her eyes. She'd summoned all her willpower not to cry in front of Lenny. Or Meade. Or especially Darby. She leaned forward and rested her elbows on the granite countertop.

Meade stood next to her, not close enough to touch, but his body heat caressed her.

Darby crossed her arms. "Meade told me something disturbing a few minutes ago. He said he kissed you."

Here it comes. Justine braced herself for Darby's wrath for getting involved with a guest.

"He said you didn't consent."

Meade didn't blame her? Wow. That was something new and different. If it had been Lenny who'd messed up, he'd find a way to point his finger at her. She had to respect Meade for his honesty, and with that respect came the impulse to protect him.

"I don't think he meant anything. His... action was more a... a reflex than anything else."

"Reflex?" Darby sounded skeptical.

"Like putting a child to bed." Justine had never tucked in anyone, although she'd been on the receiving end often enough with her grandmother: story; drink; bedtime kiss.

Meade made a choking sound, but Justine didn't look at him.

She couldn't. She needed to maintain her composure. For all she knew, Meade was married with a half-dozen children and working in the Adirondacks to escape the chaos. Which made him even more off limits than if he were merely a paying guest. Forever off limits.

The idea of him belonging to another woman depressed her, when she ought to be furious with him and even more upset with herself for wanting more from the kiss. Much more than a mere kiss.

"I doubt he felt fatherly," Darby said.

"I never assumed anything else." Justine still couldn't look at Meade, who remained silent.

"As I told Mr. Palmerton, I won't have my staff being harassed in any way by anyone," Darby stated, "and that means any guest, including Meade Godwin and his alter ego. The Write Place is a safe place to work."

Darby's statement warmed Justine. She'd been working at the retreat only a week, and already the owner put Justine's welfare ahead of paying guests. It had been too long since anyone was on her side. But Meade didn't deserve Darby's wrath.

"Mr. Godwin has been nothing but kind to me. He has never once said or done anything anyone could construe as out of line." *And considering how often he's carried me around, he's had plenty of opportunities.*

"Then why do you want to stop my job-shadowing?" Meade propped himself against the island, facing them.

"What?" Darby's head jerked. "When did you decide this?"

"Before he allegedly kissed me," Justine admitted.

"Right before Palmerton arrived," Meade said at the same time. He bared his teeth at the women.

"I don't have anything more to add to Mr. Godwin's knowledge so he can create a believable character," Justine explained. No way would she blurt out she'd changed her mind again. Meade would make a great buffer against Lenny. Yeah, she'd be using him. So what? If he was determined to be in her kitchen, he ought to be useful.

Besides, she trusted him, which surprised her. Even though Lenny had eroded her faith in her instincts, Meade had partially shored them up again when he went to Darby and confessed his transgression. He didn't apologize or make excuses. Owning up to his actions revealed a lot about his character. Nuances she liked. "He's creating a celebrity. I don't know what being a celebrity entails, but I will reconsider if he believes I have more to offer."

"I've already revoked his job-shadowing privileges," Darby said. "Meade violated my trust in him by kissing you."

"I didn't kiss her until after she fired me," Meade pointed out. "I wasn't abusing the situation."

"Oh, really?" Darby studied the two of them, as if searching for signs of impropriety.

"It wasn't really a kiss," Justine insisted. She was tempted to grab Meade by the shirt and plant one on him just to show Darby the difference between what Meade had done and what Justine wanted.

Instead, she swallowed her frustration and smiled at her boss. "And I have to admit Meade has been a big help while I'm... temporarily limited."

"Did you twist your knee again when you fell?" Darby asked. "Your ankle looks worse."

Justine repeated her lie. "I startled myself more than any-thing."

"Stop faking your wellness," Meade said. "Stop trying to be brave. Your ex isn't around. He doesn't deserve any more of your pain."

"Tell me something I don't know." *Like why you're being so nice to me.*

Meade grasped her waist and lifted her until she perched on the island. The granite chilled her butt, but if he moved his hands just a little south... No. She shouldn't be sitting on the countertop, much less thinking about... She prepared food there.

"He's not the man you deserve," Meade said, as he started to roll up her pant leg.

She slapped at his hands. The brush of his fingers against her skin conjured delicious images, but she couldn't sample those pleasures, no matter how much she wanted to. *Focus on Lenny, not on Meade or his touch. Or the way he made her insides melt and bubble.* "Stop it. Believe it or not, I figured Lenny out on my own."

"Meade, what are you doing?" Darby's sharp tone cut through Justine's defensiveness.

"You need to see this, Darby," Meade said as he eased the fabric over the swelling. He pressed his palm against the side of Justine's knee. "You need to know how much it's costing your chef to work; why she needs help doing her job right now."

So much for focusing on Lenny. He never would have concerned himself with her ability to function. His fingers on any part of her body had never made her long for more.

Darby stared at Justine's fully exposed knee. "Oh my God, how are you even walking? The swelling hasn't gone down at all."

Justine swallowed. Hard. She tried to inch away from Meade's touch but failed. "Not carefully enough, or I wouldn't have slipped on the melted snow on the floor."

Meade scowled.

"I'm not blaming you, Meade," Justine hastened to add, still protecting him. "Salome didn't take off her boots, either."

He lightly squeezed her leg as if thanking her.

"You can't work like this," Darby said. "What's the status of tonight's dinner? I smell bread baking, but what else needs to be done?"

Justine tried to ignore the heat inching upward from where Meade's hand rested to where she craved to be caressed. "The rolls come out of the oven in another minute or so." Her voice sounded husky. "The soup is ready to go. I'll freeze the leftovers in individual servings to be used later."

"No, you won't," Meade said. "I can handle that. I've been freezing meals all week."

Justine couldn't imagine what would have happened if Darby hadn't been present. Every molecule in her body whimpered with lust. If she spread her legs a little more, Meade could wedge himself between them. Her imagination splashed so deeply into the gutter she needed to disinfect the island top twice.

She heard his breath hitch, as if he were reading her mind. Or sharing her fantasy.

"Meade." Darby's voice shattered the suspension of time. The single word held a warning. "You are not one of your characters."

Meade did not need to be reminded he wasn't a hero. Elaine had pounded her disillusionment into him, often at an hourly rate. He'd tracked snow through the kitchen where Justine could slip, proving his ex's point.

Meade lifted Justine from the island top and returned her to the stool, the muscles in his arms straining as he held her away from his body. She didn't need to know how aroused he was.

Darby's presence hadn't stopped him from wanting Justine. "Stay put," he ordered.

Justine's eyes trapped him like a fly caught in their honeyed depths.

"Meade?" Darby spoke his name in a softer tone.

"What?" he absently replied.

Darby waved her hand in front of his face, breaking his connection to Justine. He blinked.

"I hate when Sal is right," Darby muttered. She grabbed Meade's arm and dragged him from the kitchen, down the hall, and into her office.

"Sal is right about what?" Meade asked once he'd regained his bearings. He needed to get back to the kitchen. Otherwise, Justine would pick up where she'd left off.

"You'll figure it out. More importantly, Justine can't keep working with her leg in such terrible shape."

"That's what I've been saying all along, but she won't listen to me."

"Cam and Heath can carry her to the third floor. She'd be forced to stay off her feet if she were stranded in the dorm."

Meade snorted. "She'd only slide down the banister and crawl to the kitchen. You've given her dream job to her, and she's not going to let anything stop her from performing her duties. And frankly, I'm just as worried about keeping her ex away from her."

Palmerton wouldn't listen to Darby any better than he listened to Justine. He struck Meade as a man who didn't respect women.

"I wish Cam was here," Darby muttered. "He'd know how to handle the ex."

"I know how to handle him. Toss him out on his ass."

"If I wasn't concerned I'd be sued for evicting a guest in a snowstorm, I would consider sending him on his way. He lied when he booked his accommodations."

"I could boot him and not get you involved."

"And he'd sue you for assault," Darby retorted. "You're not staff, only another guest."

She had a point, damn it.

He couldn't stand by and do nothing. "Why don't you leave Justine to me? I'll make sure she rests her leg. She's cooked ahead a lot, so you won't be in a bind. I've been freezing individual portions of every meal she's served, and she's included reheating instructions on every freezer bag."

"She's a godsend," Darby murmured. "What do you have in mind?"

He said nothing. She couldn't object to what she didn't know.

Darby crossed her arms over her breasts. "I told her she could trust you because I thought she could. You proved me wrong."

Darby's skeptical tone reminded him of his misstep.

"She can." He hoped. "You can."

"Really?"

"Finding your chef attractive is not a crime," he protested. He remembered a story Darby had told him shortly after Justine's arrival. "You and Cam were an instalove couple."

Not that Meade loved Justine.

He blundered on. "Sal predicted your marriage and two sons on the morning after your first date with Cam. Remy and Ozzie, right?"

Darby blushed, confirming his memory of their conversation.

The churning in Meade's brain slowed to a mere ripple. He needed to talk to Sal, not Darby, maybe even submit to one of Sal's woo-woo readings—whatever she wanted. He could ask if she practiced voodoo in addition to the rest of her hocus-pocus. He would give her a thousand bucks cash to hex Palmerton. But would her so-called mysticism work for a skeptic?

Only one way to find out.

CHAPTER 22

THE PAIN IN JUSTINE's leg nauseated her. She barely managed
to keep from falling as she removed the dinner rolls from the
oven. She could have used help. Anyone's help. Well, anyone except Lenny. All she had, though, was *Desire's Revenge*—Araminta, Lazlo, and their futile, incessant flirtation.

She collapsed on her stool to fill the bento boxes with the
evening meal.

Meade had been gone a long time. Darby must be cutting
him a new one.

Justine still couldn't wrap her brain around what had happened. Surprise topped the list. Shock. Most irritating of all, the
kiss created a wanting, left her aching with desire, because the
brush of Meade's mouth against hers wasn't enough.

**"What are you doing to me?" Araminta moaned.
She didn't understand the sensations Lazlo cre-**

ated on her skin as he pressed his mouth to the side of her throat. She prickled, like a freshly opened bottle of champagne.

Justine assured herself that Lenny's presence had intensified her reaction to Meade. She still couldn't believe Lenny had hunted her down, much less expected her to go along with his grandiose plans. She wasn't a grandiose woman. No matter how many times she told him his agenda didn't fit her vision for herself, he'd plowed past her objections. His wants were the only ones that mattered. His schemes nearly destroyed her.

A faux kiss was nothing in comparison to Lenny's duplicity.

Forget Lenny. Brooding over the past only added to the stress thrumming her nerves because of Meade's kiss. Which she would prefer to dream about, despite the danger to both her mental health and her job security.

"Does Cain make you feel this way?" Lazlo asked, his breath warm and moist against her ear. He nipped her lobe before adding, "Do you honestly think he can satisfy you?"

"What do you need?"

Justine started as Meade stepped into the kitchen. Hot soup splashed on her hand. She'd been so engrossed in comparing Lazlo to Meade she hadn't heard him return from his chat with Darby. *Nipping my earlobe, licking the soup off my hand,* or even, *I need a lot of things,* probably weren't among the answers

Meade expected, but they were the first things that came to mind. She clenched her teeth to prevent any wayward thoughts from escaping.

He stood at the end of the island watching her with an unreadable expression.

Her hand shook as she used a paper towel to clean her spill. "Are you supposed to be in the kitchen?" She hated how her voice cracked.

"I've straightened out everything with Darby, at least for the time being, so how can I help you with dinner?" Meade's voice was rough and a muscle twitched in his cheek.

Justine cleared her throat before giving him instructions for reheating the soup.

"I'm sorry I made things awkward between us," Meade said as he wrote on the freezer bags with a marker. He didn't look at her but seemed focused on his penmanship. "I never intended to make trouble for you."

"Cain respects me," Araminta protested. "He would never take the liberties you believe your name entitles you to take. All you have is your name. You have nothing else to offer."

Justine swallowed a lump in her throat. "Things between us have been awkward since we met."

"Have they? Really? We banter, and we're sarcastic, but we've never been awkward with each other. More importantly, we've never attacked each other. I think we respect each other." He finally looked at her. "I know I respect the hell out of you."

"You're splitting hairs," Justine said. She needed to keep distance between them. Otherwise, she would be lost. Meade was as dangerous to her in his own way as Lenny was. "We bicker all the time."

"I'm not splitting hairs. I am very careful with language. Words are as much my tools as your knives are yours."

She'd never considered that. Yes, words could be used as weapons—Lenny wielded them with precision—but she'd never considered them as a person's trade.

"Better my liberties than his disrespectful plans for you," Lazlo muttered.

"Can we turn off your book so we can talk?"

How unlike Lenny, who had walked in and silenced her phone because he felt whatever he had to say was more important than anything she wanted. Justine complied with Meade's request. The oven ticked as it cooled.

Meade studied her before continuing. "Writing is like cooking. I've seen you pull together unrelated parts to create meals. The order you add your ingredients matters to you. Crafting sentences, paragraphs, or a scene is the same. You reference recipes. I research careers, laws, medical facts, anything you can name. Whatever I need to make a believable story. We're not so different."

"We have fundamental differences." She pasted on her sweetest smile. "For instance, I don't eat jarred pasta sauce or fake cheese." *Or kiss people I don't know.*

Except that Meade, after only a few days, understood her better than Lenny ever had. Which wasn't difficult. She wasn't a complicated woman. Listen to books and cook food for people to enjoy. Meade had her down pat. He was her ideal man.

No. Thinking in those terms would only lead to heartache. Any relationship with Meade would be temporary. He was a guest who paid for short-term solitude. She wanted roots. A place to grow and thrive, using her definitions, not fulfilling another person's ambitions.

Their current discussion bordered on the too intimate. Time to get things back on track. Time to be professional.

"Please put one and a half cups of soup into each freezer bag," Justine said.

Meade stared at her for a moment, before giving a curt nod. "How many meals do you have in the freezer now?" he asked as he plucked the measuring cup from the dish drainer.

"Why?"

"You've been working hard." He busied himself ladling soup into the freezer bags he'd marked. "Darby thinks you should take a day off to rest your leg."

"Impossible. I've been here only a week. I'm not due any time off yet. I don't want any special treatment." She was starting to feel like a broken record.

"Darby is your boss. She could put you on disability."

Definitely not having this conversation with him. "I didn't hurt myself on the job, and I say I'm fine." She tapped on the book again.

"You do not deserve what Cain Dago has in mind for you."

Meade grimaced, then wiped all emotion from his face. "And you don't deserve what Lenny Palmerton has in mind for you."

"Take heed, Araminta. Remember Dago's chicanery."

"I have no intention of letting Lenny back into my life."

"Cain can afford my lifestyle, my expectations," Araminta faltered. "He can afford me."

"You can't afford him," Lazlo insisted.

"You were going to marry him." Meade's tone lacked expression.

As if she could ever forget that lapse in judgment.

"Maybe he has expectations," Meade continued. "I mean beyond his magic TV deal. I know it's none of my business, but why did you ever agree to marry him?"

Justine had asked herself the same question countless times in the past year. She owed herself an explanation before she offered one to Meade, who was owed nothing at all. "I had my reasons."

"You know nothing about me!" Araminta flung the dregs of her wine glass into Lazlo's face.

Araminta almost hit the nail on the head as far as Justine was concerned. She missed only because Meade did know Justine, at least better than Lenny did. "So there," Justine murmured and silenced the phone again.

"Ah, yes," Meade mused. "The good old days when women could get away with assaulting a man."

"Araminta didn't slap Lazlo's face," Justine pointed out. "Or kick him where it counts."

Meade winced. "I suppose I should consider myself lucky."

Justine raised her chin and locked gazes with Meade. "Very."

Before Meade could formulate a response, Salome breezed into the kitchen. "Are the dinner boxes ready? I want to deliver them before the weather gets worse."

"I can deliver them," Meade volunteered. "I have to get a few items from my place anyway."

He also needed to put distance between Justine and himself before he did something even stupider than what he'd plotted.

"Two meals for Solar Plexus," Sal reminded him. "And I ran into Vivid from Root Suite. She's going to weather the storm in Throat Cabin, so two meals go there, too. You should stay put once you reach your cabin. The weather promises to get worse. Oh, and Laurel did your laundry this afternoon, if you can manage to carry that along with everything else."

"Great. I'll be back, though. I need to talk with you about something."

"Sure." Sal seemed surprised by his request. "I'll probably be upstairs in the dorm."

Plodding the mile to his cabin was an exercise in self-flagellation. The wind whipped. Snow pierced his exposed flesh like an addict's needle searching for a vein. The burden of his laundry, in addition to multiple meal boxes, weighed him down. Heath had worked all afternoon to keep the lane passable, but the deepening snow turned trudging to the cabins into a true workout.

The wood in Meade's stove had crumbled to embers. He added a couple logs to the coals and coaxed the flames. His place needed to be snug and cozy for later. He planned on riding out the storm here, away from the distractions of the lodge.

And he wouldn't be alone.

He spent a solid half-hour putting away his clean clothes and brushing off his Hummer. Although the snowfall continued, the accumulation hadn't reached the danger zone yet. He needed the weather to work with him.

And Sal to cooperate.

He drove back to the lodge.

He found Justine in the kitchen, writing an inventory of frozen leftovers on the white board—koshary, japchae, sliced roast pork, falafel, a couple kinds of soup. The slow cookers were in use again.

"Where's Sal?" he asked.

"She hasn't returned from taking the dinners upstairs. She's probably done for the night." Justine sounded weary. Dark circles under her eyes emphasized the paleness of her face. Only a faded bruise remained from her head injury. She looked ready to fall on her ass. "It's been a long day."

"Why don't you sit while I run upstairs to talk to her? Then I'll help you get settled for the night. While I'm gone, write down any instructions for the next couple days, in case you get snowed in. I'll be back in a few minutes."

She nodded, as though speaking again required too much energy.

All Meade's willpower went into not kissing her forehead before he left the kitchen.

As he traipsed through the lobby, a chuckle coming from the library distracted him. A male chuckle. Unless Moss Crockett and what's-his-name from the cabins had braved the storm for a game of Parcheesi, the sound meant either Finn Upshaw... or Lenny Palmerton.

Meade detoured to peer through the open door. Palmerton. Probably waiting for a chance to ambush Justine again.

"Evening." Meade strode into the library. "Can I recommend a book for you?"

"I'm taking photos." Palmerton didn't look up from his task. "I've got a few great ideas for the TV show. The untapped potential promotion here boggles the mind."

"I distinctly recall Justine saying she isn't a celebrity chef and doesn't want to be on TV."

"What's it to you? What goes on between me and her is our business, not yours. You think kissing her will give you the inside track?" Palmerton made a rude noise. "Yeah, I overheard your confession to the owner. You want to come on the show, you gotta go through me, and that's not happening."

Meade clenched his teeth so hard he worried they would crack.

"Justine deserves to be more famous than she is," Palmerton continued to blather. "I'm the guy to launch her into superstardom. Not you. You'll never know her the way I do. She'll have a great on-air presence once she forgets the camera."

Meade believed him about Justine being a natural for the camera. He'd learned so much from her merely by observing and listening. She spoke clearly. Concisely. Took care to explain things in simple terms even a sauce-from-a-jar-eater could comprehend.

The rest of what Palmerton claimed? Bullshit.

"With her cooking for all these names—my God, Thayne Thorne and Andromeda Zeus both have books here—she can launch her TV career with a bang. I worked on a plan this afternoon after I discovered the gold mine hidden here."

"Thorne and Zeus are here for privacy, which you'd be violating."

"No such thing as bad publicity."

"You clearly don't understand the purpose of a writing retreat. The point is to get away from the shit and get the words onto the page. No one working here wants their dietary habits analyzed on TV."

Palmerton ignored Meade. "I found an autographed book by Lacey Dover. Didn't she read a poem at the last presidential inauguration?"

"You have her confused with another person, like you have Justine confused with someone else. You'd be smart to pack your bags and leave. You're not an author and you're upsetting the staff."

"Justine's future is bigger than the staff," Palmerton insisted.

"Her future is not your call. I pay to be here in order to write, not expose my food preferences to the world. Darby Winehouse created a haven for authors. What you're planning violates every premise of The Write Place." Meade reined in his temper. "I have an errand upstairs, so I'll go with you."

"I'm not finished here," Palmerton snapped at Meade.

"Would you prefer I physically haul you upstairs, or would you rather wait for the groundskeeper? He did a couple tours in Afghanistan. Army ranger. He doesn't take shit from anyone."

The threat worked, although Palmerton kept trying to justify his actions. Meade tuned him out as they crossed the quiet lobby and climbed the stairs to the second floor. He stood outside

Palmerton's suite until he heard the door lock before making his way to the third floor, where Sal practiced her hocus pocus.

Whether Palmerton stayed in his suite wouldn't matter in a few minutes.

The area at the top of the stairs served as a waiting room. Two velvet-clad chairs flanked a small round table bearing a lamp. A low-wattage bulb hid behind a fringed paisley lampshade and cast more shadow than light.

Fringed paisley also covered a larger round table, the fabric anchored in place by a crystal ball. Other accouterments of Sal's craft were haphazardly scattered—tarot decks, a tea pot surrounded by tins of tea, gemstones of every color, shape, and size, including several dangling from the rafters. In many ways, the space resembled Sal's living room. A brass dragon incense burner had replaced the candle collection, currently breathing headache inducing fragrance into the air.

"Hey Sal?" Meade called, as he crossed the faded oriental rug.

A beaded curtain rattled as Sal emerged from the shadows. A silky robe in shades of deep peacock and crimson clung to her body. Meade mentally filed the description for later use.

"What do you want, Meade?"

She sounded stuffy, as if she'd been crying. The shadows hid her face, so he couldn't confirm his impression. Her tears weren't his business, anyway.

"I need a favor."

"The customer is always right." Her words came out flat and lifeless. He'd never seen her as dejected.

Not his manuscript, not his typos.

"You might not think so when I tell you what I want to do."

CHAPTER 23

Justine was giving the center island a final polish with disinfecting spray when Meade returned to the kitchen.

"Looks like you're done making magic for the day. Good. We should get going." Meade strode across the room and snagged her jacket from the hook by the back door.

Magic. Meade got it. Lenny never had.

"What's going on with Lenny?" If he cost her this job, she would destroy him. Publicly. Loudly. With lots of fanfare. Then she'd disappear. She would change her name, buy a new phone—something she should have done a year ago—and relocate off the grid.

She could beg Meade to create a new identity for her. Unless he wrote nonfiction, he ought to be good at fabricating a character. Only her career couldn't change. Her essence. She needed to feed people the same way she needed to breathe.

"I'll tell you later," Meade promised. "I want to take advantage of the lull in the storm, so let's get going. Sal said she'd deal with your bag."

"I don't understand." His vagueness confused her.

Meade avoided her gaze as he held out her coat. "The weather is supposed to get worse. Did you write out your meal plans for the next couple days?"

Tomorrow's breakfast oatmeal simmered in the slow cookers. A tray of ham and broccoli stromboli chilled in the refrigerator next to two large pans of mac-and-cheese. She'd taped cooking and serving instructions to everything. Meals for the rest of the week consisted of repeats of previous meals.

"I still don't understand."

Meade shook her coat as if to hurry her along. "We have to settle in for the duration of the storm. The snow is going to pick up again in a bit, and you need a break."

"I've already got a sprain."

"Ha. Break, sprain, I get it. I meant from the kitchen. I don't want Palmerton to find you."

"Right." She and Meade were on the same page there.

Justine extended her swollen ankle. "Footwear is still an issue."

"We'll deal with it, just like we've managed so far."

We. His use of the word comforted her, even if he didn't mean anything personal. After being abandoned by Lenny when she'd most needed support, Meade's attitude meant a lot to her. His presence in the kitchen while she worked—pretending to job-shadow her—helped her, whether or not she wanted his assistance.

Strange how Lenny's arrival changed her perception of Meade.

Stop. Meade's kindness didn't mean anything except he was a nice person. A good person. She'd lost sight of basic decency after Lenny screwed her over. Even that clandestine kiss, the one that left her yearning for more, was nothing other than a friendly gesture.

Her sexual attraction to Meade couldn't matter. Sticking to the heroes in romance novels was safer. If she wanted a warm body to cuddle, she'd get a cat. Or a hot water bottle. Gran always claimed a woman without a man was like a fish without a bicycle.

"Do you always have such a positive attitude?" she asked as she wound her scarf across her throat.

"Nope. I tend to live by the seat of my pants."

"You must be an optimist, because you believe everything will eventually be okay."

"If you say so." He slid his arm beneath her thighs. "Ready?"

Justine wrapped her arms around his neck. "Yes."

JUSTINE PEGGED HIM ALL wrong. He didn't possess a positive attitude except with regard to his work. Since his stories succeeded without him micromanaging them, he never bothered to question his process. Hell, he didn't even have the foresight to warm up the Hummer before depositing Justine inside.

"You're driving to my cabin? I'm too heavy, right? You're tired of toting me around."

"You're no heavier than a shovel full of snow," he said as he twisted the key in the ignition. The engine caught right away. He switched on the heater. "Give me a minute to brush off the truck."

The wind howling unimpeded across the frozen lake gathered frigid fierceness.

By the time he'd returned to the cab, heat seeped from the vents.

"Why are we getting on the highway? My cabin is in the other direction." Justine asked as Meade pulled onto Route 73.

He heard the wariness in her voice.

"I have an errand to run before I get you settled in." She would be pissed at him, but he figured she wouldn't retaliate in a public setting.

"Where are we going?"

"Lake Placid. Ever visited? Nice place. Site of two Winter Olympics."

"I grocery shopped last week with Salome. And I researched the area before I accepted the job. Like I researched the authors, Rumpelstiltskin. What's in Lake Placid that's so urgent that you have to take me tonight?"

"You'll see." His answer wasn't intended to satisfy her. He merely wanted to delay having her freak out as long as possible, because she would flip out on him, and he didn't want to risk having her pull a knife while he drove. Yes, he knew she had her knives, because she'd grabbed her tote bag on the way out the door. She didn't need them. Her sharp words and the tone with which she wielded them were weapons enough, but she never left her tools behind.

She leaned forward in her seat and held her hands to the heater vents, and he relaxed.

Meade couldn't recall the last time he'd been this comfortable while alone with a female–working with Justine in the kitchen didn't count. Even the night he and Justine had spent together after he'd rescued her had unnerved him because he'd had the strangest urge to protect her from Heath.

He was out of practice when it came to relationships with the fairer sex. He hadn't befriended a woman in years, probably since before his divorce. The gender terrified him, and he frequently feared his fandom would overwhelm him. He'd had to hire an assistant to keep up with the mail. Strange women were under the impression that he understood them, that he knew what they wanted. Ha. He didn't even know what *he* wanted. He certainly hadn't known what his wife wanted. He was better off without her. Without anyone.

So his attraction to Justine baffled him. His extremely good-looking agent didn't tempt him, and his sexy editor, a shark disguised as a mama bear, terrified him. Sal never appealed to him nor had any of the women authors at The Write Place ever inspired even a twinge of lust. Until Justine.

He wondered if finally ridding himself of his obligations to Elaine had freed him to explore new possibilities. Justine was the first woman he'd seen after meeting with his attorney, and his inner alpha male had roared to life when he'd tossed her over his shoulder and hauled her through a storm to his man cave. She'd assumed the feminine role by cooking for him even though she was injured. They'd played their parts perfectly—if they'd been characters in a romance novel from the 1980s. Oh boy, a fresh plot should Andromeda ever decide to write another book.

His brain swirled. He glanced at Justine. She looked out the window, the dashboard light illuminating the line of her cheek in the darkness.

"I don't suppose you're taking me to the library so I can apply for a local card."

"A great idea, but no."

"Well, we can't be headed to the grocery store. No boots." She paused as she let her words sink in. "I would not be welcome without boots or shoes anywhere except—" She twisted in her seat to face him. "No. You wouldn't."

"I'm not a mind reader. What wouldn't I do?"

"Are you trying to make me lose my job?"

He caught a hint of panic in her voice.

"First off, Darby is not going to fire you because you're hurt. Secondly, I'm trying to help you. If you don't let your knee heal, how are you going to manage in the long run?"

Her inhalation was as sharp as one of her blades.

"I can't go to the doctor. Urgent Care. Whatever." Her voice broke. "My insurance won't cover an MRI."

Why wasn't he surprised? "Your refusal to take care of yourself has been about money?"

"Insurance. I don't have any," she admitted.

Surprised? No, shocked. "You don't qualify for subsidized insurance from the state?"

"The so-called affordable monthly premiums are too high for my austere, post-financial-ruin budget."

"So you cut out superfluous expenses. Like health insurance." Meade was getting a clearer picture of her situation. "And replacing the tires on your car."

She turned away again, apparently fascinated by the snow-laden evergreens lining the highway. "I was lucky I could buy the gas to get here."

He wanted to hit something. He yearned to pick her up, wrap her in his arms, and protect her from the wicked world. Traveling as far as she had in her joke of a car was a testament to God's existence, a theory Meade frequently questioned.

He bit the inside of his cheek to keep from lambasting her. "Not quite. Not lucky enough to stay out of that ditch."

"No," Justine corrected. "I blame that moose, looming out of the snow like a monster emerging from the mist in an old black-and-white horror movie. Scared the stuffing out of me."

"Ah. You must have a guardian moose," he said, as he continued to scan the area ahead of them. Moose and deer were both problems.

"What?"

"If I hadn't stopped for a moose standing in the middle of the road, I never would have seen your flashers. You might still be in the ditch."

"Great. St. Lawrence is a moose."

"No, St. Lawrence is a river, a county, and university." Meade cited the Adirondack connections. "He is not a moose."

"St. Lawrence is the patron saint of chefs, sommeliers, cooking, and comedians," Justine insisted. "My grandmother gave me a medal for luck. I hung it from the mirror in my car. She liked the idea of a saint protecting both chefs and comedians. And because the moose interfered with my journey, then guided you to me, St. Lawrence must be a moose. Or else Gran reincarnated as one." Justine sighed before adding, "I miss her. She believed in me. I mean, truly believed in me. Not like Lenny believing I could make us rich and famous."

"You know," he said, "I've heard Palmerton's side of the story. What's yours?"

He sensed rather than saw her flinch.

"Lenny lies. He's good at rearranging the truth. He should write fiction."

"I can always do a search on you while you're with the doctor. The internet is a marvelous tool. In fact, I might be able to get a signal right now." He fumbled to take his phone from his coat pocket. "Hey, Siri?"

Nothing. The weather probably dampened the cell signals.

"See?" Justine said. "There's nothing more to tell. Just untwist anything coming out of Lenny's mouth. Please keep your eyes on the road."

"My ex-wife dragged me out to Brooklyn to eat at Just Food." To tell him she wanted a divorce.

"Is that why she's your ex?" She paused. "Sorry. None of my business."

Ouch. "We married young, before we knew what we wanted from life."

"And after you grew up, you discovered you didn't want each other?"

Fucking hell. "Ouch. Why do you bother with your knives?"

"Sorry. Lenny does this to me. Maybe I should Google *you* on the internet." She pulled her phone out of her pocket. "Hey Siri, who is Meade Godwin?"

Nothing.

"Siri doesn't listen to me either. Nobody does." She slipped the phone into her coat pocket.

Meade refocused on his driving. "I listen to you. I hear you perfectly. You want to go back to the lodge or the cabin you share with Sal instead of to Urgent Care. You want to work for Darby. You don't want to return to New York with your ex, and you definitely don't want to be a celebrity chef. How am I doing?"

"Three Michelin stars. Congrats, Rumpelstiltskin."

Meade squinted through the windshield. The falling snow tried to hypnotize him. "Here's the thing. I'm helping you achieve your goals by helping you get better so you can work for Darby. Until your leg heals—"

"I know," she interrupted. "The conundrum is I can't afford Urgent Care."

"You can't afford not to take care of your injury. I'll front you the money."

She verbally jabbed him again. "I am not a charity case or a hobby."

"You're a classically trained chef, I know, and I'm lucky you're letting me job shadow you. Consider this payment for the honor." He couldn't keep the sarcasm from his tone. She'd thrown those facts in his face often enough during the past week.

She said nothing.

His patience, stretched by driving with poor visibility, snapped. "You might think I'm being as much of a bully as Palmerton, but if you can't see the difference, I'm writing the scene all wrong."

"I'm not one of your characters, and my life isn't yours to mock in a book."

"Mock? I have nothing but respect for you. Which is why I'm not going to allow you to continue sabotaging yourself."

"Allow me?" Her voice rose, ending in a squeal like the wipers against the windshield.

Meade stole another peek at her. Her profile remained inscrutable in the dim dashboard light. "Consider me the current incarnation of St. Lawrence."

"Funny, but I think I'd rather blame the moose."

CHAPTER 24

How the Puck was she supposed to fill out the paperwork Urgent Care required? Justine had no insurance, no emergency contact, and no next of kin. A deadbeat ex didn't count. She sat in a wheelchair with a clipboard of forms and gripped the provided pen as she considered inserting Lenny's name as guarantor of payment.

Or Meade's. He'd abducted her, driven her to the center, then vanished after securing the wheelchair. Billing him for her treatment would serve him right. After all, he'd offered.

She would never pull such a stunt. She didn't have Lenny's flair for chicanery, such as mixing horseradish and spicy mustard with green food coloring, then labeling the concoction wasabi on the menu.

Besides, Meade's real name might not be Meade Godwin. He probably used a pseudonym while at The Write Place. Every single guest could have a secret identity. Meade might really be

Andromeda Zeus, for all she knew. He certainly looked the part of a romance hero and had even swept her off her feet more than once—literally—but he couldn't charm his way out of a pastry bag, let alone make millions of female readers swoon.

Darby Winehouse became her emergency contact. Next of kin? Blank. If her heroin-smoking parents spawned other offspring, she wasn't aware of them. She wrote her own name in the space for a guarantor. She'd probably have to sell a kidney to pay the bill.

Once she'd finished the paperwork, she set the clipboard on the reception counter and pulled out her phone. Internet access meant she could investigate the man who'd created this embarrassing scenario.

Her search engine claimed Meade Godwin didn't exist unless his real name was Godwin Meade Pratt Swift, the Viscount of Carlingford, who'd died in 1864. She tried different spellings of both Meade's first and surnames with the same results.

Granted, her research skills were basic, and she disliked typing on a phone, but how could an adult in the US elude an internet search in the twenty-first century?

Wait. The agent person who'd invaded the kitchen claimed to represent Meade. India something. Meade should have been listed on her website, if she had one. His picture might be next to his pen name on the agency's page. The idea was worth checking out.

Justine typed in "literary agent India," and there she was, India Snodgrass, complete with a photo confirming Justine had found the right person.

"What's going on?" Meade strode through the front door and crossed the waiting room.

Bad timing. She'd just clicked on India's "Authors Represented" tab. She slipped her phone into her coat pocket. "I'm waiting to be called in. Where have you been? I thought you'd abandoned me."

Cold air emanated off him as he gripped the handles on the wheelchair and rolled her away from the reception area.

"Parking. I couldn't leave my Hummer out front." He stopped at a seating group next to a space for the wheelchair. "Let's get your coat off. You won't need it in the examining room."

She tried to free her phone from her pocket, but Meade was too quick with his help. He flung her coat onto the chair beside him. Before she could protest, a woman in pale blue scrubs stood in an inner doorway and called her name.

Meade pointed at Justine as he said, "I'll keep an eye on your stuff." He plucked her tote from her lap and tossed it on her coat.

"Hold on. I need my—"

"Your knives? I'm surprised you got into the building with them."

The scrub-clad woman—Heather Beck, RN, according to her name badge—whisked Justine away before she could argue.

"Do you want your husband to come back with you?" Nurse Heather asked.

Justine choked. "Not my husband, not even my boyfriend. In fact, I was just on the internet trying to find out who he is."

"A random stranger you picked up on the side of the road?" Nurse Heather sounded confused. She opened the door to an examination room.

"He picked *me* up," Justine admitted, recalling how Meade had carried her through the deep snow to his cabin. "Last Friday. My car slid off the road, and I hurt my knee."

Nurse Heather's eyes widened as she helped Justine onto the examining table. "He's been holding you prisoner for a week?"

"No, he rescued me. I'm the new chef at the writing retreat where he's staying. Everything worked out."

"Oh. You were lucky," Nurse Heather conceded. "Let's get you set for the doctor to examine the knee."

"Yes, I was. I am," she replied as Nurse Heather helped her squirm out of her chef pants.

Nurse Heather draped a paper sheet across Justine's lap. "Your rescuer sounds like a hero in a romance story."

Justine's cheeks grew warm. "Yeah, I guess."

Meade as her hero evoked a scenario she didn't want to consider, not as a character in the spicy subgenres she preferred. He definitely had the smoldering sexy thing going on.

"The doctor will be right in," Nurse Heather said, and exited the room.

Admit it, Justine chided herself. *You've been attracted to Meade almost from the beginning. Not only his body, but also his kindness. His decency.* His apparent integrity still made her uncomfortable. Paranoia kept her waiting for payback time. What did he want from her? Simply job-shadowing her made no sense.

Sex? She wasn't anybody's idea of arm candy. Still, he'd sort of kissed her that afternoon.

Her girl bits clenched. She'd never repaid anyone for anything with her body. She refused to change her moral compass simply because the guy in question melted her from the inside out. Yet no matter how much she snarked at him to keep the distance between them, his compassion trumped her prickliness.

How did one calculate the value of niceness?

She couldn't. She didn't even trust it.

Reality check. Lenny damaged her ability to put her faith in anyone, and her instincts were no longer reliable. She'd met Lenny shortly after her grandmother had passed. She'd been depressed. Vulnerable. He'd offered his alleged support, although hindsight clarified that misconception.

Her new mantra? No more making decisions while traumatized. The bankruptcy ranked right up there with Gran's death. Justine had learned a hard lesson. She could only depend on herself. Compassion proved to be either an illusion or a scam. Stop expecting, stop accepting. Goodwill was either a place to drop off used, discarded items, or—according to old Christmas carols—serving people who had less. No more second-hand offerings for her. She didn't need anyone's pity. She didn't have less because she still possessed herself. Priority one? Protecting her self-worth. From everyone.

Including Meade Godwin.

Especially Meade. His temporary status in her life meant nothing in the long run. He'd finish writing his book and return to wherever he lived, to the world in which he belonged. Possibly to a second wife and family, or a serious girlfriend. Or boyfriend. The retreat wasn't his reality.

The chef position at The Write Place was her future. The right place for her.

As soon as Justine and the nurse were out of sight, Meade sauntered to reception. "I want to make arrangements to pay Justine Macko's bill."

The woman behind the desk delightedly took his credit card information. Justine would be pissed, but he'd deal with her tantrum when she found out. She shouldn't have to suffer because her ex was an asshole.

Mission accomplished. Meade returned to the chair where he'd left Justine's belongings. He transferred them to the magazine-filled table next to the chair and sat.

Typing Justine's name into his search engine revealed how much of an asshole Lenny Palmerton truly was. Several articles laid out the Just Food scandal in staggering detail. If half of what Meade read were true, Palmerton ought to be strung up by his balls. He'd whitewashed the situation when he'd related the story to Meade. The piece of shit minimized the serious nature of the health code violations.

Meade's regard for Justine shot up.

Although no one had gotten sick from eating wild venison in her restaurant, people sued anyway. Sure, bankruptcy put a stay on personal injury lawsuits, but several other claims were still pending. The restaurant's insurance should have handled any payouts. Except, Meade learned, the insurance had lapsed due to nonpayment.

He clenched his teeth. He was willing to bet every cent Andromeda had earned on the Navy SEALS series that Palmerton had been in charge of the restaurant's finances. No wonder Justine had pawned her engagement ring instead of flinging it in Palmerton's face when she'd declared bankruptcy. She'd probably paid for it.

The woman continued to amaze him. She didn't collapse, hide out, or try to reinvent herself after Lenny had done his best to destroy her. No crying that a man had done her wrong. Nope. She'd chosen to take the lessons she'd learned and move forward with what she loved doing. On bald tires. During a snowstorm. All to reclaim her passion.

Meade understood passion. Not the kind that involved getting naked, but the unquenchable need to create. To get out of bed and approach one's work without dread. He understood that what she did in the kitchen was just as creative as what he did at his computer. She was as much of an artist as he was.

Palmerton ought to be held liable for trying to extinguish her light. He needed to pay for what he'd done to Justine.

The story begged for Meade to write it, but he refused to tap Justine's troubles to advance his career. Palmerton had used her enough. No, Meade—with Sal's assistance—planned to help her. Although he'd debated covering her legal fees, he'd decided that, for now, he risked enough of her wrath by paying for this Urgent Care bill. Throwing money at her wasn't the solution. Not for a person like Justine.

Meade's two-fold plan would keep Justine off her leg and hide her from Palmerton.

Palmerton. Who tracked Justine to St. Huberts and The Write Place via the GPS on her phone.

Time to ditch the phone.

Meade eyed her brown leather tote. The bag booby trapped with her knives. Then he remembered she'd been holding her phone when he'd returned from the parking lot. She'd dropped it into her coat pocket, not her tote. He fumbled with the garment, and the phone slid into his lap.

Thumbing off the phone and removing the battery were simple. Locating a hiding place took a little more ingenuity, but he ended up slipping them beneath the phony moss in a planter sporting a fake tree.

Let Palmerton try to stalk Justine now.

Bonus: no more suffering through *Desire's Revenge*.

He sat back in his chair and continued to cyber stalk Justine while he had internet access.

Half an hour later, the nurse wheeled Justine to the waiting room. "She's all set," the nurse chirped.

Justine clutched several papers in her hand. Judging by her expression, she was not happy.

He was not surprised. He suppressed a smile as he stood and handed her coat to her. "Diagnosis?"

"Exactly what Heath and Cam Winehouse diagnosed. This visit was a waste of time. Stay off the leg at least a week. Ice packs. Every single *oeuf*ing thing I'm already doing."

Yeah, she was not in a good mood. And things were going to get worse. Nor was it the time to remind her that staying off the leg meant not working, but the question had to be asked: "Do you have a doctor's note for Darby?"

Behind her, the nurse nodded.

"I'm not in kindergarten," Justine snapped.

It would be just like her to destroy the note and keep on working.

He held open her tote. "Put your paperwork in here. I'm going to brush off the car before we head back to the retreat, and since I'm the one carrying you, I'll take your bag with me now."

Justine stuffed the papers into the tote.

The storm had regained its force while they'd been inside. Several inches of snow blanketed the Hummer. He ran the engine while he cleared away the accumulation.

As he waited for the chill in the interior of the Hummer to fade before he pulled around to collect Justine—and while he still had a cell phone signal—he called The Write Place. Sal answered.

"It's Meade. I'm glad you picked up instead of Darby."

"She went home while she still could," Sal replied. "What's happening?"

"Heath and Cam were right about Justine's leg. She sprained her knee, and the doctor has disabled her for a week. She has a doctor's excuse for Darby, unless she chucks the paperwork before we get back."

"If you can find a way, take a picture with your phone and email the photo to Darby," Sal suggested.

Shit. He did not want to rifle through Justine's bag. "I have her tote with me now."

"Then you won't have a problem. Everything is set on my end," Sal continued. "Justine prepared meals for the cabins in case of another storm, so no one questioned the extra deliveries. Your fridge and freezer are stocked for two for the next several days. You left your laptop in the kitchen, so I grabbed that, too. Will you be back soon? The weather is getting worse."

"Yeah, I'm warming up the car before I get her."

"Be careful driving. A good chef is hard to find."

"Thanks a lot."

Sal laughed. "I'll see you after the storm ends." She disconnected the call.

Meade pulled the documents from Justine's tote, reading only enough to find the note for Justine's employer. Sal's clever suggestion didn't make snooping in Justine's bag sit right with him. He took and sent a photo to the retreat's email address, reminding himself the whole time he was invading Justine's privacy to protect her.

He drove to the front of the building. Justine waited in the wheelchair, her coat on and her scarf wrapped around her throat. She'd jammed her hands in her coat pockets.

"I can't find my phone," she greeted him. "The nurse checked where you were sitting, and she couldn't find it either."

"Did you put it in your bag?" Good thing he'd hidden the phone as well as he had. He lifted Justine from the wheelchair.

"No. I never do, because things get lost in there. I distinctly recall putting it in my coat pocket."

"Where else would it be? You said the nurse checked around my chair. I suppose you could frisk me." He settled her in the passenger seat.

Good thing for the cold temperature, because the idea of Justine running her hands over his body... presented a scene to put in his book.

He couldn't dwell on his lust now. Driving required all his attention. The visibility had deteriorated while they were in Lake Placid. The storm's furious assault surpassed the day he'd found Justine in the ditch. Snow filled the air like static on his grandparents' old television set.

What should have been a half-hour drive stretched to forty-five minutes. An hour. The tension in his chest didn't ease until he pulled into the retreat's lane.

Heath had plowed the parking spot next to his cabin in the not-too-distant past.

"Why are you stopping here?" Justine asked.

"Because this is my cabin. I guess you didn't get a good look at it the last time I brought you here, but yeah, welcome to my home sweet home while I'm at The Write Place."

"Yours. Not mine."

Meade killed the engine. "End of the line, Justine."

"You plan on carrying me to my cabin?"

Meade didn't bother to answer. He unlatched his seatbelt and climbed out. Snow billowed above his ankles as he rounded the vehicle to fetch Justine.

He opened her door and released her seatbelt. "Come on. Let's go."

"Where are you taking me?"

He gathered her close. "I'm putting you to bed where you can't sneak off and work."

"Put me down."

"Should I drop you in the snow?" The wind tried to steal his breath.

"Don't be ridiculous."

He lowered his head as Justine buried her face against his chest. The few yards between where he parked and the door to his cabin felt like the length of a football field.

"What's going on?" she asked once they were inside. "Is Heath coming for me on a snowmobile or the tractor?"

Meade deposited her on the bench by the door, a replay of the previous week. "No. You're staying here."

Justine stilled, much the same as Meade imagined a deer would, scenting danger, her brown eyes wide, her expression alarmed. "You're not funny."

"No," he agreed, "but abducting you is the only way I can think of, short of putting you in the hospital, to keep you off your leg and give your knee a rest. If I have to tie you to the bed for the next seven days, you will not be walking anywhere."

CHAPTER 25

Tied to the bed? Justine's skin prickled. Alpha males were great in fiction. In real life, not so much. As in not at all. The threat of being snowed in with Meade for a week should have frightened her. Any normal woman would be terrified after his ultimatum. Wouldn't they?

She couldn't let him see how appealing she found the idea. "You can't be serious."

Meade started unlacing his boots. "As a heart attack."

"You can't do this. It's... it's kidnapping or something."

He toed off the first boot. "Maybe. Take off your coat. Make yourself at home."

She clutched the front of her coat as if she could hermetically seal the garment to her body. "Is Darby in on your plan?"

"Not exactly." He started on his second boot. "Palmerton can't find you here."

"He tracked my location by phone," Justine reminded Meade. "Speaking of which." She reached for her bag. Groping in the tote's dark depths yielded nothing.

Meade removed his second boot, then shed his jacket. "Come on. Get your coat off. You're going to bed."

"I can't find my phone."

"You don't need your phone. No cell service here, remember?"

"I'm not going to bed with you." *Not from lack of wanting.* Her nipples tingled, tightened. Her insides clenched. She hated how much she wanted him to kiss her as if she were a glass of fine wine to sniff, sip, savor. As if he craved more. Yet the kiss he'd planted on her had been annoyingly non-sexual. Insultingly so. She hated that she couldn't sort out the messages, couldn't read what was happening here.

"I didn't say 'we'," Meade pointed out. "I'm sleeping on the futon in the loft, just like last week. You can get out of bed to use the bathroom. That's it. If you try anything else, I swear I'll tie you down. You're off your leg for a week."

"Don't be ridiculous. Who's going to cook? You? I refuse to—"

"Eat sauce from a jar. I know. Meals have been taken care of, along with your clothes. Thank God not every female on staff is as stubborn as you are. Sal knows the customer is always right. The customer, in this case, would be me."

"Salome knows where I am? She *gave* me to you?" So much for their budding friendship, the traitor.

Meade ignored her outrage. "Sal delivered frozen leftovers to all the cabins while we were gone. You were smart to prepare ahead for the storm. Darby is going to be impressed with your foresight."

"Meade, I can't—"

"You don't have a choice." His tone remained calm, but firm. "Someone has to take care of you if you won't take care of yourself."

Her temper flared. "I'm the one who takes care of people. My job—no, my destiny—is feeding them. I don't expect you to understand." Lenny certainly hadn't. Why should Meade be any different?

"Apparently, caring for you is my destiny." Meade sounded almost bored. "Yeah, you probably deserve better, but I'm what you've got."

"The Urgent Care nurse thinks you're a dashing knight on a white horse," she told him. "Too bad I don't need one. Otherwise, I'd be out of luck."

"You sure would, because I'm nobody's hero. Never claimed to be." He lifted her from the bench.

Justine longed to cling to him, skin-to-skin, olive oil on bread, as he cradled her against his chest. "Then why are you acting like one?"

He snorted as he headed toward the bedroom. "You clearly haven't read enough romance novels."

"I knew it. You *are* a romance author. How else would you know about romance heroes?"

Meade kicked aside a suitcase leaning against the bed. "I know enough." He dropped her onto the mattress. "For instance, if we were in a romance novel, would you be fully clothed in my bed?"

As if that situation couldn't be easily remedied. But those thoughts led to dangerous territory. She had to be practical. Realistic. Her continued employment at The Write Place depended on her professionalism... if she even had a future at the retreat after this stunt.

"Why can't I stay off my leg at the lodge or my cabin?"

Meade lifted the suitcase and set it next to her. "A, you don't have a bed in the lodge."

Okay, that was valid, but she did have a room in the cabin she was supposed to share with Salome; the place where he'd pretended to kiss her only hours earlier. Or had the *faux* kiss meant so little to him that he'd forgotten the details?

He opened the bureau's middle drawer. "B, Palmerton is still skulking around. I wouldn't put it past the asshole to stalk Sal, hoping to find you."

This far too reasonable point turned her insides to mush. Yes, Justine had considered using Meade as a buffer to Lenny. In the kitchen, a less intimate place than this isolated cabin. Compared to Lenny, Meade was a sanctuary—but that didn't make him any less a hazard to her heart. Now he'd appointed himself the role of her protector against Lenny. Who was going to protect her from him?

He tossed gray sweatpants and a gray t-shirt on the bed, then slammed the drawer shut. "And C, nobody trusts you to follow doctor's orders."

Which would not be an issue if she were in her own space, stranded by a snowstorm a quarter of a mile from the lodge. What could she do there except lounge about? She didn't even have her phone so she could listen to her book. She might go stir crazy enough to beg Lenny to take her back to Brooklyn—if he were sneaky enough to track her down—confirming Meade's point B. "Who's nobody?"

"Me," Meade admitted. "Darby and Sal, too, but mostly me, because I'm the one who's been watching you refuse to take care of yourself because you have some bug up your ass about keeping your job."

He jerked his head toward the suitcase as he snatched up the clothes he'd thrown on the bed. "Sal packed a few of your belongings. Change into something comfortable enough to make icing your leg easy. I'll be back in a few minutes."

As he swapped his jeans for sweatpants, Meade pondered Justine's claim that the Urgent Care nurse had called him a hero. Talk about boggling the mind. He'd tried. He'd failed. Spectacularly.

He checked the refrigerator to confirm that Sal had stocked enough meals for two people over the next few days and wondered if the gods were offering him a second chance. Either that or demons were messing with his head.

His money was on the demons. What had he been thinking when he arranged to be snowed in with Justine? This wasn't the plot of one of Andromeda's novels. He and Justine were flesh and blood people, and given the way he felt about her, flesh was the last thing he should have on his mind. But it was too late to pivot, and all the excuses he'd spouted were still valid.

After he'd started a pot of coffee and stoked the fire, he figured he'd given Justine enough time to change. He knocked on the closed bedroom door. "Are you decent?"

"Yes." She sounded petulant.

"Good." He opened the door. She wore pale purple flannel printed with steaming green mugs. She'd pulled the bed's orange comforter across her lap. He figured her outfit meant she'd finished giving him grief. Tonight, anyway.

"Satisfied?" She lifted her chin as if to dare him to argue.

No way would he answer that question because he wouldn't be satisfied until his fingers were tangled in her hair as he kissed her, until her legs were draped over his shoulders and she moaned his name as he tasted her, or until her thighs were clamped against his torso as he—

Don't go there.

He leaned against the doorjamb, arms crossed over his chest and wished he hadn't changed out of his jeans. Sweatpants revealed too much. "Here's our story: as far as anyone except Sal is concerned, I took you to Urgent Care in Lake Placid, then stashed you in a hotel room because it's the only way to force you to stay off your leg."

"I don't like being forced," she muttered. "It smacks of your need to plunder and loot."

Meade uncrossed his arms and jammed his fists into his pockets. "You think I'm a villain because I wanted your leg looked at? Thanks a lot. I might not be a hero but making me out to be a bad guy is just wrong."

Plus it hurt. A lot. Purposely stranding them together might not be his best idea, even though Andromeda heartily approved, but most of his motive was pure.

"Are you not trying to control me by holding me hostage?"

Meade summoned his inner macho and snorted. "I pity anyone who tries to control you. You'd poison them if you didn't skewer them first. I'm shocked Palmerton is intact."

"Then why am I here?"

So I can take care of you. But he couldn't tell her that. It sounded too... wussy. Maybe he wasn't a hero, but he wasn't a wimp, either.

He opted for the rest of the truth. "So you can heal. I want you operating at full power. God help me, I like you."

Her jaw dropped. Her lower lip trembled.

"I like you a lot," he admitted. "Maybe too much."

Her eyes widened until they resembled shot glasses brimming with whiskey.

Confessing his attraction embarrassed him, but the words kept flowing. "I want to really kiss you. This afternoon? That wasn't a kiss. I didn't taste you, and I wonder what you taste like. Your mouth. Your skin." *Body parts better left unnamed.*

He imagined the smutty details he wanted to say to her, the words he kept bottled inside, except when he was at the keyboard. The desire that ruined his sleep. The erotic scenarios he shouldn't be thinking, much less discussing with her.

Swallowing wasn't the only hard thing. His sweatpants betrayed him.

"I like you, too," she admitted in a low voice. "And I wish you really had kissed me."

Her words were a sucker punch to his gut. She wanted him. This crazy lust was taunting both of them. For one moment, one all-too-brief lapse, he conjured more fantasies—her soft gasps against his ear as he thrust into her; her strong fingers clutching his shoulders; her internal spasms as her climax coaxed him to orgasm; the aftermath of love, when she was limp and warm in his arms.

He adjusted his stance, hoping to conceal his erection. "Damn it, Justine. Don't you understand? We can't get involved."

"I know. Being stranded here with you during the storm scares the stuffing out of me because I'm afraid of what will happen—I'm not afraid of you, but of me. Us."

The sadness in her voice nearly undid him. Because he was afraid of them together, too. If he didn't watch himself, he'd be quoting his damn work in progress to her. His truth. His fucking goddamn emotions.

He was in so much trouble.

He fought his lightheadedness and told himself to man up. "I think about sex with you all the time. But don't worry. I'm not going to touch you. Sex would only make things more awkward between us. It complicates everything."

He tried to laugh, but the sound that emerged was something he didn't recognize. "Trust me, I know. The last time I had sex with my muse, I ended up married to her. Not happening again."

Memories of Elaine should have squelched his lust for Justine. No such luck.

Justine's chin jerked and her eyes narrowed. "Your ex-wife was your muse?"

"Not important."

"The Puck it's not. How is turning me into your muse any different from Lenny trying to franchise me?"

"A muse is an inspiration. A franchise is a money-making venture." He forced a smile. "You do inspire me."

"You still plan to make money off me."

If she was trying to piss him off, it was working. Thank God.

"No, I plan to make money off a book I write. My work, not yours. Big difference."

"I knew I never should have let you into my kitchen," she muttered.

"I'm not Palmerton. I'm not asking you to do anything you don't want to do, and I'm not asking you to change. I'm not asking jack-shit from you, except to stay off your fucking leg."

CHAPTER 26

JUSTINE GLARED AT MEADE'S retreating back. He might not be Lenny, thank Child, Puck, and Ramsey, but they had at least one thing in common: running away the minute the situation started to simmer.

"What kind of books do you write?" She'd seen the front of his sweatpants and wavered between being flattered by his condition and irritated he'd fled. If she focused on that frustration, she could ignore how turned on she was by the thought of a real kiss from him. Maybe. Her internal muscles were still clenching. Her skin prickled. If he touched her, she would implode.

"Doesn't matter," he tossed over his shoulder.

"What's your pen name? What kind of books do you write?" she shouted after him. "Don't you think your *oeuf*ing muse ought to have a clue?"

"What difference does my genre make? I write for a living, but what I churn out doesn't define me, not the way cooking matters to you." He faced her again, his blue eyes as bright as a gas flame in the gloom of the cabin.

She kept her attention fixed on his face because... well, because of his arousal. Checking him out seemed... rude. Provocative. They'd already agreed to ignore whatever this thing was between them, even though neither one of them was doing a very good job.

"And I know nothing about you except you're a classically trained chef who merely wants to feed people," he continued. "Oh, and your ex-partner is a rat you should have poisoned."

Even the dim light couldn't hide how his knuckles whitened where he gripped the doorjamb. His chest shuddered as he deeply inhaled. "Here's the thing." He cleared his throat. "I wasn't talking about me and you, not really. I was, uh, channeling the hero in my new book."

The words sliced at her. "What do you mean?"

"Like I said. You inspire me. I'm a writer. I'm supposed to make a reader want what I'm peddling." He sounded as though he were choking. "Good to know I haven't lost my mojo."

"What do you write? Porn?"

He jerked upright and released the door frame. The blue flame in his eyes flared as if she'd thrown grease on the burner.

"No."

"Then why are you ashamed of what you write?"

"Who said I'm ashamed?"

"You act as if you were judged for whatever you do, the same as I'm supposed to be embarrassed for listening to romance."

Time to refocus their conversation. The kind of books he wrote didn't matter, unless he followed through on his threat to Lenny and put her name in the acknowledgements. But they could hash that out later. "Which reminds me, my phone must have fallen out when you tossed my bag in your truck. I need it."

He could use a cooling off, judging by the way his sweatpants tented. Tackling snowdrifts for her phone ought to do the trick. Payback for claiming his seductive words were merely passages he pulled from the book he was writing.

Instead, he narrowed his eyes. "I'm not going out in the storm to search for your phone. You don't need it."

Her chest tightened. Her audio book player was only one of the apps on her phone. She'd been planning future menus, writing shopping lists—no internet required for many apps to be useful for her. "I beg to differ. If I'm going to be stuck in your bed for the next week, I can't stare at the ceiling. I need things to occupy my time." *You.* "Like listening to my book."

"You haven't finished the book yet?"

"I keep getting interrupted, but I could finish the book this week if I had my phone."

Meade hesitated before repeating his refusal to brave the storm. "Have you tried reading a book the old-fashioned way?" he asked, before vanishing from her sight.

Now what did he have up his sleeve?

She had to stop thinking of him in terms of potential. Sexually. His impeccable logic resembled her own. Abstinence shouldn't be an issue. They were on the same page.

Except the bed linens smelled like him, spice and citrus, and whatever his body chemistry did to his soap. Delicious. If she recreated his unique aroma in the kitchen, she would make a fortune. Not that she would share. She wanted to keep the fragrance close. Personal.

He returned with a shopping bag filled with paperback books. "Here you go. Sal thought of everything. I guess Darby made her assistant manager for a reason."

She couldn't remember the last time she'd relaxed with a physical book. She usually listened while she worked, multi-tasking, because her plate overflowed on a regular basis. The past week proved the point, with her time spent preparing for another snowstorm so the guests in the cabins wouldn't go hungry or have to subsist on substandard fare.

Meade spilled the books onto the mattress next to her. "I see Sal sent lots of romance to keep you busy."

Justine selected a paperback. "Andromeda Zeus, *Web of Deceit*. I hope *Desire's Revenge* is in here."

"Nope."

"Did you look? Or did you steal the copy for your own private collection?" She couldn't resist a sly smile, complete with waggling eyebrows. "I mean, everyone here is awfully familiar with the story. They must have multiple copies in the library."

Meade squirmed. Then he scowled. "I don't need to steal books."

"She packed almost all Andromeda Zeus books," Justine observed as she pawed through the pile. "Oh. Wait. Here's a

Dublin Kennedy mystery. Oh, and a Tudor York historical romance. Tudor York sounds like a pen name. What do you think?"

"I think authors use pen names for lots of reasons, usually to protect their privacy."

A concept she appreciated. "I can relate."

Meade did his snort noise again. "I read the online news covering your scandal while you were with the doctor. Trust me, you were lucky compared to other stuff I've seen."

"You don't get to judge my experiences," she reminded him. She lifted her chin, daring him to contradict her. "The situation invaded my privacy. I'd better not pick up your next book and find you've shredded my dignity or my life on the pages."

His lips parted. Pure evil glinted in his teeth. "You'd need to know my pen name."

Meade enjoyed how Justine's face flashed her conflicting emotions. Her reactions eased his tension. The urge to strip her naked and bury himself deep inside her subsided. His lust didn't vanish. No, his desire went underground, lurking instead of dominating.

She chose another book, read the title, then placed it in the bag.

He decided to reassure her. "You don't know my pen name because no one values privacy more than I do." *Just ask my ex-wife.* "Why would I do to you what I wouldn't want done to me? I would never write anything to paint you in a bad light or embarrass you."

Her attention remained on repacking the books.

"If I were going to skewer anyone, I would aim for Palmerton. Not you." *Never you.*

"Fine," she muttered.

"Do you want anything before I head upstairs?" Their conversation was pointless. The sooner he delved into his story, the sooner he'd banish his inappropriate reactions to Justine. "A glass of water for next to the bed?"

"I'm good." Her voice retained a chill.

"Then goodnight."

He escaped before he surrendered to stupid impulse—crawling into bed with her topped the list

He decided to skip the bourbon. Alcohol would only sharpen the teeth of his desire and numb his restraint. Pounding his lust onto the hard drive via keyboard was a better choice. A safer existence. Bonus: his book would get written. Colleen Eaton, Basil Graham, and Colby Quince would come alive on the page, as unlike Justine, Heath, and himself as possible.

Heath? Since Palmerton's arrival, Meade had forgotten about the wounded soldier in his story. If he was going to dip into the why-choose subgenre, it wasn't going to be one woman

with multiple men, written by Andromeda. Andre Jove, however—

Maybe Andromeda could have the wounded soldier being
court martialed for killing the ex, which would clear the way
for the hero and solve his love triangle problem.

Meade carried his laptop to the loft. The metal rings clattered on the rod as he drew the heavy, quilted privacy curtain
across the opening. He booted his computer and got to work.

Two thousand pulled-from-his-guts words later, he yawned.
His jaw cracked with the effort. Meade preferred post-mid-
night writing sessions. Job-shadowing Justine messed with his
sleep patterns; caring for her might throw them completely off
kilter.

He stood. Stretched. More joints popped and snapped like
his favorite breakfast cereal when doused with milk. He hated
getting old. His body protested every hour he'd hunched over a
keyboard. Trudging through snow and hauling Justine around
didn't count as a true workout.

He drew back the curtain a couple feet. A wall of heat greeted
him. Even so, he needed to tend the stove and check on Justine.

The bedroom was dark. He assumed Justine slept. Sal had
banked the fire to last until morning, leaving Meade nothing
to do except get back to work. Luckily, writing didn't always
require typing words. At times, thinking produced more story.

He stood at the window and peered into the night. The icy
BBs had morphed into giant white flakes tumbling from the
sky, unfurling like a lace curtain or bridal veil.

Bridal veil? Where in the hell had that come from? Oh yeah. The manuscript. Of course. Andromeda wrote romance. The happily-ever-after genre usually included a wedding, either on the page or in the offing. Had he ever used the imagery of snow as lace before? He didn't remember. Another reason to ditch Andromeda. He didn't want to be the author who kept repeating himself.

Hah. He'd ask Justine to keep an eye out for the phrase while she read his backlist—if he could figure out how without revealing his pen name.

A rustling behind him alerted him to Justine's presence. "What are you doing up?"

"Bathroom," Justine muttered as she limped to her destination. The door closed firmly behind her.

Since she was awake, she might as well ice the knee for a few minutes. He mentally prepared to battle with her as he fixed an ice pack. The toilet flushed. Pipes rattled as water flowed through the faucet. He waited with an icepack and dishtowel until she emerged.

She looked at the towel, then him. Shrugged.

"Couch or bed?" he asked.

She ought to be grateful he gave her a choice.

"Sofa." She reached for the icepack. "If I had my phone, I would set a timer. Since I don't, you're on duty."

"I volunteered," he reminded her.

"Why?" She stretched out her leg and wrapped her bare knee with the towel. The motion exposed her thigh. Her naked thigh.

The flannel sleep shirt barely covered her, at least not from the point of view of a man who... who... who what? Lusted after her?

"Why don't I get you a blanket?" he hoarsely asked.

"Because it's hotter than a pizza oven in here." She brushed a hank of hair away from her damp forehead. "Is your offer of a glass of water still open?"

"Of course."

"As cold as possible, please."

He took his time.

He handed the glass to her, and she held it against her cheek before bringing it to her mouth. "Thank you," she said, after several gulps. "Do you have to burn the stove so hot?"

"You ought to be in the loft," Meade muttered.

"No thanks." Justine took another drink. "I'm sorry I'm displacing you, but you volunteered."

Meade didn't trust himself to speak.

Justine set the glass on the coffee table. "You're a throwback, aren't you?"

"What's that supposed to mean?" He purposely inserted a growl in his tone.

Her lips tilted up at the corners. "You're an old-fashioned gentleman."

He debated whether to be flattered or insulted. "Again, what the hell are you insinuating?"

"You're nice. You have a wide streak of... honor."

He studied the ceiling instead of facing her. A dust-beaded cobweb draped across an exposed beam captivated him. "Go back to bed, Justine. Leave the ice pack."

CHAPTER 27

DAY ONE OF JUSTINE'S incarceration dragged. She dozed. Stared at the ceiling. She had nothing to do except read, a pastime Meade reminded her of each time he arrived with an icepack for her leg. If she had her phone, she could have played solitaire. He continued to refuse to go out to his Hummer and search for it, although he made trips to the woodpile on the porch.

"Why don't you give me one of your books to read?" She didn't want to overdose on romances, afraid too much would dilute her pleasure in reading them.

He'd snorted.

By day two, cabin fever had set in. She wasn't used to inaction. Even after Just Food's closing, she'd kept busy dealing with the fallout. Bankruptcy. Job hunting.

Meade carried her to the sofa, where she peered out the windows at the mesmerizing snowfall. She gave him a pass on retrieving her phone from his vehicle while the sky continued to unload on them. She had to be content reading paperbacks while he worked.

He descended from the loft and joined her for meals. He made sure she had a fresh ice pack every couple of hours. They conversed, Meade asking chef-related questions or her opinion about the books she read. Her reading particularly interested him, as if he were a professor planning a pop quiz on the works of Andromeda Zeus.

His probing made her uncomfortable. Her crazy imagination plugged his image into the love scenes, replacing the hero who'd planted an impassioned kiss on the heroine with Meade. The transformation complicated her fantasy, especially when Meade solicited her opinion.

"Have you considered switching to writing romance?" she asked. "You have a heroic mindset."

The look he gave her defied interpretation. Her knee wasn't the only body part needing ice. The prose turned her on. *Meade* turned her on.

On the third morning, Justine decided her flannel sleep shirt had to go. The fabric was limp from her perspiration and smelled sour. She refused to put on that *oeuf*ing garment again after taking a sponge bath. She searched Meade's bureau drawers until she found a t-shirt, which protected her modesty by hanging to her knees. Being a guy, he probably wouldn't notice that she'd pilfered it.

She made the mistake of using his soap to scrub herself clean at the bathroom sink. Well, not scrub. The terry wash cloth was just nubby enough for her to imagine it was Meade's hand spreading the fragrant lather down the side of her neck, caressing her collar bone, fondling her breasts, moving lower, across her belly... and lower still. The scent clung to her skin. Not even drying herself neutralized it. No, the coarse towel became Meade's unshaven cheeks and chin, as his tongue lapped every drop of water from her body.

Donning his t-shirt intensified her sense of being embraced by him.

She really needed a break from reading romance novels.

She wobbled to the main room, where she reclined on the sofa. Meade must have heard her in the bathroom because a steaming mug of coffee was waiting next to her book on the coffee table. Other than refusing to look for her phone, he excelled at pampering her. No wonder she kept viewing him as a hero, despite his insistence that he lacked the necessary qualities.

She liked being pampered. By Meade.

Since she didn't see him, she figured he was working in his office. *Good.* Less distracting for her. She sipped the coffee, then settled back to immerse herself in the spicy story Andromeda Zeus had written.

Two pages later, the door opened, and Meade stomped into the room along with air cold enough to flash-freeze boiling water. He dumped his armload of snow-crusted firewood onto the floor, then slammed the door.

Exactly like the survivalist mountain man in the story she was reading.

"Do you have to burn the stove so hot all the time?" She plucked the already-damp cotton of her t-shirt away from her chest and blamed the burst of frigid air for her puckered nipples.

"Can't let the pipes freeze." He stamped his feet, dislodging clumps of snow from the bottoms of his jeans.

"I'm not suggesting you let the fire go out, just die down a bit." *To smolder. Like me.* "You wouldn't have to make as many trips outside because we wouldn't be using as much wood."

A mountain man would know that, would know there were better ways of staying warm than roasting them in dry heat. Except Meade wasn't her mountain man.

"Guess what? I figured that part out all by myself," he grumbled as he pulled off his jacket and hung it on a peg near the door.

She ought to be reading her romance, not fixating on the broadness of Meade's shoulders—shoulders she knew too well from being draped across them—as he unbuttoned his flannel shirt.

She pressed a finger against the wildly fluttering pulse in her throat, but the pressure did no good. "I'm glad you're smarter than you act." Bantering came too easily to her now that she'd spent two days absorbing the flirtatious snark at which Andromeda Zeus excelled.

Meade took off the shirt and flung it on the newel, as if he were a Chippendales dancer or auditioning for the next installment of *Magic Mike*. He had the body for the part. The blueberry-colored waffle Henley that he wore beneath the flannel clung to muscles he shouldn't have from sitting at a computer all day. The man had stamina. He'd carried her a mile in a storm, for Puck's sake.

She picked up her coffee and finished it. Thinking about Meade's endurance was as unsafe as any other thoughts he inspired. She was better off reading her book.

Except Meade continued to distract her when he sat on the bench and began unlacing his boots. She'd noticed his big, thick fingers before, when he typed on his laptop. They should not be as agile as they were. He undid the bootlaces as deftly as Lazlo had loosened Araminta's stays in *Desire's Revenge*.

Justine wondered what those fingers would feel like on her. In her.

Meade stood. Despite his efforts, the cuffs of his jeans remained covered with clotted snow. "Since you're not using the bedroom, I'm going in there to change."

"Don't forget to lock the door behind you. In case I decide to make a fool of myself," Justine quipped. Oh, Puck, if he ever found out how close to the truth her laughingly stated words were, she would be forced to take her chances in the storm and hike back to the main lodge on her bad knee.

Meade stared at her for a few unblinking, unnerving seconds before averting his gaze.

Justine squeezed her eyes shut. She didn't know what had gotten into her. Her mood had to be triggered by the books. Flirting didn't come naturally to her. She prided herself on her professional behavior. She'd never teased a man in her life. Her past romantic relationships were grounded in... boredom.

No. Her current reading material put sex in her brain. Successful relationships required mutual respect, not sexual attraction. Two years ago, she would have pointed to her life with Lenny as a perfect example.

She exhaled. Lately, she'd speculated if she'd ever felt anything for Lenny except relief for his handling—or mishandling—the non-cooking side of Just Food. Their sex life had been... adequate. Not earth shattering, but enough for her.

Maybe she hadn't expected enough, secure in her belief that the romance novels she consumed were fantasy, not reality.

She placed her book on the coffee table and swung her feet to the floor. Resting her leg for two days had reduced the swelling in her knee. She owed Meade... a fabulous meal for forcing her to obey doctor's orders. Nothing more. She slowly climbed to her feet and headed for the kitchen to refill her mug.

The bedroom door opened. Her bare foot landed in a half-melted puddle of snow. She slipped, twisting her knee. The dregs of her coffee splashed to the floor, followed by the mug itself. She would have fallen if Meade hadn't caught her. Awkwardly.

Very awkwardly.

One hand clasped her waist. The other landed on her breast. Her nipple immediately responded to his touch. The hem of the t-shirt rode up, exposing her undies.

Meade froze. Justine would have sworn paralysis set in, except for the embarrassing reaction in her body. Something in her brain went click, click, click, like the electric ignition on a gas stove trying to spark. Any second, she would whoosh.

MEADE DIDN'T KNOW WHAT to do. He was tangled in a wet dream or the best fantasy of his life. Or Andromeda had decided to commandeer and narrate his reality.

"What are you doing off the couch?" Speaking through his tight throat hurt.

"I need more coffee."

"You couldn't wait?"

"No."

Either his imagination worked overtime, or she arched, ever so slightly, pressing her breast against his hand. Her eyes were wide and liquid. Her lips were parted, as though daring him to kiss her, to slip his tongue into the warm, damp recesses of her mouth and devour her like a man who'd gone without nourishment for far too long.

His sweatpants betrayed how much he wanted her. Why had he opted to wear clothing intent on betraying his desire whenever he got within a foot of her? Oh yeah. Quick, easy, comfortable. Except she deserved much more than quick and easy and comfortable.

She leaned into his touch, and just that slight movement, that small hint of her possible surrender had him battling to breathe. She snuggled even closer. Oh, God, her bare, her naked, her bare-naked thigh rested against his bare-naked forearm, her impossibly silky skin a hot caress all its own. Her t-shirt had crept—

Wait, that was his t-shirt. Possession gripped him, and his descriptors fled. They didn't matter.

He brushed his thumb against the tight point of her nipple. She shuddered. Inhaled sharply, then slowly exhaled his name.

Her coffee-scented breath fluttered against his face. He brushed his mouth against hers, catching a hint of her essence hiding behind the caffeine.

Her fingers combed through the hair on the back of his head as she pulled him closer still. Her tongue traced the contours of his lips.

He lost... everything. Control. Sense of time. Sense of decorum and right and wrong and place and everything except the woman in his arms. Somehow they were on the couch, and she was under him—finally, finally under him—pressing against him as if trying to absorb him.

He couldn't recall ever being kissed with such enthusiasm. Such demand. Not that his brain remembered anything, held any thought except the urge to possess this woman.

He abandoned her mouth. Scraped his unshaven cheeks along her throat to her breast and that needy, needy nipple. Pulled the puckered flesh into his mouth, tasting her through the worn cotton of her t-shirt.

Her soft whimper only spurred him on.

Her hands, so tiny but so strong, slid beneath the waists of his sweatpants and boxers. Her thumbs hooked under the elastic and tugged.

He could take a hint. He rolled away long enough to yank the garments down his ass to his thighs, freeing his cock. Freeing him. No more constraints. He could claim this woman he had wanted for so long.

She claimed him first, her fingers circling his erection and stroking.

His clumsy hands shoved her t-shirt to her waist, then jerked her panties out of his way. He ran one of his thick, inept fingers through her wetness to make sure she was ready for him.

Oh, she was ready.

She splayed her legs, and he settled between them. He pushed into her. She was warm and snug and welcoming and grateful and giving, the epitome of every romance heroine he'd ever written. He thrust as if his existence depended on joining with her, becoming one with her, his perfect fantasy, what he'd been searching for his entire life.

Her thighs clamped his ribs; her body mimicking his rhythm. Following his lead. Dissolving when he dissolved.

He rested his forehead against hers as he gulped in much-needed oxygen. He was crushing her, but his body needed to reassemble itself, separate from her, and reconnect to his brain before he could function again.

Eventually he raised himself on his arms. He peered at her, unsure of what to expect.

What he saw hit him. Hit him hard. Harder than he'd ever imagined anything could hit him.

He saw his future. He saw forever.

Chapter 28

Justine sprawled on the sofa, trying to recapture her composure. Meade fled to the bathroom without speaking. Words were unnecessary. Unnecessary? She couldn't even think in words. A barrage of emotions she was too befuddled to name chased language away.

She sat up and tugged the t-shirt over her butt.

She heard water running, pipes rattling, then silence. The bathroom door opened. Meade emerged and handed her a warm, wet cloth before turning away and finding the view from the frost-etched window more alluring than her.

Or he was giving her privacy to wipe away the evidence of their... interlude.

He remained silent, as if regretting what had happened between them. As if he were ashamed he'd succumbed to their mutual neediness.

Except she refused to be ashamed. She wouldn't let him get away with wallowing in whatever nonsense muted him.

"If I'd said no, you would have stopped." Her voice creaked. She crumpled the damp cloth in her fist and dropped it onto the coffee table. "You listen to me."

His head jerked up, gaze meeting hers. An unreadable emotion flared in the depths of his eyes.

She rejected whatever blame was about to be splattered around like an uncovered bowl of marinara in a microwave. They were adults and responsible for their actions. "I wanted what happened as much as you did."

"I didn't use a condom."

Oh.

"I don't—my ex took care of contraception," Meade continued, his cheeks brightening with pink. "And I tested negative for STDs after we split."

Her first reaction insisted this particular conversation should have happened before the action. She didn't want to consider the deeper truth he'd revealed: he hadn't been with anyone since his divorce.

At least she could reassure him. "I visited the free clinic after Lenny left. I'm clean. And I have an IUD."

Meade shakily exhaled. "I would have, I mean—"

"It's a non-issue, Meade."

His Adam's apple bobbed in his throat. "I can't think clearly around you. My brain cells take a nose-dive south, along with my blood."

At least he didn't blame her.

"Same." She wished she could get up, wrap her arms around his waist, and rest her cheek against his back. "Why are you beating yourself up? We're consenting adults."

"I feel as though I took advantage of you." He sounded miserable. "Darby told you I could be trusted, and I violated that trust."

The man was pushing himself through an emotional meat grinder for no reason.

"I didn't say no," she reminded him. "I didn't tell you to stop or try to stop you." *I enthusiastically participated and anytime you want to get your head out of your butt, here I am.*

He peered at her, as if trying to pry into her brain for the truth. Then he shook his head.

"I'm sorry you regret what happened." Okay, she hadn't meant to apologize for anything, but Meade obviously suffered for nothing. "I don't."

"You think I regret—?" He snorted, as only he could do. "Oh, no. I only regret not taking more time with you, and that whatever this is between us will mess up your job here."

Oh yeah. Her job. The one she not only needed but loved. Meade's respect for her priorities warmed her.

"Then what are you doing over there?" She patted the sofa cushion next to her. The scene of their crime.

He cleared his throat. "And I'm really grateful you didn't pull a knife on me."

"There's always time later, especially if you give me a good reason."

He stepped closer. "And what would constitute a good reason?"

"Let's start with being too dense to understand that what happened a few minutes ago wasn't a bad thing. Worrying that I'm going to run screaming to Darby. Shall I go on?"

"Not yet." And with the ease he so frequently demonstrated with her, he plucked her off the sofa and into his arms. "Let's take this discussion to the bedroom."

Once they reached the bedroom, they sent their clothes fluttering to the floor. Meade stretched her out on the mattress and stared. "What do you like?"

"You."

"I like you, too, but how do you like to be touched?" He ran his thumb under her bottom lip.

"I won't know until you touch me. How do you like to be touched?" Justine brushed her fingers through the patch of wiry hair curling between his pecs. His skin was warm beneath her palms. The man had muscles, but she'd yet to see him work out. How did a desk jockey maintain such a physique?

"How can you not know what feels good to you?" His eyes burned bright above her.

"Touch me. I'll let you know what works for me."

Meade rolled away from her and sat up. "Are you trying to tell me you'd never climaxed before?"

Justine laughed. "You flatter yourself. Deservedly so, but for the wrong reasons. I like sex, but it's not high on my list of priorities."

"Except while you read romance novels."

"The sex is part of why I enjoy them." Embarrassing to admit. She dragged her fingertips across one of his nipples, which tightened into a hard nub.

She'd acquired a trick or two from her steamy book habit.

"You do realize you've challenged me." His hoarse voice belied his lazy smile.

"No challenge. We're learning about each other." She struggled to keep the questioning note out of her voice. Learning, then saying goodbye. Meade wasn't permanent, and she needed the stability of her job. She would see him the next time he returned to The Write Place to finish a book and possibly resume their affair. If either of them wanted to.

The many reasons why a physical relationship with him was a bad idea flitted through her brain.

Until then, they were stranded together.

"I finally get the answers to everything I've wondered about you." Meade's husky tone drew chills. He trailed his fingers across her breasts, her ribs, her belly. Lower. "I've been imagining you naked and in my bed, almost from the first. I'm glad you don't shave or wax. I like knowing I'm with a woman, not a child. Points for you."

Justine's cheeks heated. "Oh? You're keeping score?"

He chuckled, low and throaty. "I've compiled a mental list of everything I intend to discover about your body."

His plan sounded good to her.

"First, though, I want to kiss you."

Meade tried to control the trembling in his hands. His fantasies of the past week were coming true, and he didn't want to rush Justine. He'd already wham-bammed her. Not a good start. Not when she was like a perfectly written novel he needed to read and cherish one word at a time.

He stretched out beside her and cupped her cheek in his palm. His lips brushed hers. He'd tried to devour her earlier, and consuming her drove him at the time, but now was different. Now he wanted her to wallow in sex with him and make the intimacy important. Now the pace mattered, and that pace had to be slow. Languid. Attentive to her.

Her lips were soft. Plump. He drew the lower one into his mouth and gently sucked. Although their bodies rested against each other, he didn't grope. Instead, he held her face steady as he savored her mouth. His fingers tangled in her hair.

He'd forgotten how much he enjoyed kissing. He did not consider foreplay an annoying preliminary to getting laid. Meade loved the intimacy of sharing breath, exchanging tastes, being close enough to imprint Justine's unique aroma into his psyche, making her a permanent part of him, no matter what happened in the future.

He could have been kissing her for a week; he needed to make up for lost time. Needed to stockpile the memories for future solitary days and nights, snowbound or sweltering in summer. If only it were possible to absorb the traits that attracted him to her—her fearlessness, her sense of worth, her awareness of her essential identity, and the meaning of her life. Her self-assurance. She was one of the strongest women he'd ever met, and by far the most intriguing. She'd defined herself and woe to anyone who tried to rewrite her script.

Meade wanted to plagiarize it.

Justine's mouth was a prayer. A banquet. A symphony. A safe place in a threatening environment. He released her lower lip and eased his tongue inside, tracing the outer contours before seeking a deeper connection.

"Mm," she hummed and wiggled closer to him, except no closer existed unless he worked his way inside her again. Which was a fine idea. A very fine idea.

He released her hair and dragged his fingers along her cheek. The side of her neck. Barely paused to tweak a nipple before skimming down her ribs and her hip. He burrowed his hand between their bodies, confirming her readiness for him matched his for her.

Justine rolled onto her back, pulling him with her. Every part of his body except one turned to putty where she touched him. Every bit of his strength gathered in his dick. Justine's hand joined his, her fingers warm and flexible as she ensured his readiness. Her legs splayed, knees rising. She guided him home.

Home. He'd been homeless his whole life and never realized the lack.

CHAPTER 29

"SHOWER SEX ISN'T A good idea." Justine hated sharing a shower. Elbows in the nose, not enough space to breathe—her list of reasons didn't matter to Meade.

"Who mentioned sex? I'm here to prop you up." His size claimed most of the space in the compact shower stall. If she slipped, his body would cushion her fall.

He kept his word. Wet and naked equaled temptation, but he helped her wash her hair and held her as she lathered her body with his citrus-and-spice soap. He didn't offer physical assistance when she cleansed her breasts or between her legs, but his grip on her ribs tightened as if he was preventing his hands from joining hers as she scrubbed herself, and the heat in his gaze promised he would inspect her efforts once they were out of the shower.

Well, he wasn't the only one who could use slow, wet heat to tenderize something tough until it fell apart. His turn was coming.

Their conversation consisted of logistics. "Move a little." "Let me rinse your hair." Nothing overtly sexual, and all the more sensual for the lack.

His ablutions were quick, but still more intimate than anything she'd ever shared with anyone. She wasn't plotting how quickly she could leave, dry off, and get dressed. Instead, she watched his hands, those fingers that had fascinated her almost from day one, work the suds through his chest hair, around his balls and semi-erect penis. And how was he still semi-erect? She thought they'd taken care of that not-so-little situation.

After Meade finally shut off the water, he told her to wait. He stepped outside the stall, returning a moment later with an oversized orange bath sheet. He swaddled her before carrying her to the main room. The heat from the woodstove caressed her damp skin and dripping hair.

He planted a kiss on the top of her head as he placed her on the sofa. He vanished into the bedroom.

She closed her eyes. Being thoroughly clean again felt marvelous.

Meade returned, wearing sweatpants and carrying a fresh t-shirt for her, as well as her hairbrush. He hadn't shaved in a few days, and the dark scruff on his cheeks and chin lent him a menacing air that failed to fool Justine.

She just didn't know the future of their... situation.

She pulled on the t-shirt, then picked up her hairbrush.

Meade covered her hand with his. "Let me."

He propped her between his legs and gently began dragging the brush through her tangled hair. Droplets of cool water fled the strands as the bristles approached. His bare chest warmed her back.

"What now?" Justine mused aloud.

Meade paused. "What about now?"

She gestured toward the window. The snow tapered off. Their retreat from reality was drawing to a close. Soon someone would deliver a meal or two and discover her in Meade's cabin.

"The real world is coming for us." If nothing else, she regretted wasting two days of not opening herself to what Meade offered.

Meade used his fingers to separate a tangle, tugging lightly at her scalp. "The real world," he repeated.

"Do you regret what happened?" He'd had time to reconsider, and she needed to know.

He answered immediately. "No."

"Any ideas about what we do going forward?" She didn't have a spontaneous cell in her body. After her recent past, she craved security. Not the "we-bumped-uglies-you-must-marry-me" kind of security, but—

"No." His fingers tightened in her hair.

She'd never felt as fragile as she did at that moment. Even in her bleakest hour after the Just Food debacle, she'd found inner strength to draw on. Courage to face the next obstacle.

Apparently she'd depleted her reservoir of nerves. Or thrown them away along with her common sense. She'd broken the first rule: she'd gotten involved with a guest. Darby now possessed valid reasons to fire her.

"You're thinking too hard," Meade said, as he resumed brushing her hair. "Don't."

"Easy for you to say. Eventually you're leaving. I want to keep working here."

His thighs tightened around her ribs. "And you will. I told you. Darby thinks you're in a hotel in Lake Placid, following doctor's orders to stay off your leg."

WHY DID JUSTINE WANT to talk things to death? Why couldn't she simply accept a relationship without forecasting emotions as if they were weather? The last thing Meade wanted to do was analyze their relationship or wish away this winterlude.

He inhaled deeply, feeling smug when he caught the scent of his soap mingling with her essence. If he were a hero in one of his books, he'd claim he'd marked his territory. He wished it were true. Except Justine would never be any man's territory.

In many ways, that was a relief. Defining her wasn't his responsibility.

This... thing with Justine was so new, so fresh, he didn't want to examine it, didn't want to tally orgasms, didn't want to inventory her physical responses to put them in a book. He simply wanted to enjoy her. Not the sex, the woman. Justine herself. He dreamed of spending forever sitting here like this, snug in their cabin in the woods, the snow isolating them from civilization. He loved brushing out her maple-syrup-colored hair to let the heat from the woodstove dry the strands. Talking to her was easy. He could be himself. Sex was a bonus. An essential bonus. But even if he hadn't made love to her, he would still cherish these stolen moments as some of the best in his life.

Taking care of someone who didn't demand his soul was easy.

The variety of emotions making love to her had triggered amazed him. The next time might reveal the origins of the universe. Didn't matter. Darby Winehouse's reaction didn't matter. Only Justine mattered. Justine with him. He didn't care for how long. Time stamps and labels didn't belong on feelings. He made a living spinning tales of love and romance and happily ever after, and he still had no clue what those things were, or if they even existed. All he knew, at that moment, was that he needed Justine as desperately as he needed his heart to beat.

His craving wasn't related to *Karleen's Cuisine*. And if he included any of his new insight into a story, India would drop him as a client. Or pitch his books to a paranormal line.

Not important. Everything he'd learned in the past couple hours was private. Extremely personal. So intensely emotional he didn't know if he would ever grasp his whole connection to

Justine. Until he absorbed what had happened, he could not, would not, let her go.

Justine cleared her throat. "This conversation belongs in the we-should-have-discussed-before-we-fell-into-bed category, but what happened is out of character for me."

"Same." He debated whether to admit she was only the second woman with whom he'd been intimate.

Justine blundered on. "At first, I assumed the books I've been reading aroused me, you know?"

"Yes." In the early days, when he'd started writing, he'd been plagued by the same problem.

"But I've been listening to romance novels for years. They've never sparked as intense a reaction in me before. You're the reason, not the books."

She'd been having the same effect on him since the first night.

"I'm not assuming we have a future. I don't expect anything," she added.

He set her brush on the coffee table. "I don't bed hop."

"Yeah, I figured as much when you told me you were tested after your divorce, and you don't pack condoms. Now I'm telling you that I, well, I respect myself too much to waste my... intimacy."

He slipped his arms around her waist. "One of the most attractive things about you is your self-respect." She didn't recognize the power of her sense of self-worth.

A faint rumble of an engine outside snagged his attention. The storm's weakening marked the end of their hiatus from reality.

"Sounds like Heath is clearing the lane to the main lodge."

Justine tensed ever so slightly, but Meade's attunement to her ran deeply enough to turn her reaction into a punch to his gut.

Re-entry meant confronting the immediate future, exactly what he didn't want to face. He braced himself. "How should we play this?"

She inched away from him. "Play?"

Okay. He should have chosen a better word. He rested his hand on her stomach, not wanting to lose the physical connection. "Sal will be descending on us soon. Do you want our relationship to be open, or should we hide our involvement?"

"What do you think?"

"Not my call. You're the one who works here. Staff members are your co-workers. People whose respect you want." His brain rejected any thought other than *Justine*. He only wanted to carry her back to bed and spend the day, the week, the next month eating her food and making love to her. He couldn't envision a future beyond that perfection.

"We tell the truth."

CHAPTER 30

"THE TRUTH?" MEADE ECHOED. "Truth has facets."

Justine wished she could stand and put distance between her and Meade. "Don't split hairs. I endured enough dishonesty from Lenny to last me a lifetime. I will not lie to Darby."

"I don't want to lie to her either."

Right. Justine had forgotten Meade had gone immediately to Darby to confess their kiss. That alone ignited deeper emotion toward him.

"And if there are repercussions—negative ones—I'm prepared to do right by you," Meade continued.

"Do right by me? What is that supposed to mean?"

"I'll make sure you're taken care of."

His words snuffed the spark. "I don't expect, want, or need to be taken care of."

"I know. That's why I enjoy pampering you."

She tried to crawl to the other end of the sofa, but Meade tightened his legs, effectively trapping her. "You're trying to control me."

"No. Never. Your uncontrollability is part of why I'm attracted to you."

She wanted to believe him, but being stranded in his cabin told a different story. He'd tricked her. Second thoughts about everything they'd done tumbled into her head, mirroring the snow outside dumping from the sky. The effect chilled her. Suffocated her.

She'd let her body rule her emotions. Her fault. Binge-reading romance novels lulled her into thinking... no, not thinking. Feeling. Lusting. She'd been stupid. *Oeufing* naïve.

"You're worrying too loud," Meade murmured. "I get why you're suspicious of ulterior motives—I googled you and Palmerton while we were at Urgent Care. You have every right to question everything, including me. But remember—you want your job at The Write Place. All I'm trying to do is make sure you're well enough to handle the work. I'm helping you, not controlling you."

He relaxed his grip on her. Swung his feet to the floor and stood. "If working here is not what you want, well, that's a different discussion for another time. Right now? I'm going to put on a shirt, then go upstairs to work. That way, when someone descends on us, they can't jump to conclusions."

He padded into the bedroom.

She needed to put on her big girl panties. Every word emerging from his mouth made sense. Lenny had scraped her raw enough that she'd forgotten how to trust her own instincts. Meade's mixed messages didn't help. Why didn't he consult her before driving her to Urgent Care? Before he'd stranded her in his cabin to not only rest her leg but also to hide her from Lenny? She refused to dismiss her problems with the high-handed way Meade steamrolled through his agenda, especially involving her.

He had controlled her from the moment he rescued her from the ditch. Drying her hair was only the latest instance of—she wasn't sure if it was manipulation or pampering. All she knew was that his behavior had the power to hurt her, especially now, after their incredible intimacy. She'd never experienced sex so... spiritually. She'd never expected anything more from the act than a quick climax to release tension. The romance novels she read weren't documentaries. Too many book characters confused orgasm for love. Connection didn't matter, not true, deep connection.

She'd never appreciated the difference until Meade.

He emerged from the bedroom wearing an ice-blue t-shirt printed with *Peace, Love, and the Oxford Comma*. Justine's throat closed. She wanted to stand behind him, slip her arms around his waist, and rest her cheek against his broad back. She longed to believe in him. Trust him.

He'd been taking care of her from the moment they'd met. He took the worst she could dish out, and still he'd stuck.

Even so, she did not want to love him.

Yes, he wanted something from her, but what he wanted reflected his regard for her. He didn't consider her a utensil. He appreciated her mind. Respected her reputation. And knew how to kiss.

No, no, no. Kissing only added to her confusion. Mouth on mouth only sucked out her common sense.

"What?" he asked, as if reading the turmoil in her brain.

"The books aren't to blame," she blurted.

He closed his eyes for a moment, as if praying. "I know," he said after he opened them again. "Well, maybe partly the books."

He understood what she meant without having her elaborate. Meade perceived her in ways Lenny never tried to plumb.

Nothing made sense to her. "You didn't read the books. You only knew what I told you, and I never mentioned their effect on me."

Emotions in a spectrum of red usually seen in ripening berries flitted across his face. He opened his mouth as though to speak.

A knock on the door distracted him.

She hadn't noticed the sound of the plow growing louder. Meade occupied all her senses. Now the vehicle rumbled like a hungry giant's stomach outside the cabin.

Meade's questioning facial expression morphed to neutral as he headed for the door.

MEADE'S GUTS TURNED TO slush. He should have confessed he'd written the books Justine had been reading. She'd given him the perfect opportunity, but he'd lost the chance when reality knocked. She wouldn't appreciate learning the truth later in their relationship.

Because yeah, he wanted a relationship with her. They'd manage, despite their circumstances. He welcomed the challenge.

He opened the door. The snowfall may have tapered to a few drifting flakes, but the vicious cold had intensified.

Heath stomped inside. His insulated snowsuit cast frigid air into the room. He whipped off his ski mask, sending bits of crusty ice flying.

"Would you like a cup of coffee?" Justine called from the couch.

Heath peered around Meade. "Godwin's been hiding you? Your boyfriend thinks you were abducted by the Abominable Snowman."

"Sal knew she was here," Meade said before realizing his statement might land Sal in hot water.

"Figures," Heath muttered, then smirked at Meade.

"I'm hiding from my ex," Justine explained.

"Darby thinks you're in a hotel in Lake Placid, resting your leg per doctor's orders."

"Well, I am resting my leg, too. I have a note from my doctor to give to her." Justine sounded anxious.

Meade's guts refroze.

Heath changed the subject. "I'm checking the cabins to make sure everyone survived and to see how you're doing on supplies."

"We're good," Meade said.

"Okay." Heath jerked his ski mask into place and left.

Meade waited until he heard the plow rumble away before telling Justine, "We need to talk."

Her eyes widened. "When a person says 'we need to talk' using that tone of voice, it's never good news. You're married, right? Or are involved in a serious relationship?"

"No! What kind of asshole do you think I am?" Yeah, he admitted to being an asshole, but he was a faithful asshole. He sat at the opposite end of the couch.

"I don't think you're a jerk," she replied.

"I'd like to keep it that way," he muttered. "You might change your mind after I tell you what I've done. Two things. One minor, the other fairly significant."

She scowled. "Do I get to choose the order?"

"Nope." He had to admit to his crimes in his own way. "I emailed a picture of your doctor's note to Darby while I warmed up the car at Urgent Care."

Justine's lips thinned. Her nostrils flared. "You searched my bag."

"Yes, but I swear, I didn't touch anything else. My many bad habits don't include poking into people's private stuff. I value my privacy and respect other people's."

"More of you doing what you believe is best for me?" The look she gave him could have secured the polar ice caps for the next millennium.

"I don't want you to lose your job, and Darby needed to know your status."

"So you didn't take my phone?"

Damn. He'd forgotten her phone. One more reason for her to be pissed. Three sins to confess. "I did not remove your phone from your bag. I didn't touch anything except the paperwork from Urgent Care."

She stared at him. Didn't speak.

"Your phone fell out of your coat pocket and—" He choked on the twisted version of the truth he'd planned to tell her. He couldn't lie to her. "I hid your phone at Urgent Care."

"You had no right to do that." A second millennium's worth of permafrost resided in her tone.

"No, I didn't. Except that's how Palmerton tracked you, and I don't want him to find you."

"His phone won't work here. No cell service, remember?"

"No *reliable* cell service," he corrected. "Sometimes I can get bars in the loft. But I also didn't want to risk your ex finding out about the diner ten miles up the road where there's free Wi-Fi. I didn't want him going there to track you down in your alleged hotel room."

"You took my phone to protect me?"

Meade wadded his fingers into his palms to keep from touching her. "Yes."

"And me listening to a romance novel without ear buds had nothing to do with why you stole my phone? Did you ever stop to think that I might use my apps for a lot of things?"

"I shut it off and found a safe place to hide it. Even if Palmerton traces the GPS to the medical center, he won't have an easy time finding the exact location."

"Gee, thanks."

Her sarcasm pleased him. He found the habit... endearing. Since he'd never heard her be snide with anyone else, he hoped it was her love language for him.

Oh shit.

Love language indeed. Well, time to fuck that up.

He uncurled his fists and tried to relax. He couldn't anticipate her reaction to his next revelation.

"I don't blame you for being pissed at me," he said, trying to soften the coming blow. "If someone did those things to me, I'd be furious. I had no right to interfere, even though I only intended to help. I have no excuse, except... well, my head hasn't been screwed on straight since I met with my lawyer. The day I found you in the ditch."

"Now you're bringing in lawyers? Should I contact mine?"

She didn't have a lawyer. According to the online articles he'd read, she'd used Legal Aid to help her with her woes. Meade had debated hiring a more experienced attorney to sue the hell out of Palmerton on Justine's behalf when he'd learned the facts.

No. That would be interfering again, similar to when he'd paid Urgent Care. *Oh shit.* A fourth crime. At his current rate, she would never let him get within a hundred feet of her, much less touch her again.

"That's two, but judging by the expression on your face, you're not done."

"Nope," he admitted. She deserved nothing less than his complete honesty. He wanted no more secrets between them. "Two more things."

"You started out with two," she reminded him.

"Okay, I'm a bigger asshole than I thought." Her feet, with their cherry-colored toenails, rested next to his thigh. He lifted her left foot and started massaging the arch. He'd researched the process for one of his books but never practiced what he'd learned.

Besides, if he held the foot, she couldn't kick him.

"I paid your Urgent Care bill." He dug his thumb into the flesh below her big toe.

Her low moan didn't displace her glare.

"I don't consider you a charity case or a hobby. I fronted the money, and I expect to be repaid." He rubbed her arch. "And I don't mean with sex. I respect you too damn much to think you'd barter your body."

He softened his tone. "I want you to be with me because you want to be with me, not because you think you owe me." He lifted her foot as he bent and gently kissed the top.

She tried to pull away. "I am so angry with you right now."

At least she wasn't screaming at him the way she'd shrieked at Palmerton.

Her control was a good thing, right? Palmerton triggered powerful emotion in Justine. Meade wanted the same, only on the positive end of the spectrum.

His actions were to blame for complicating his relationship with Justine. He'd never expected to… develop feelings for her. Intense feelings. Strange new emotions.

"What I want doesn't matter to you at all," she continued as she struggled with him for control of her foot.

"What you want is all that matters to me," he argued. "Your wants are my motivation for doing what I did. Not the short term, but the long term. You want your job at The Write Place. You don't want Palmerton in your life. Or have I misunderstood you?"

Meade fought to keep his irritation from commandeering the conversation. "You really want to believe his promises? His grand plans for your future? You only slept with me because you'd been reading steamy books?"

Her foot jerked. "Lenny is history. Out of my life. And the books had nothing to do with what happened between us. They're only stories. Make believe. I trusted you."

Only stories. Not the yearnings penned in the blood from his opened veins. "I have never lied to you."

"Lies of omission," she shot back.

At least she believed him. His annoyance dropped a notch.

"Okay, hit me with your last confession." Her voice hardened. The pliancy of the foot in his hand turned rigid. "Or are you going to add two more instances of deceitful behavior on your part?"

CHAPTER 31

IF JUSTINE COULD GET her foot free from Meade's grasp, she'd kick him in his ego: his crotch. But she didn't have the strength to wrench free from him. Her willpower was otherwise occupied, fighting tears of rage, struggling not to unleash the fury rattling her entire body, and rerouting the urge to lunge toward him and claw at his eyes. Too bad her knives were across the room.

She was *oeuf*ing tired of men making decisions for her. Only she knew and decided what she wanted. How Pucking presumptuous of Meade to take charge, as though she didn't have a functioning brain cell.

He was no better than Lenny.

She refused to cry. After Lenny, she'd made a vow to herself: no more man-induced weeping for her.

"I'm waiting." She hated how her voice rasped, betraying the depth of her anger.

He dug both his thumbs into the arch of her foot.

She swallowed a moan.

His body tensed. "My last confession has nothing to do with you, but something I want you to know about me."

"Rumpelstiltskin reveals all?" she sneered.

His icy blue eyes fixed on her face, as if trying to perform laser surgery on her brain. "Something like that."

His dark brows drew together when another knock on the door interrupted them. "Why did the storm have to end?" he muttered.

She agreed, but she wouldn't tell him. The past couple of days, isolated from the world and obligation, had provided a much-needed respite for her. She hadn't realized how tightly wound she'd been about her life. Her failures.

Meade released her foot and padded to the door. Salome slipped inside. Insulated food delivery bags filled her arms.

"I brought more rations," she greeted them. "How are you two doing? Justine, have you forgiven me for setting you up?"

"No," Justine replied. She didn't blame Salome because she'd indulged in sex with Meade. The forced proximity, however, was entirely Salome's doing.

"You will." Salome sounded confident. "Your ex has no idea where you are. He has harassed the guests in the lodge, irritated Darby—who's already in a crappy mood because Cam is on a search-and-rescue mission because an idiot tourist didn't listen to the weather report. Your ex has driven me to consider doctoring his meals with every purgative herb I can put my hands on.”

“Might do him good,” Meade muttered. “The asshole is full of shit.”

“Exactly my logic,” Salome serenely agreed.

“Don’t you dare taint my food,” Justine said, pride in her craft overriding everything.

“He knows your cooking,” Salome reminded her. “You don’t need to impress him.”

Valid point. Then Justine remembered she was mad at Salome for helping strand her in Meade’s cabin during the snowstorm. “I have a bone to pick with you.” Bone? Try an entire blue whale skeleton.

Salome’s bright turquoise eyes fixed on Justine. “You will thank me later. I brought more food for you. You’ll have a lot to do once you’re back on your feet. We’re close to depleting the stockpile you left in the freezer.”

“That’s what they were meant for.”

“And you were scathingly brilliant to plan for a storm. Darby is quite impressed with you.” Salome held out her arms. “Here, Meade. Take the top two bags. They’re for you. Do you have any used bags ready for me to take back?”

He glowered at her as he took the meal delivery.

“Okay, I won’t wait. I sense enough tension in the air here without me adding to it.”

“You interrupted a serious conversation,” Meade admitted, as he carried the frozen meals to the kitchen.

"Exposing your sins?" Salome sounded as if she were joking about Meade doing wrong.

"Yes," he admitted.

"Romance novels aren't sins. What some readers do while reading them might be, though."

Justine's throat closed. She'd accused him of being a romance author before, and he'd danced around giving a straight answer. Now he dashed to the living room, standing between her and Salome.

"Pseudonyms aren't a crime, unless you're using the false name to break the law." Salome chuckled. "The only law Andromeda Zeus has broken is the law of averages—how many times a man can make love to a woman in one night. Gives us women unrealistic expectations."

SHIT, OH SHIT, OH shit. Shit!

"Shit." No other word fit. "Fuck" seemed inappropriate, given the topic.

Justine stared at him, eyes wide, mouth agape.

Meade triggered similar responses in a lot of women lately.

"Tell me I'm jumping to conclusions." Justine's hoarse voice was barely audible.

"Uh-oh," Sal said. "Did I just...?"

"Yup," Meade confirmed. "You beat me to the punchline."

"Meade. I'm so sorry."

Sal acted genuinely contrite, but Sal didn't concern Meade. He didn't spare her a glance. He took two steps toward the couch. Toward Justine.

Who raised her hands to stop him.

"I was about to tell you." Meade hoped she believed him.

"I was making a joke when I packed all his books for you to read," Sal added. "I never—"

"You're not helping," Meade snapped. "You should leave. Now."

"She should stay," Justine said in that small, scary tone.

"I'd better go," Sal said. "We'll talk later, Justine. It's not as bad as you—"

"Get out!" Meade roared.

Sal slipped out the door.

He couldn't remember the last time he'd raised his voice. Helplessness sludged through his veins and clogged every cell in his body. Of all his crimes against Justine, his alter ego should have been the least, because keeping his pen name secret had nothing to do with her.

Sure, the rest of the staff knew the name he published under. Andromeda Zeus shouldn't matter. He was going to kill her off anyway.

But the author mattered to Justine. He'd loved listening to her opinions on the stories he'd penned. He'd felt good about his work for the first time in ages. She'd restored his confidence without knowing how he desperately needed the boost.

Oh, hell, she'd healed him.

And that was priceless. To him. But at what cost to her?

He stood at the end of the couch and studied her face. A log in the woodstove popped, loud as a gunshot in the stillness.

"If I were one of your heroines, like Araminta, I would toss a cup of hot coffee in your face or dump a bucket of melted snow in your lap. Or Charlotte in *Web of Deceit*—didn't she shove her lying beau into an icy lake? I'm pretty sure Darby told me there's a lake out there. You must have been laughing your head off," she finally said.

"Never. Not once. Laughing didn't occur to me."

She averted her face. "All those things you said to me... earlier... before..." Her voice cracked. "Taking inventory to include in your book?"

"No. I was too wrapped up in my feelings, my emotions, to pay attention to anything except the awe of being with you."

"Words are *oeuf*ing easy for you."

On the page, yeah. In real life? Not so much. Still, he had to try.

"Why can't you believe a man—or anyone—would want you for being you? Not to franchise you as a chef, not to turn you into a heroine in a spicy romance novel, but simply to be with you because you're worth being with?"

She hunched her shoulders around her ears, as if trying to crumple her body and hide.

He eased himself onto the foot of the couch. "If I'm going to reveal all my secrets to you, then you should know you're only the second woman I've been intimate with."

No reaction.

"I've never wanted to be with anyone else."

"Not much need when you write what you do."

"What? Do you think I masturbate while I'm writing?" He snorted. "I wish I could. Paying extra for the hardcover would solve a lot of problems."

"I'm an idiot." The couch back muffled her voice. "The truth was in front of me, and I didn't want to see it."

"You're not an idiot. I was going to tell you my pen name when Sal interrupted."

"Joke's on you instead of me."

"No joke, Justine." He blocked the urge to pull her into his lap. Cradle her against his chest. Comfort her.

"I don't know why I'm upset. Your pen name shouldn't matter."

He thought he heard a sniffle. Oh God. If Justine was crying—he'd fortified his heart against female tears. Used them to fill the moat protecting his soul. He'd take Justine's knives over her weeping any time.

"You have a hard time trusting men, and you were starting to trust me. Which is why I planned to tell you about Andromeda before Sal interrupted."

He eased off the couch and sat on the floor next to Justine. Icy air seeped up from the crawl space beneath the cabin and through the rust-colored rug, chilling his ass. "I confessed every instance I interfered, but I didn't tell you what I considered doing. Like contacting my lawyer while we were in Lake Placid so he could get rid of the contracts Lenny signed allegedly on your behalf."

Justine's spine stiffened.

"Or creating a trust fund to handle any additional lawsuits from the health department issue. I read how Palmerton let your insurance lapse." No insurance meant no coverage for future lawsuits.

She twisted until she faced him. The skin around her eyes was dry. Not red. No sign of tears anywhere. He found the mood in their honeyed depths unreadable.

"I am willing to do both those things and more if they help you get what you want." He lifted his hand to brush away a strand of hair clinging to her cheek, then changed his mind. He would not touch her without her permission. "I'm not making the offer to appease you or show off. I care about you and have the financial means to… protect you. Or help you thwart Palmerton."

"I don't need you or anyone to help me—"

"I know." He kept his tone soft. "You have no idea how sexy your independence is."

CHAPTER 32

"Sexy?" Justine refused to meet Meade's gaze. She studied the hand resting atop his propped knee. His thick fingers were at odds with the keys on a laptop computer, but she'd seen him type. Watched him create magic with his prose. Experienced him summoning magic within her body.

She was half in love with those fingers.

He'd dumped a lot of info on her. A secret pen name wasn't a crime. She didn't blame him. She even understood. A man writing romance needed protection. They weren't married, much less in a serious relationship. They were... oil and vinegar. Compatible only when shaken vigorously. Still, she ought to be furious he'd hidden her phone and high-handedly paid for her Urgent Care visit.

And she was angry. She'd trusted him with her reactions and emotions when they'd discussed his books. Not suspecting he'd written the stories, she'd exposed more of herself during their conversations than she'd ever shared with Lenny. She'd told Meade from the get-go she didn't want her life showing up in his novels. Their intimacy intensified her concerns.

"I've found you sexy since the first night when you pulled a knife on me," Meade admitted.

Shocked, she lifted her gaze from his hands to his face. The truth gobsmacked her. "You weren't job shadowing me for your book."

The realization felt... creepy.

"Yes, I was. I had no idea what to write for Andromeda's swan song until I met you. The shadowing was genuine, as well as an excuse to help you get around. Be with you. Get to know you better, and not only for character development."

Character development? Did he mean he didn't see her as real?

Then his words penetrated.

"Andromeda's swan song? You're quitting writing? Why?" His confession shocked her as much as learning his pen name had. "Never mind. Your reasons aren't my business, but please consider how the world will be a sadder place without Andromeda Zeus novels."

His lips thinned into a grim line. "Andromeda is finishing out a three-book contract, then I'm retiring her. I have another pen name in mind, bought the dot com web domain, brainstormed a few story ideas. My agent isn't supportive of Andromeda's demise, but my reasons are valid."

He ought to be happier if he really wanted a new career.

"My ex gets a percentage of all Andromeda Zeus royalties, past, present, and future." A muscle in his jaw twitched.

"That's not right."

"My last couple books didn't do well. Part of me doesn't want the final one to succeed, either."

He might as well have struck her. She swallowed the hurt. "Gee. Should I be insulted?"

"No. India—you met her—says the last title has to be the best book I've ever written, to show another agent I still have the mojo to hit the best-seller lists. In fact, she identified you as my ideal reader and suggested I talk to you."

Another reason to isolate her. Used again. Guess she'd earned the money he'd paid Urgent Care, working as his consultant. Still, trading her emotions for medical services weighed more in his favor.

Except he'd been facing his own difficulties, and Justine had been clueless. She'd been too intent on her own misery to stop and consider Meade might have his own ulterior motives for helping her.

The man possessed layers she'd never imagined. More in common with her than she would have guessed. He'd been honest with her. She should respect his openness.

"Another agent?" she asked, to prove she'd been listening, not merely hearing. "Is yours quitting the business?"

It was easier to pick his brain than examine her conflicting emotions about him. And despite all of his underhanded behavior, she cared. Not only about Andromeda Zeus, but also the man behind the name.

The pulsing in his jaw increased. He unclenched his teeth to answer. "She says she doesn't represent and won't represent the book genre I'm switching to."

Made sense, like not hiring a master sushi chef for an Italian restaurant.

"Can't you just change your pen name? You're a great romance author. As a reader, as a fan, I would hate to lose you. Why do you want to change?"

"I want to grow as an author. I want respect." His tone turned bitter.

"From whom?"

"Everyone."

"You're a best-selling author. Your readers respect you. Your agent respects your fan base. I assume your publisher respects the money coming in from all those book sales. Or aren't your readers worthy of your devotion?"

He reacted as if she'd slapped him.

She took a wild guess. "Or are you angling for your ex-wife's respect?"

ELAINE'S RESPECT? JUSTINE POSED one of the most ridiculous theories Meade had ever heard.

"No, I don't want to keep paying her with money earned by books she mocks. Books she finds contemptuous. Why should she benefit from a career she sneers at?"

Justine's reaction convinced him he had to continue revealing his ugly truths. "Okay. Yes. I'll admit I want to stick it to her." He shouldn't have been relieved by the confession but being honest with a person who didn't have a financial stake in his decision felt wonderful.

"You didn't leave her. She left you."

"We separated by mutual decision. We no longer wanted the same life."

"She gave up first. Did you ever tell her what you wanted?"

"Does that matter?" He didn't care. He'd spent the final years of the marriage listening to Elaine bitch about what she wanted. His needs never entered her mind.

Legal verification that his plan to retire Andromeda Zeus wouldn't violate his spousal support agreement had freed him. Another person's expectations no longer weighed on him. Until India pissed in his bourbon. Yet his agent's negative response to his proposal spurred him to write a better book, and he was proud of the words he'd fed into the manuscript thus far.

"Yes, not telling her matters. Women aren't mind readers."

What the fuck? "You're taking my ex's side?"

"No!" Justine sounded appalled. "Not at all. What you want should be all that matters as far as your career goes, but she couldn't support you if she didn't know what you wanted."

"What I wanted never mattered. I explained to her why I, as a man, wanted to keep my identity a secret. You know what she said?" Elaine's response still irritated him. "And I quote, 'Let me be Andromeda's face.'"

"Ouch."

"As if I would let her represent me to the world while she called what I wrote smut and porn... all throbbing cocks and heaving bosoms."

Justine winced. "She didn't respect your craft."

"Or me."

"I let Lenny box me into a situation that wasn't a good fit for me, and I never admitted how much I resented the restaurant until I no longer had the weight slung around my neck. I felt as if I'd lost a walk-in freezer from my chest. Do you really hate writing romance?"

Right now, Meade only hated the continued floundering in water over the dam. He wanted two things: no more money going to his ex, and Justine naked and under him, and not necessarily in that order. He'd settle for kissing her. But no. She insisted on tinkering with his head.

"You've had two years to reconsider your career after your marriage ended. Are you going to let your anger at her keep you from doing what you really want to do?"

"I told my agent what I want to write, and she blew me off." He knew he sounded petulant, like a child not getting his own way.

Justine inhaled deeply, briefly closed her eyes before she exhaled, then glued him with her honey gaze. "I'm not aware of all your circumstances. But I do know you want to abandon hope and happy endings. You must have believed in them at some point, or you wouldn't have started writing romance in the first place."

"When I met Elaine in college, she read a lot of romance novels. When she got mono, I decided to convince her to have sex with me by writing a steamy love story and reading a scene or chapter to her every day." Meade muttered.

"Eww." Justine wrinkled her nose. "I can't decide if that's sweet or disgusting."

"I was young and let my little head do my thinking."

When he'd decided to confess all to Justine, he hadn't meant to include everything currently spewing from his mouth. Honestly? He hadn't been aware of how much venom poisoned his brain, how frequently Elaine still pushed the buttons she'd installed.

"Who came up with the idea to give her your royalties?"

"She did."

"And you agreed? Why?"

"To get rid of her. Elaine wasn't the only one who was unhappy in our marriage." He'd been miserable. "The difference is I didn't fuck anybody else."

God, that felt good to admit. Confession really was good for the soul.

Now that he'd started, he couldn't stop. "I was tired of listening to her bitch because I used a pen name. No release parties or book signings or any of the accolades she decided were a best-selling author's due. The fame and glamor she wanted reflected onto her. Alimony in the form of royalties was the only way to force her to keep her mouth shut about the pen name. If she ever tells anyone she'd been married to Andromeda Zeus, she forfeits everything, including half of what she's received to date."

"Blackmail."

"A small price to pay for my privacy," he corrected.

"And what would happen if people found out Andromeda Zeus is a man?"

"You didn't handle the truth well," he pointed out.

"Not because you're a man, but because I bared my soul to you about your books. I told you stuff I might not have said had I suspected they might show up in a future novel. I'm handling your secret okay now. Except for my disappointment."

"Disappointing women is a talent I have. Don't worry. I'm not writing romance after this book. Your secrets are safe with me." The same as he knew his secrets were safe with her.

He'd missed having a friend in whom to confide. A person whose opinion mattered to him—a person he didn't pay to have an opinion. His was a solitary profession. His desire to keep his identity a secret intensified his isolation. Friends from college gradually fell away. He hadn't seen or spoken to his sister since their mother's funeral, mostly because she and Elaine loathed each other. He had no excuse for the past two years indifference except he'd gotten out of the habit of being a brother.

Justine wasn't done with him.

"If you disappointed women, no one would pre-order your next release. No one would buy your books. The secret to your success is that you never disappoint."

"The books are fiction. Not real." Creating what he considered to be the ideal woman.

"The pleasure we get from reading your stories is real. Very real. Why do you think I listen while I'm working? No matter how bleak the situation, knowing the problems will work out in the end keeps me going."

She pulled his hand off his knee and squeezed his fingers. "Women would flock to you because you're a man who gets what women want."

She touched him. She'd reached for him first. Meade took her gesture as permission to twine his fingers with hers. He needed the connection to her. The physical link. The steadfast intent she represented. Justine required no one to define her. No one to validate her. She was her own anchor, and latching onto her persistence served as a lifeline for him.

But Justine still hadn't finished picking at his head. His scars. His scabs. "Are you going to let your ex steal your dream?"

"What if being a romance author wasn't my dream?" His gut clenched, as if to keep him from exposing his most vile, terrifying fear. "What if my career fulfilled her desire instead of mine?"

Chapter 33

Meade clutched Justine's fingers so tightly he cut off the blood circulation. She didn't try to free herself. Something was happening here. Something important.

Meade claimed to hate writing romance. He was an adult. He could make his own decisions about his future. People urged her not to close Just Food, despite the scandal and lawsuits. She hadn't admitted how much she disliked running a restaurant until bankruptcy freed her. Knowing what she did, she had no business trying to change Meade's mind.

"I'm sorry you're not getting the support you want," she finally said. "Other than stop nagging you, what can I do to help?"

She would have melted in relief if anyone had made her a similar offer during her darkest times. Or two weeks ago.

The hard expression on his face dissolved. He appeared... vulnerable.

The idea pierced her, because Meade never showed weakness. His strength had assisted her through her worst injuries, propped her up so she could keep her job. To see him floundering bothered her.

"You're listening. You're not judging. That's enough." He tightened his grip on her fingers until she feared he would crush the bones.

He buried his face in the blanket covering her legs. His warm, humid breath through the fabric caressed her skin.

Child, Puck, and Ramsey, she'd slept with Andromeda Zeus. She'd had sex with one of the most famous romance authors in the world. And she wanted him again, despite knowing getting involved with him would only lead to heartbreak.

They sat entwined in silence for several minutes, the only sounds in the room the occasional pop of the woodstove and the distant motorized growl of Heath rearranging the snow.

A tentative knock on the door interrupted their calm.

Meade lifted his head, a scowl firmly imbedded on his face. "Now who the fuck thinks my cabin is Grand Central Station?"

He climbed to his feet and padded to the door. "India? What are you doing here?"

His beautiful, statuesque agent slipped inside and stomped the snow from her boots. "Geez, Meade. When I suggested you talk to the chef, I meant take her for a hike in the woods or have coffee in the library, not hold her hostage during a blizzard." She sat on the bench and pulled off her boots.

"Make yourself at home." Meade's sarcasm had no apparent effect on India. "If I'd known I'd be hosting an open house, I would have ordered hors d'oeuvres from the kitchen."

"I'm not staying long," India assured him. "Cabin fever, of all things. Doesn't it figure? I'm here to work without distractions, but as soon as I was stuck in the building, I craved the outdoors."

Once her boots were off, she unzipped her puffy quilted coat and wandered further into the cabin. "Hey, Justine. India Snodgrass. Meade's agent. We met in the kitchen last week. You've got everyone at the lodge in a tither."

Uh-oh. "Yes. I remember you. We discussed romance novels." *And you're the one who suggested Meade pick my brain.*

India's lips curved. "I ate at Just Food a few times. It's a shame you closed."

"When it's time to move on, it's time to move on." Justine didn't refer only to her failed restaurant.

She knew Meade caught her subtle dig when the corners of his mouth twitched upward.

"Your fiancé and business partner said you have bigger things in mind," India continued.

What the Puck was Lenny doing? Regaling all the guests with his version of she-done-me-wrong? "I don't have a fiancé, and my former business partner skipped town after his illegal actions were uncovered."

India's left eyebrow soared to her forehead. "The power of point of view," she murmured. "Meade, take note."

"What do you want, India?" Meade demanded.

"Well, I overheard the assistant manager and the groundskeeper—Heath Remington. Isn't that a great name? You should use it in a book. Anyway, they were arguing because she helped you hold the chef captive during the storm. He was furious because she interfered and asked when she was going to grow up and accept her tarot cards and crystals were bullshit excuses for avoiding life. Whew!" India mimed wiping her forehead. "If you don't want this plot for your next book, I'll give it to another client."

India's prevarication did not satisfy Meade. "Why are you here?"

"The chef's ex—has anyone told him he's an ex?—was knocking on doors looking for her, spouting off about the Abominable Snowman and kidnapping. Everyone in the main lodge is now aware of Justine's past and how she's currently missing. That's when I overheard the argument. I wanted to see if what Heath said was true—if you had kidnapped her and was holding her prisoner."

Justine's stomach knotted. Naturally Lenny would mess up everything again. She found her voice and raised her arms. "Look. No shackles. Lenny Palmerton loves drama."

"You're not here against your will? Meade didn't trick you—or seduce you—into staying for the duration of the storm?"

"Why she's here is none of your business," Meade pointed out.

"Excuse me? You're my client and that makes you my business," India reminded him. "I suggested you talk to her. I would hate for you to have misconstrued my meaning."

"I'm an adult woman," Justine interrupted. "No one, except Darby Winehouse, has the right to ask me what I'm doing."

"I've been writing. In fact, let me put the manuscript on a flash drive for you to read. In your suite." Meade's tone remained stony. "I'll be right back."

He climbed the stairs to the loft.

As soon as he stepped out of sight, India plopped onto the sofa next to Justine. "I don't know what's going on here." The agent spoke in a hushed tone. "You should be aware that his ex-wife gutted him. Completely eviscerated him."

Justine loathed being trapped by gossip. "What does she have to do with me?"

"Elaine made him cynical. He didn't deserve what she did to him. She undermined both his talent and his belief in himself. Now he plans to write everything Elaine wanted him to write, and trust me, Meade can't pull it off. He wouldn't know how to create that kind of asshole character, much less bring one to life on the page."

Justine's throat ached. "Not my banquet, not my burned toast points."

Okay, she owed Meade for his kindness and support. However, she drew the line at interference in his career. "Despite what you believe is going on between us, Meade is his own man. If he needs to prove his worth as an author to himself, that's his business."

India's storm-colored eyes steadied on Justine. "The house-keeper mentioned she'd loaded you up with Andromeda Zeus romance novels to read. I know you've listened to at least one audio book he's written. He has magic. Don't you see?"

India's determination to do to Meade what Lenny attempted to do to her annoyed the stuffing out of Justine. "Isn't how he practices his magic his decision?"

Sure, she wanted Andromeda Zeus—Meade—to continue supplying her with reading material, but not if the price included a piece of his soul. He was the only one who should make that decision. Romance novels flooded bookstore shelves. Most weren't as good as Andromeda's—Meade's—oh, making the distinction in her mind would take time. If he made the shift away from romance, she'd have to keep reading until she found an author to replace him. Other readers would do the same.

"I have no influence on Meade, nor do I want to," Justine said. "He's the only one who can decide what's right for him."

India's eyebrows flexed again. "You have more influence than you realize."

"Why would you believe something so absurd?"

"I've been his agent since the beginning. I've never seen him behave like this before."

"Have you ever listened to him?"

"Did he tell you his plans?" India countered.

"No." Justine still reeled from his earlier confessions.

"He wants to write toxic males doing toxic things to shallow women and emerging triumphant for being an asshole." Contempt colored every syllable India spoke. "He wants to transfer his anger at his ex onto the page and make himself the winner."

"He won when he got away from her," Justine pointed out. She needed time to process India's revelations.

"You know that, and I know that, but he—"

"Is the author." Meade stomped down the stairs. "Managing his career."

"The book you pitched is everything Elaine pestered you to write," India accused.

"Clearly you had no idea what she wanted. She thought I should write like Moss Crockett or John Grisham. Dan Brown. What part of my pitch sounded like a James Patterson plot to you?"

"She wanted you to write best-selling—"

"She wants to be married to a celebrity. She wants to be feted as a muse. Me using a secret pen name couldn't give her that."

"She offered to be Andromeda's face," Justine said. "Trashing your books could have been a ploy to make you write under your own name. That way, she could claim credit as your muse. India is right. You are doing what she wanted."

"Except now she can't benefit from my work." He sounded smug.

MEADE FOCUSED HIS ANGER on India. Everything he'd overheard her say infuriated him. He dropped a flash drive onto her lap. "Here's the work-in-progress. Knock yourself out. And show yourself the door."

He hated the way India had presented his plans to Justine, giving her a totally inaccurate picture. He needed to clarify his intentions with her... Justine, not India. Justine's opinion mattered.

Before he could, the cabin door crashed open, and Lenny Palmerton whirled into the room like a snow devil. "What the fuck, Justine? I thought you'd been eaten by a polar bear."

"What the fuck," Meade echoed, "are you doing here?"

"Tracking down my fiancée! I have been crazy with worry." Palmerton crossed the room in a few strides, trailing snow along the way. "I can't believe he's holding you prisoner."

Justine winced and burrowed deeper into the corner of the sofa. "I'm not a prisoner. Meade has been caring for me." Her chin jutted. "He's been pampering me."

Palmerton didn't catch the accusation lurking in her tone.

"As soon as I get you back to the main lodge, I'm calling the police or whatever passes for law and order in this godforsaken place," Palmerton continued, as if she hadn't spoken.

"Go ahead," Meade goaded. "Then I can have you arrested. Breaking, entering, and trespassing, for starters. I'm renting this cabin until the end of March, which means I'm the tenant, and you burst in here without knocking and threatened to abduct my house guest."

"You've found your inspiration for the protagonist for the first book with your new pen name," India murmured. "Take notes."

"Go away, Lenny." Justine sounded weary. "The storm is over. You can leave. Go back to your world."

"I'm not leaving without you. We have meetings set up—"

"*You* have meetings scheduled," Justine corrected. "I'm not part of your schemes. Good luck breaking the news to whomever."

Palmerton grabbed Justine's upper arms and shook her as he shouted in her face. "We've signed contracts! You're not going to fuck me on this!"

Meade didn't think. He merely reacted. He seized Palmerton and threw him against the door. Palmerton slumped to the floor.

India shrieked and gathered her legs to her chest.

"Be fucking grateful I don't throw you into the stove," Meade growled as he hoisted Palmerton from the floor by the front of his jacket. "Be grateful your sorry fucking ass isn't in the middle of the lake right now."

Blood roared in Meade's ears, drowning out every other sound. He pulled Palmerton closer until they were nearly nose to nose. "If you ever put a finger on Justine again, I will break every fucking bone in both your fucking hands. Now get the fuck out of my cabin."

He released Palmerton long enough to open the door, then heaved Palmerton onto the porch. Every nerve in Meade's body tingled and sparked as if they were electrical wires short-circuiting. His fingertips should be hissing and sizzling like fireworks. He couldn't pull enough air into his lungs.

He slammed the door, then braced his back against the panel. All he saw was Justine, huddled on the couch, her aged-bourbon eyes wide, her full lips parted. The edges of his vision hazed, as though smoke from the woodstove invaded his skull.

"You were very heroic, à la Andromeda Zeus." India's voice penetrated the din in his head. She had the nerve to clap her hands.

Meade blinked. The room swam into focus. He was breathing as heavily as if he'd run a marathon. Two sets of female eyes fixed on him. Only Justine's mattered.

"Are you all right?" he asked her.

She nodded.

He'd probably terrified her with his shitstorm, but Palmerton had no business putting his hands on Justine. She had to realize Meade only wanted to protect her.

Oh hell, now that the adrenaline surge subsided and his right mind came out of hiding, he admitted he'd scared himself with the intensity of his reaction. No wonder Justine stared at him as if he'd sprouted a second head.

Meade scrubbed his cheeks with his palms. His innards were starting to shake. He wasn't a violent man, but Palmerton summoned his latent caveman.

His legs were going to fold beneath him. Meade sank to the bench next to the door.

India's gaze flitted between Justine and Meade. "What am I missing here? I thought you were picking her brain."

Meade swallowed. His dry throat craved a drink, but the coffee pot and his bottle of Knob Creek were too far away. "I think you need to leave," he said to India, his voice hoarse.

CHAPTER 34

JUSTINE'S VOICE WOULDN'T WORK. Her brain stuttered, unable to concentrate. Words required focus. She was grateful she reclined on a sofa, propped on her bottom, her back, and left side; otherwise, she might have fallen because... because... Meade. Lenny. She wondered if Lenny had been hurt when Meade had catapulted him out the door, but nothing left inside her gave a Puck. Maybe India's departure would thaw the numbness shrouding Justine's brain.

On the other hand, she might never recover.

Which was ridiculous. She'd recovered from the Just Food disaster. Gran had always insisted she was a resilient soul.

Her thoughts continued to skitter across her brain like water drops on hot olive oil. She simply needed a minute. An hour, if not a day or week or year, to process the enormity of this day's holy Puck moments.

Her gaze drifted to Meade, who sat on the bench by the front door, looking shellshocked. If not for the audience, she would have crawled to him and curled up in his lap. Wrapped her arms around him. Made him marinara sauce from scratch.

"Can adults get shaken baby syndrome?" India asked, peering into Justine's eyes.

"Shaken baby?" Justine wanted to swat her away because she blocked Justine's view of Meade.

"Yeah," India said. "The way your ex was shaking you..."

Right. Lenny attacked her. He never had before. Not physically.

"She hit her head last week when she had her accident." Meade stood, looking unsteady, and took a hesitant step toward her. "Heath or Cam should check her again."

"I'll go back to the lodge and let someone know what happened." India climbed to her feet.

"Great idea." Meade wobbled to the other end of the sofa and collapsed.

"Don't bother," Justine managed to rasp out. 'I'm fine."

They ignored her.

Why did everyone focus on her when Meade needed attention?

Only the popping of the fire and the rustling of India's movements as she pulled on her boots and coat broke the silence, followed by the closing of the door behind her.

They were alone.

"Mmm...Meade?" The first letter of his name hummed on her lips.

His head tilted enough for her to see his eyes, wide and wandering until his gaze landed on her.

"I wanted to kill him." His voice creaked, mimicking the hinge on the woodstove door. "He touched you, and I—"

"You stopped him."

Meade blinked rapidly. His gaze dropped to his hands, resting palms up on his knees.

His big, strong hands with those thick, clever fingers. Hands and fingers she wanted on her again. It never occurred to her to be frightened by his physical display of anger or wonder if someday the force of that rage would touch her. He'd been protecting *her*. Defending *her*, just as he had from the moment they met. Helping her make her dream stay real. His methods were definitely questionable, but his motivations were pure.

For the first time since Gran's death, she had a safe place. How could she stay angry at him?

Quiet descended on the cabin after India departed. Justine wasn't speaking to him, and he didn't blame her. He'd probably terrified her. He was shocked she hadn't begged India to help her back to the main lodge.

A log in the stove collapsed, overly loud in the silence. Meade usually preferred quiet. Some authors listened to music while they wrote. Not him. Justine's stillness, however, nibbled at him, eroding the edges of his composure.

She had to be the one to initiate a reconnection. Everything that transpired should have destroyed whatever illusions she held about him. A spectacular crash and burn.

He stole a glance at her and found her gazing at him, the way prey would keep its eye on the hunter. A lump rose in his throat. He required several attempts before he could swallow.

She lifted her hand, as if to reach for him, but changed her mind. Her bare foot brushed his inner thigh. His muscles tensed as he braced for a kick in the balls. Instead, she rubbed her sole against his sweatpants.

He let his fingertips feather the top of her foot, studying her face for any sign of rejection. Revulsion.

Her lips parted, and the expression in her eyes softened. Moisture shimmered on her lashes. Signs, he decided, her anger was thawing.

"You see," he said, his voice cracking from disuse and bottled-up emotion, "Cain Dago is an alias. One of many he used."

Justine blinked.

Meade didn't know how to say what he wanted in a way that wasn't dangerous, so he used the language, the scenario most comfortable to him. "Dago would marry fair English virgins and take them to the continent on their wedding trips... without consummating the marriage. He would secure the dowries, then claim the brides died of a foreign fever while on their honeymoon."

Justine's lips parted even more. Her eyes widened.

"Dago was a greedy bastard. He would sell his virgin brides to maharajas in India. He sold Lazlo's cousin Beatrix in such a manner. Lazlo found her dying in the brothel where the maharaja sent her after he tired of her. Lazlo made it his life's work to stop Cain Dago. But Lazlo foolishly falls in love with Araminta. Women always prefer bad boys." *Heath.* "The wounded soldier."

"How does the story end?" Justine asked, her voice warbling. "I only got as far as Araminta flinging her wine in Lazlo's face."

"The duke initiates an in-depth investigation into Lazlo's allegations and learns Lazlo was telling the truth. The duke forbids Araminta from seeing Dago. Dago tries to kidnap Araminta, but Lazlo thwarts the attempt. They duel. Lazlo kills Dago but is also wounded. The duke reminds Araminta how Lazlo offered up himself as a husband to save her from a fate worse than death. He didn't want her to endure what his cousin had suffered. The duke grants Lazlo permission to court Araminta, who has been nursing him back to health. She accepts Lazlo is the better man, especially after he tells her he doesn't want her dowry. He wants only for her to be safe to live her own best life, and that he hopes he is part of that best life."

"Why do I feel as if you've hidden a message in the recap?"

Meade shrugged. "I wrote the book years ago. My first one. Even back then, I found retreating into my fictional world easier than addressing the herds of elephants in the room."

At some point in his recitation, they'd clasped hands. He didn't recall who had initiated the contact, but he appreciated the connection.

"Manifesting the ending you want?" Justine asked.

Manifesting. A good word. He nodded.

"What ending do you want in our case?"

The words were a body blow—not a slap to his face, but a punch to his gut. At least his insides stopped their adrenaline-deprived trembling.

"You."

She flinched as if the same fist struck her.

He climbed to his feet, then lifted Justine from the couch. She offered no resistance. Once he reached the bedroom, he gently placed her on the bed and reclined beside her. He clasped her hand again.

He had no more words to give her. Their fingers tangled, hers slender and dexterous, his bulky and clumsy. She gifted him with her stillness. After the confessions, the yelling, all the conversations careening around, the stillness created a respite. He was talked out. His brain required silence to work, the same as Justine needed to listen to romance novels to cook.

Justine released his hand and rolled onto her side, facing away from him. She snuggled her butt against him, as if inviting him to spoon her.

He draped an arm across her waist. If he were writing this scene in a book, they would have finished having sex or were planning to. He didn't remember the last time he lay on a bed merely holding a woman. The lack of anxiety, the absence of urgency to fuck, soothed him. He appreciated being still and quiet with a person with whom he shared respect. He'd never shared such deep relaxation and trust with anyone.

Revealing his crimes to Justine had been important to him. He dealt with lies in the form of fiction every working moment—and if the falsehoods weren't the words on the page, his agent and editor generated them to bolster his output. Even an author as successful as Andromeda Zeus played the games. He enjoyed the games; otherwise, he wouldn't want to continue writing. But this, this pocket of nothingness comforted him in unfamiliar ways.

Yes, too much remained unresolved between him and Justine. She had every right to be pissed he'd taken her phone and had gone behind her back to pay for her Urgent Care visit. But now his chicanery was out in the open. Nothing he'd done put her at risk. Not one of his actions was illegal... except the phone thing. He doubted she would press charges.

Meade could lie with Justine forever—not pre-or-post-coital, but quiet, with no demands, no agenda, wrapped around the woman he loved.

Loved?

Where had that come from?

He met Justine barely two weeks ago. Sure, several of his characters suffered from instalove, but not him. Tropes—those familiar story motifs so loved by readers—were strictly business, not a way of life. At least not his. Were they anyone's reality? He wrote the fantasy of happily ever after, but the brass ring remained out of his reach. Maybe no one ever grabbed it. Yet his sales figures confirmed that people continued their quest for happiness. People buying a dream. People plunking down their hard-earned money for his version of hope, when in reality he had no hope to give. But just now, in this moment, he would take contentment.

CHAPTER 35

JUSTINE FIGURED SHE OUGHT to be angrier at Meade. He was another example of a man going behind her back because he thought he knew better than she did. Except she believed him when he claimed he'd only had her future interests in mind. Her interests, not what he wanted her interests to be.

Oh yeah. His being her favorite romance author didn't hurt. She didn't blame him for keeping his identity hidden from her—as part of the world population, not only Justine Macko. He claimed he would have revealed his pen name if Salome hadn't beaten him to the punchline. If Justine's memory served, he'd been on the verge of a confession. Her recollections were hazy, overshadowed by Lenny's scene—and by Meade's reaction.

It wasn't in her to stay angry with a man who ventured beyond lip service and who was as stunned by his rage response as she'd been.

His arm across her body anchored her to the mattress, but not to prevent her escape. The contact was more a gauge to make sure she was okay. Unless she misread his intentions.

A pounding on the cabin door broke into her ruminations.

Meade's arm tensed. "Wait here."

As if she wanted to be in any other place.

She recognized Darby's voice, but although the male voice who also spoke sounded familiar, his identity escaped her.

"I'll get her."

Meade's terse tone warned Justine that something displeased him.

He stalked into the bedroom. "Darby is here with Deputy King. They want to know if you want to press assault charges against Palmerton. I guess India didn't leave out anything when she tattled on us."

Justine flinched.

"It's your choice," Meade continued. "But I think you should."

"Don't make this about me." Justine spoke in a low voice.

Meade cocked his head. "I'm not. Palmerton did."

She wanted to contradict him, but once again, Lenny had cornered her.

"Let's get this over with." She did not want to face her boss while she was staying with one of the guests, but Lenny had taken that choice away from her. At least she'd showered so she didn't reek of sex.

Meade helped her hobble to the main room, then settled her on the sofa.

"What is going on?" Darby stood in her sock feet near the table. Her arms were crossed, and a scowl pleated her face.

Thank Child, Ramsey, and Puck, her focus was on Meade.

"Why is my chef languishing in your cabin instead of a hotel room in Lake Placid like Sal told me?"

"So I can wait on her and make sure she stays off the leg," Meade replied.

He perched on the arm of the sofa near Justine's head, as if he were making up for not protecting her from Lenny's attack. As if to protect her from her boss.

"So fatherly of you." Darby's sarcasm was as thick as the snow on the ground.

"How did you find out Justine was staying with me?" Meade's tone remained conversational.

"Your agent was kind enough to fill me in on the situation. Then Sal confirmed her part in your little charade."

Justine said nothing.

Darby approached the sofa and finally spoke directly to her. "Your leg looks better."

"She hasn't been standing around a kitchen cooking," Meade said.

"I love standing around a kitchen cooking," Justine reminded him. "Embracing my destiny is very freeing." She stopped herself from adding, "*You ought to try it.*"

"Well," Darby interrupted, "I'm glad resting the knee worked, but I'm here for another reason. This is Deputy Dylan King from the sheriff's department."

"We met last week," Justine said.

Deputy King dipped his head in acknowledgment. He held a pocket-sized spiral notebook and a mechanical pencil. "Ms.—er, Chef Macko, according to a witness, one Leonard Palmerton assaulted you this afternoon. Can you tell me what happened?"

Justine swallowed her sigh. Would she ever be free of Lenny? Her arms still ached where he'd gripped them. Her neck hurt, and her head throbbed. She briefly recited her version of events.

"Mrs. Winehouse said you don't have an order of protection against him." King continued scratching in his notepad.

"Until today, I never considered he would physically harm me." She tried to remember if she'd made herself clear earlier. To Meade. "I never would have put up with physical abuse."

"You believed you were in danger today?"

"Believed?" Justine laughed. "He grabbed me and started shaking me. My neck is stiff now—"

"Whiplash," Meade muttered. He lurched to his feet and started pacing.

"—And my head aches."

"Any bruising?" King's hazel eyes fixed intently on Justine. She blinked. "I haven't looked," she confessed.

"Why don't you check now?" King suggested.

"Uh, um, sure." Her cheeks heated. She wasn't wearing anything under Meade's t-shirt.

"Let's go in the bathroom," Darby offered. "I'll help. Bring your cell phone in case you need to take photos."

Justine glared at Meade as she stood. "My phone is missing. I'm not worried. I doubt he left any bruises. But I'll check, just to—" *get you off my case* "—ease your mind."

"How are you holding up?" Darby asked once the two of them were safely behind the closed bathroom door. "I didn't get a chance to ask you earlier."

Justine faced the mirror above the sink, flipped her hair back, and discovered Meade's earlier kisses had left beard-burn along the side of her neck. Her face heated. Hopefully Darby wouldn't notice. "From Lenny? I've already survived him."

"I meant Meade." Darby's cocoa brown eyes, reflected in the mirror, searched Justine's face as if scavenging for clues, before her gaze dropped to Justine's throat. "Yeah. Meade."

Justine slipped the neckline of the over-sized t-shirt off her left shoulder. A pattern of mulberry-colored contusions marred the pale skin of her upper arm. "Not Meade's fingers," she whispered.

Darby swore. "How's the other side?"

Baring her right side revealed a matching set of bruises.

"You need to press charges. Meade and his agent are witnesses. Due to state hospitality laws, I can't do it, even though you're my employee. Dylan can take pictures for evidence of the assault with his phone." Darby planned everything. "I'll make sure your modesty isn't compromised."

"Damn it!" Meade wished he'd had the balls to hurt Palmerton. The livid bruises on Justine's biceps infuriated him. He'd stopped pacing when he saw the damage Palmerton had inflicted on Justine. He wanted to gather her into his arms again and try to atone for not tossing Palmerton from his cabin sooner.

"You said your neck is stiff?" King asked as he snapped photos of the damage on Justine's arms with his cell phone.

She nodded, wincing as she did.

"Have it checked out at Urgent Care, along with the bruises," King suggested. "More evidence."

"I'll drive you," Meade volunteered through clenched teeth, then added, because he knew she would need more incentive: "We can look for your cell phone."

Justine narrowed her eyes and scowled in his direction before diverting her attention to King. "Won't the photos you took suffice?"

"Yes. But you need to have your neck checked. Whiplash is nothing to mess with. It can get worse over time. If you seek immediate medical attention, you'll have something on file for your insurance claim."

"*My* insurance claim," Darby interjected. "You were hurt at work."

"I wasn't on duty," Justine pointed out.

"On medical leave," Darby countered. "And still on my property. As I told you before, The Write Place is a safe place to work. Plus, you hit your head last week, so you really ought to be looked at."

Thank goodness Darby sided with him, Meade thought, no matter how much he'd irritated her.

"If my symptoms get worse, I'll consider it," Justine agreed.

Meade glared at her. He'd gotten intimately familiar with her prevarication tactics. "Clearly being shaken caused a brain injury. You're going to Urgent Care. Then you're going to press charges and get a restraining order."

"I would press charges, but I can't." Darby brought her fist down on the arm of the couch. "Damn it. Leonard Palmerton assaulted my chef. I ought to be able to have him arrested."

"You're doing everything by the book," King assured Darby. "You reported the assault and are cooperating with us."

"I should have evicted him the moment I found out who he was. Or when he kept harassing Justine in the kitchen."

Meade appreciated Darby's persistence. Her shouldering of what she considered her responsibility made forcing Justine to take care of herself easier for him. "I'm going to sue Palmerton's ass for breaking and entering."

"You can't," Darby said. "You're a guest, not an owner or tenant."

"What?" Meade couldn't believe his ears. "That's the stupidest thing I've ever heard."

Darby shrugged. "I don't make the laws, I only obey them."

"Having your injuries on record at Urgent Care would help toward an order of protection against Palmerton," King pointed out.

That was it. Meade was ready to lift her and carry her, kicking and screaming, into Lake Placid.

"All right!" Justine sounded exasperated. "I'll press assault charges."

"Go to Urgent Care," King advised. "Get checked out. The more evidence you have supporting you, the easier proving your case will be. In the meantime, any idea where Palmerton is?"

CHAPTER 36

"I SUPPOSE YOU THINK you're clever," Justine said to Meade as his Hummer hurtled through the clear, frigid night toward Lake Placid.

"No," he replied. "I'm exhausted. Getting pissed at Palmerton physically drained me. Add shoveling out the car and dealing with your cute but stubborn ass, it's a wonder I'm upright."

"I would have helped dig out," Justine reminded him. She wore jeans—which, miracle of miracles, now fit over her leg—and Darby's son's outgrown boots. Brushing the snow from the Hummer windows wouldn't have reinjured her knee and would have given Meade a chance to admire her butt while clad in jeans.

"Right, and I'd end up hauling you around again, and I'm too damn tired." He glanced at her. "The only place I want to carry you is to bed."

Justine settled back in her seat and peered out the window. She'd never seen as many stars at one time. The sky looked as though the snowstorm had relocated to heaven.

The multitude of things she wanted to say to Meade tumbled through her brain, yet she hesitated to speak of any of them. How could she pin him down until she straightened out her own thoughts? Or rather, admitted and accepted her feelings for him; the emotions that sex had either revealed or further confused. She hated when romance heroines confused orgasms for love, and she worried she'd fallen into the same trap.

Who fell in love after a week? Crazy people, that's who. She wasn't crazy. Practicality was her middle name, so she shouldn't be head over heels for Meade. But she was. She'd loved him before they'd made love; she'd loved him before learning he was the man behind her favorite author.

Loving him didn't mean she wasn't furious with him. Hiding her phone smacked of abusive control. She'd employed a server whose partner regularly took her phone in order to isolate her. But every one of Justine's instincts echoed Meade's reasoning: Lenny used the device to stalk her, so get rid of the phone. Her intuition and tangled emotions insisted she believe Meade, that he had no agenda other than simply being a nice guy trying to help, but Lenny had made her paranoid as well as battering her faith in humanity. Remembering that not everyone hid an ulterior motive was a challenge. The world had been simpler when she'd believed in human decency.

"You're steaming up the windshield with all your angst," Meade growled a few miles later.

"It would be worse if I were talking," Justine pointed out. "I don't want to distract you. I have a healthy fear of moose meeting metal."

"You could always cook the meat."

"Um, no. I've already gotten into trouble for cooking wild game and charging people to eat it. Not going to happen again."

"How did Palmerton manage that?" Meade's grim tone bespoke a simmering anger.

"Legally, I was the sole proprietor. Mine was the only name on the paperwork." She grimaced. "I trusted him.

"I'm sorry. On behalf of honest men everywhere, I am truly sorry."

"Honest men?" Justine forced a snicker. Yeah, she wanted to believe him but worried she couldn't survive another betrayal.

"I have no more secrets from you," Meade assured her.

Except for how he felt about her or where he expected their relationship to go. Had she merely been a convenient, near-naked woman in his cabin during a blizzard? Okay, he'd connived with Salome to strand them together. A point in his favor. And Justine was definitely not convenient. He'd had to work for her trust.

He'd assured her he wouldn't abuse that trust, but lapses could happen. Wouldn't it be easier for him to transfer what had transpired between them to the page than to create female capitulation from scratch? His heroine was, after all, modeled on

Justine, who came with a readymade plot: Justine's moments and emotions; her longing for intimacy that Meade had tapped into. Magic.

Puck. When had sex become magical for her? After she'd gotten naked with a romance author. Except she hadn't known his secret identity at the time.

"I want to settle something before we get to Urgent Care." Meade cleared his throat. "I'm paying for the visit. Consider the money part of my lawsuit against Palmerton."

She couldn't stop him, so she didn't bother quarreling about it. "Fine."

"No argument? Palmerton *did* scramble your brains."

"Ha. Ha. Very funny." She twisted in her seat to face him. "Someone paying my way is an unfamiliar experience."

Meade winced, then squared his shoulders. "It's time someone looked out for you."

"I'm not used to having a guardian angel. I'm not handling your involvement well," she admitted.

"I wish you would get used to me in your life." He reached across the console to take her hand. They both wore gloves, but the contact seemed more intimate than had they been skin-to-skin.

"I should be allowed to make my own decisions."

"Agreed."

"Without being nagged into doing what everyone else wants me to do," she clarified.

"You're so focused on what you want—and that's not a bad thing—you can't see what you need to get there," Meade pointed out. "Apparently that's where I come in."

His logic was sound, and she hated it. Simply looking at her leg and ankle proved that three days of elevation lessened the swelling. She wore jeans. She had boots on her feet. None of that would have happened without his interference. "Okay," she said.

"I'm not trying to control you or tell you what to do with your career."

"Gee, thanks." She couldn't keep the sarcasm out of her tone. She'd had plenty of time to consider everything he'd said to her and in the name of every great chef past, present and future, Meade was right. Which meant she was wrong, and she was so tired of being wrong. "I appreciate your restraint."

Meade frowned, as if surprised by her response. "Being checked for potential whiplash and having the bruises on your arms examined is one more step in getting—"

"Rid of Lenny once and for all. I get it, Meade. Really. I do."

"And you're not going to throw my high-handed interference up in my face twenty years down the road? Twenty years? Was he implying they had a future? She felt as if he'd just handed her a sticky cinnamon bun still warm from the oven. She had to swallow a lump in her throat before answering. "Nope. Your unforgivable sins are fake Parmesan and sauce from a jar."

He laughed. "Because only food matters?"

"You shouldn't settle for inferior substitutes." Like he had with his ex-wife, and she had with Lenny. Okay, so she wasn't always wrong. She was right about this. "You deserve the real thing."

MEADE DID NOT WANT to have this conversation with Justine while driving the dark, twisted road to Lake Placid. The sentiments were better suited to a snuggled-together-in-bed afternoon. He mentally composed the setting: candles, wine, all the romantic accouterments.

Except he hated that scenario. To start, the props were clichés and, as Justine pointed out, he shouldn't settle for less than what he truly wanted.

Truth be told, he didn't care for wine. He doubted he'd sipped a drop since his divorce. Candles? A fire-hazard. Scented candles? Gave him a headache. Why did romance have to be so... so... formulaic? All he needed was Justine naked, in bed, sighing with pleasure. Occasionally screaming his name or giggling at awkward moments. Or in his kitchen, making sure he ate well. Sometimes listening to him work out a plot problem without judgment. Even brainstorming.

Justine. Not a generic, faceless heroine he'd conjured to appease his readers. Oh, his readers deserved what they paid for, and he happily gave them the experience they craved. But his job didn't extend to his bed. To his personal relationships. To his life.

"And you don't deserve the genuine article?" Meade asked.

"Yeah. I do. That's why I'm at The Write Place. This job is the career path I always wanted. At times, I can't believe I let myself be talked into a situation that was so wrong for me."

"Found yourself in a life you didn't want? I'm familiar with the feeling."

"What are we doing, having come-to-Jesus moments with each other?"

"You and I have a lot in common." Meade admitted. "Besides, you're easy to talk to, even while you're giving me grief. Your sarcasm comes uncomfortably close to the truth."

Way too often.

He didn't know when to stop talking. "Your honesty is refreshing."

"Oh." She turned away from him as if to focus on the yellow fast-food arches that marked the edge of town. "I don't want to be your conscience any more than I want to be your muse."

"You only want to cook for me."

She didn't answer right away. When she did, her words surprised him.

"When you took me to your cabin after the last time we visited Urgent Care, I told you I was afraid of what would happen between us. I was right to be afraid."

The lump of emotion suddenly clumping in his throat made speaking difficult. He focused on maneuvering through the village. "I scare you?"

"Yes." She didn't elaborate.

Well, hell. What was he supposed to do with her confession? Her fear annoyed him because he'd been himself with her. He hadn't bothered to summon a persona. The one secret he'd kept from her had nothing to do with his identity as a man.

He went on the defensive. "I'll admit I should have behaved better with Palmerton this afternoon."

"You think pulling Lenny off me scared me?"

He dared a glance in her direction as he pulled into the Urgent Care lot. She was staring at him again. "My reaction scared me," he confessed. "For all my bluster, I am not a physically aggressive man."

"Maybe scare isn't the word I want," she said. "Wary? You know words better than I do, so I could be getting it wrong. You make me nervous because, if I let you, you'll upend my world. Worse than Lenny did. Much worse."

"I don't want to disturb your world." He spoke between clenched teeth. How could he be worse than that sniveling piece of shit? He hesitated before adding, "I'd like to be part of your life."

Right. Way to sound like a jerk. A pathetic loser.

"It's too soon," she whispered.

Too soon? Nearly two weeks had passed since he'd rescued her from the ditch. Two weeks spent getting to know her. Two weeks being fascinated by her and envying how intimately she knew herself. How he'd suppressed his desire to make love to her until that morning was nothing short of a miracle.

She was his miracle.

CHAPTER 37

JUSTINE STARED AT THE screen of her phone. The number of emails cluttering the inbox shocked her. Other than the library notice that her books had been automatically returned—thank Child, Puck, and Ramsey for Meade and his spoilers—everything was from Lenny.

Although she'd emptied her voicemail box when she'd gone grocery shopping with Salome, he'd filled that again, too. More trying to bully her into doing what he wanted.

"Anything urgent?" Meade asked.

"Just Lenny." There was no one else, but Meade didn't need to know how alone in the world she really was. She started deleting the messages without listening to them.

"Wait," Meade cautioned. "You should keep everything. It's evidence he's been harassing you."

"But my inboxes are full," Justine protested.

"Are you expecting an important call?"

Oh, that question hurt. She had no family or support networks. Lenny had used her workaholic tendencies to isolate her from her friends. To control her.

And again, Meade was right. On two fronts. Her phone was proof of Lenny's harassment. Even worse? There was no one left to call her.

"You can always get another phone with a different number," Meade suggested when she didn't answer. "A throwaway, pay-as-you-go phone."

The phone she held in her hand contained all that remained of her old life. There were memories she didn't want to lose. Business connections that might come in handy in the future. Recipe ideas. Meal plans. Contact information for the few friends Lenny hadn't offended and who might want to hear from her again. The final voice message from Gran before she'd died.

At least Meade hadn't offered to buy her another smartphone, complete with bells and whistles, and put her on his service plan. Never doing that again. She'd learned her lesson the hard way.

"Or I can block Lenny's phone number and email address," she countered. She should have done that before instead of merely deleting his attempts to contact her. "I wouldn't be able to download and listen to library books on a pay-as-you-go phone."

"He could still track you. Besides, the cops may want your phone."

Oh, Puck. Gran was dead. Hearing her voice again would only make Justine cry. Right? She handed the phone to Meade. "You should have left it hidden and told the cops where to look."

He returned it to her. "I never intended to cut you off from your life, only hide you from Palmerton. If you have friends or family to call, call them. Tell them you're getting a new phone with a different number and to keep an eye out for my phone number when you send your updated contact information."

"And should I tell them who you are?"

"I'm Meade Godwin." He leveled his gaze on her as though daring her to contradict him.

Oh, double Puck. He'd trusted her with his secret and here she was, being a rotten egg. She needed to stop sniping at him. He'd offered her a reasonable solution and a way to preserve her last contact with her grandmother. He was only trying to help her. He relied on her discretion.

Meade Godwin, one of the good guys.

She would not betray him. "Right."

"If you have messages you want to save, email them to yourself. Same with any photos or documents."

The photos of Gran the last time they'd been together were precious. She'd never considered the need to save them to a safe place before. Thank Child, Puck, and Ramsey for Meade.

Justine had barely made a dent in emailing her files when Deputy King arrived. He acknowledged them as he strolled to the reception area before joining them

"I told them you're here because you're a crime victim." King said. "In the meantime, we can't locate Palmerton. He checked out of The Write Place. We've issued a BOLO for his vehicle."

"Be on the lookout," Meade mansplained.

"I know what BOLO means. I read a lot," Justine reminded him.

"Any ideas where Palmerton might be?" King asked.

"Lenny mentioned meetings in the city. New York," Justine offered.

King took out his two-way radio and shared the information with the person on the other end.

A nurse called Justine's name a moment later. Her leg ached, but she refused to request a wheelchair. The walk to the examination room wasn't that long.

Neither was the examination. Another time and money suck. Another body part to ice. Another reason to swallow ibuprofen. Another doctor—not the one she'd seen before—who suggested she resume normal activity after resting a couple days.

Right. All while staying off my leg.

She'd figure out a way. Didn't she always? She deserved a James Beard Award for improvising life.

Her irritation mellowed when she saw Meade waiting for her in the lobby. She'd known he'd be there, but his solid presence still managed to amaze her. In a good way. The best way. He was a person who wouldn't vanish the moment things got uncomfortable. Dependable and sexy, an unbeatable combination. If only they had a future together.

She'd just have to take what she could get. This moment. If they were lucky, another day or two, but even that wasn't a given now that everyone knew where she was.

King interrupted her musing. "Godwin mentioned Palmerton left threatening voicemail and email messages on your cell phone. Can you access them for me?"

"I haven't read or listened to anything. I only know he filled my inboxes with hundreds of messages since last Sunday night."

"Harassment," Meade muttered. "Stalking her."

King shot him a look, which Meade returned, his arms crossed and jaw jutting out.

Oh boy. Antler wars.

Meade, she reminded herself, only wanted to protect her.

Instead of going toe-to-toe with King, Meade ought to open his arms and catch her in a tight embrace. She wanted his arms around her and to hug him back. Not cling to him. He knew that about her. He understood that holding each other didn't mean smothering. He understood her in ways no one had since Gran.

Her breath hitched. Was it possible he loved her?

"THIS ISN'T ONE OF your books," Justine reminded Meade as they headed for his car.

His temper threatened to erupt. Every time he'd tried to point out where Palmerton had crossed a legal line, King had countered with some lame-ass explanation to dismiss Meade's theory. *"Palmerton probably didn't know the cell service at The Write Place is spotty." "He sounds like a concerned man trying to locate his fiancée, not a stalker."*

Did the law have to wait for Palmerton to knock Justine on the head with a hammer—or worse—before acting?

"Things take time," Justine continued. "Nothing can happen until they find Lenny, and he's real good at making himself scarce when he's in trouble."

Her breath formed white clouds that hung in the air like empty dialog bubbles in a comic strip. Her gait grew more uneven with every step.

Meade shoved one wadded fist into his jacket pocket and wrapped his free arm around her waist so she wouldn't fall on the slick walkway. "I get that things take time. Doesn't mean I have to like it." The frigid air froze the inside of his nostrils. "Besides, if this was one of my books, you'd have taken your big ass knife to him. Justine Macko, Warrior Chef."

"Please don't put that in your book."

"Why not? My heroines are strong, and you're one of the strongest women I've ever known."

Strongest, bravest, smartest, most caring—the perfect heroine. The perfect woman. At least for him. She wasn't faultless, but she was comfortable with her flaws. And his. Even if he never wrote another romance, Justine would always be his gold standard.

And a man valued and protected his gold standard. That's why Palmerton pissed him off. The leech needed to repay Justine for everything he'd caused her to lose. Meade was going to do everything he could to make sure that happened.

There was just one problem.

If Palmerton hadn't fucked with Justine, Meade might never have met her.

His breath caught. *What if he'd never met her?*

He opened the Hummer door and boosted Justine inside.

Unthinkable, he thought as he rounded the front of the vehicle.

He'd asked himself the same question about Elaine, but the answers were as different as the women. As different as life and death.

Justine was life. She gave his life meaning. Not his writing, although she'd provided a breath of fresh air there, too, but his existence. She expected nothing from him, but continued to give, including giving him grief. Yet her comments weren't about diminishing him, but clarification.

The instant Palmerton grabbed her arms, Meade had surged past all the boundaries he'd set on his emotions. His emotions? Hell, every boundary in his life. He was stalking uncharted territory and behaving like one of his over-the-top alpha heroes. Didn't make the sentiments any less real. He recognized them because he'd written them too many times to ignore.

He was in love with Justine Macko.

How could that even be possible?

CHAPTER 38

"WHY ARE WE STOPPING here?" Justine asked as Meade pulled up next to the back door of The Write Place lodge.

"I want more of the beef and barley soup."

"Am I going to have to install a lock on the freezer?" Justine asked, half-joking. "Guests raiding the kitchen after hours are going to mess with my inventory. Do you sneak food often?"

"Nope. Meals were never worth filching before. I'll be only a second. I'll leave the car running for the heat." He leaned across the console and gave her a quick kiss on her mouth before he climbed out.

What was she going to do about him? She loved him, but she didn't trust herself. Everything was so new. Fragile. And she still didn't know how he felt. He—

The passenger door opened on a blast of frigid air, and someone grabbed her arm.

Justine screamed as she was dragged from the Hummer. Her bad knee banged against the door opening.

"I knew if I hung around long enough, you'd be back." Lenny said. "Why you moved to Siberia is beyond me. Damn near froze my nuts off waiting for you."

Justine tried to wrest her arm from Lenny's grip. He held her too tightly. She slipped while struggling and twisted her knee again. The fall freed her, but she couldn't get up to run or climb back in the Hummer.

He jerked her upright.

She lurched against the Hummer, hoping to trigger the alarm. She lacked the weight or momentum to trip it.

"Come on, let's go." He tugged on her arm.

The tote with her knives was in the Hummer. Meade would find it when he came back and know she hadn't willingly left. She was on her own, unless someone heard her scream. Meade wasn't the only guest in the lodge. Writers working. Meade's agent. Salome, with her cordless phone.

"I told you." Justine barely managed to speak. "I'm not going anywhere with you."

"You are not going to ruin me," Lenny snarled. "You don't belong here, and the sooner you accept it, the better off you'll be. We'll both be."

"Help!" she shouted. "Lenny's trying to—"
She never saw his fist coming.
"Shut up or I'll have to hit you again."

She tasted blood. She spit into the snow. "How will you explain the bruising to your TV exec friends?"

"You let me worry about that. Just do what I tell you for a fucking change." He left the plowed portion of the lane, still hauling her in his wake.

"If you leave the path, you'll get lost. Salome told me people vanish in these woods and are never seen again." Hopefully the deep snow would numb the ache in her leg and leave a trail for Meade—anyone—to follow. She spat more blood onto the ground.

"Oh, please." Lenny's contempt rang in the still air.

"Where are you taking me?"

"My car is parked off what passes for the main drag, not far. Don't worry."

A pack of coyotes answered.

"Are those wolves?" He sounded worried.

Justine didn't correct him. *Let him be afraid.* She stumbled in Lenny's wake as he tried to slog through a drift.

The snow trapped them, stalling their progress.

A loud snapping noise startled her, followed by a whoosh as something heavy fell to the ground. Hunters? At night? What if she and Lenny were mistaken for deer? She choked on the impulse to laugh. Venison would always be her downfall. Now would be a good time for St. Lawrence the Moose, protector of cooks and comedians, to come to her rescue.

"Justine!" Meade's voice sounded close enough to comfort her.

"Here!" she replied, risking another taste of Lenny's knuckle sandwich. "It's Lenny!"

"What do you want him for?" Lenny asked. "He's only using you."

"Like you?" she snapped. "I'd rather be a character in a best-selling book than what you did or what you have planned for me."

"You think he's innocent?" Lenny's venom filled her with chills that pierced deeper than the frigid night, delving into her very marrow. "You forget. I overheard him talking to the owner about you. About how he kissed you without your consent. About how he wants to buy a cabin from her and will even marry you to procure a permanent residency here."

Her heart stopped. Arteries clogged as her blood turned to icy sludge and swelling the muscle until the ballooning ache filled her entire chest.

"He's lying!" Meade sounded closer now.

She didn't care what Meade's motive for rescuing her was, as long as he helped her get away from Lenny. She'd worry about his intentions later.

A narrow beam of light bobbed closer. *Hey Siri. Lumos,* Meade had ordered right before he found her in the ditch that first day. He would find her again.

Lenny floundered in the snow. He lost his grip on her arm.

Justine tumbled onto her butt.

"Heath! I got them!"

Meade had come with reinforcements.

Which was all fine and well, except Lenny was her problem. What kind of heroine waited for the hero to rescue her? Well, she wasn't a character in a book. Meade claimed her independence was sexy. Now would be a good time to prove him right. If only she had her knives—or two working legs.

"They're headed for the lake," Heath replied. He sounded closer

The lake. Hadn't she just that afternoon reminded Meade that one of his feisty heroines had shoved a lying, cheating suitor into a half-frozen lake? Except it was too cold for Nippletop Lake to be anything but solid ice.

But Araminta had tossed a glass of wine at Lazlo, and Justine had threatened Meade with hot coffee or—

She dug her hand into the drift and formed a loosely packed ball. "Fuck you, Lenny!" she yelled as she flung the snow in Lenny's face.

FEAR CLUTCHED AT MEADE. From the second he'd heard Justine scream, to finding the Hummer's passenger door wide open, a vice grip clamped his lungs. His breath rasped in and out, as loud as a blizzard wind.

He didn't need a light to follow their trail. Palmerton had to be dumber than dog shit to not realize he left tracks in the snow.

"Who screamed?" Heath materialized from the darkness.

"Palmerton snatched Justine."

"Sal!" Heath shouted. "Call the cops!"

Heath needed no other explanation. He switched on his Maglite and surged into the snow. Meade took the other side of the fresh ruts. An enormous branch from a pine tree had fallen from the weight of the snow, forcing Heath to detour and putting Meade in the lead.

If anything happened to Justine... He didn't know how to finish that thought. Life without her was unimaginable. If Palmerton hurt her, Meade wouldn't be able to stop himself from inflicting bodily injury this time. Nobody messed with his woman. Justine was his woman.

He called out for her. When she answered, the tension in his chest loosened. Her conversation with Palmerton carried in the still night air. The crap the man was trying to sell Justine further infuriated Meade. The flashlight on his cellphone picked out Justine's hair, dark against the pristine white landscape.

"He's lying!" Meade shouted.

Palmerton fought a snowdrift like a dinosaur in the La Brea Tar Pits, while trying to wipe off the snow Justine continued to fling at him and sputtering the whole time.

Heath could handle Palmerton. Meade squatted next to Justine. "Are you okay? How's your leg?"

He aimed his light at her. She blinked before averting her face. Everything inside him froze.

"Is that blood?" He played the light along her mouth and jaw. "Palmerton hit you?"

Heath caught up. "Christ Jesus," he muttered as his light illuminated Justine's face. "He do that to you?"

Justine's throat muscles worked as she swallowed.

Heath hauled Palmerton out of the drift by the front of his coat. "We don't hit women around here, asshole." He planted his fist in Palmerton's solar plexus.

Palmerton doubled over and puked on Heath's boots, prompting colorful curses from Heath. "Let's go, fuck wad." He glanced at Meade. "You got her?"

Forever, if she'll have me.

But all he said was, "Yep," as he pulled her into his arms.

CHAPTER 39

JUSTINE SPRAWLED ON A sofa in front of the massive fireplace in the lobby of The Write Place main lodge, holding an icepack against her jaw with another draped across her knee. The fire burned hot and bright. Salome had provided dry clothes, which helped dispel the chill, but the heat emanating from the open hearth embraced Justine inside and out. All that was missing was a nice cinnamon and clove potpourri simmering over the flames to add to the cozy ambience.

Oh, and Lenny's departure.

The room teemed with people focused on her. Darby hovered. Her husband Cam had handcuffed Lenny and guarded him until Deputy King could arrive. Salome dispensed cups of herbal tea while offering crystals for healing and detailing her plans to cleanse Lenny's former suite of any bad juju he'd left behind. Heath glowered at Salome. Even Laurel, the housekeeper, offered her rooms to Justine since she was leaving for the evening.

The Write Place staff was a family, the perfect example of the workplace atmosphere Justine had wanted at Just Food but had failed to achieve. She didn't deserve their concern, but here they were, rallied around her. They believed in her when she'd done nothing to earn their support.

All she knew for certain was that she didn't want to lose this. Yes, she'd screwed up by getting involved with Meade, but Salome had been complicit. That had to count for something.

And Meade? He sat on the floor next to her, periodically touching her free hand as if to reassure himself she was really safe.

The question was safe from whom?

The words Lenny had flung at her about Meade's ulterior motives festered. Had Meade seduced her to secure a permanent residency at The Write Place? Her stomach churned, even though she didn't want to believe the worst of Meade. But Lenny had tried to marry her to use as a springboard to fame and fortune. Once burned, twice shy. Lenny could be merely reflecting his own intentions onto his rival. Classic Lenny.

Her doubts lingered.

She couldn't think about them, not now. Nor could she confront Meade yet, not with everyone else smothering her with their worry.

Oh, and Lenny's presence.

Lenny kept trying to justify what he'd done until Heath told him to shut his *oeuf*ing mouth or he'd break his jaw. Well, not *oeuf*ing, but close enough.

Deputy King arrived, bringing questions, demanding answers, trading forest ranger handcuffs for sheriff department restraints, and taking more photos with his phone, this time of Justine's injured mouth. Lenny departed with him, secured in the backseat of the sheriff department's cruiser.

The fire crackled. No one spoke for several minutes.

Meade broke the silence. "Palmerton lied to you about the cabin."

"I don't want to talk about this now." Justine averted her face. She couldn't bear having her humiliation blasted to her co-workers and boss.

"Yes, now. While the Winehouses and Sal are here to back me up. You probably misunderstood—"

"Lenny was pretty clear."

"What's going on?" Darby asked.

"Apparently Palmerton overheard our conversation about kissing Justine without her consent," Meade explained.

Darby's brows drew together. "And?"

"We also had our usual discussion where I offer to buy Sacral Cabin."

"Oh Goddess," Salome said. "You've been asking about Sacral for years."

"How many times have we told you?" Cam inserted. "We're not selling."

They'd just confirmed her worst fear: Meade wanted to live full-time at The Write Place and had offered to marry her so he could. The truth hurt. A lot.

"Well, I am serious," Meade said. "I want to live here. But suggesting I marry Justine was—"

She was going to be sick.

"Wait, what?" Salome's head swiveled from Meade, to Justine, and back again. "You suggested marrying Justine so you could live in staff housing?"

"He asked what would happen if he married Justine," Darby explained in a dry voice. "And he was... sincere. That's when I first began to suspect—"

"I keep telling you," Salome interrupted.

"Not this shit again," Cam muttered.

"I was right about you and Darby," Salome insisted. "And I'm right about Justine and Meade."

Justine swallowed her nausea. "Right about what?"

"Sal believes she's a psychic matchmaker," Cam replied.

"You and Meade." Salome's innocent and earnest tone matched her glowing face. She appeared illuminated by an inner light. "You're meant to be together."

"What?" Meade spoke at the same time as Justine.

He sounded as shocked as Justine felt. Shocked, and in Justine's case, warm and squishy. Hopeful.

"Look at it this way. If Meade wanted to marry someone just to live here, why hasn't he ever proposed to me?" Salome asked.

"Because you're fucking nuts," Heath muttered. He shook his head and stalked from the room.

"I never proposed to you because you and I don't have that kind of relationship. I've already had one lousy marriage. If I ever wed again, well, you're not it for me. No offense, Sal."

"None taken."

"But you're right." Meade clasped Justine's hand and rose to his knees. His blue eyes bore into hers, as if drilling for her very soul. "Justine Macko, would you do me the great honor—"

"You can't steal my chef." Darby interrupted, sounding pissed.

Meade never intended to pop the question in front of everyone. A marriage proposal should be intimate. Private. Because the feelings involved were intensely personal. His emotions were a scrambled mess, but Palmerton's latest stunt clarified Meade's vision and forced him to acknowledge exactly how deeply he cared for Justine. He loved her, damn it. He didn't want to waste another second of not having her in his life.

Justine looked as if she wanted to burst into tears.

Okay, he was doing this all wrong. His timing was off, but Lenny's accusation exposed the final elephant in the room. How anyone had misconstrued his conversation with Darby confused him. He'd meant his offer to marry Justine, he realized now, even though he'd freaked out as he'd spoken the words. The idea of being connected to her calmed him. His gut reaction had been *yes, marry her*. The panic had been about relinquishing his new freedom from his ex, not Justine. Never Justine.

"You know," Sal said. "I could move to the third-floor dorm, then Justine and Meade can live in the assistant manager's cabin. Me being on site makes more sense than having me live a quarter mile away. Darby doesn't lose her chef, and Meade gets to stay and write."

"Wait a minute," Justine said. "Don't I get a say?"

"Absolutely." Meade refused to let anyone talk Justine into a situation she didn't want. Between him and Palmerton, they'd already done enough to last her a lifetime. "Yours is the only say that matters."

Say yes. Say you'll marry me. If not marriage, then live with me. Say you love me.

"I love—"

Yes!

"—working here."

Meade's heart dropped to his stomach.

"I don't want to do anything to jeopardize that."

Her maple-honey eyes abandoned Darby to lock on him.

The intensity with which she watched him should have made him uncomfortable but instead renewed his hope.

Of course she wasn't going to spill her guts in front of her boss and co-workers.

"Can we go back to your place?" she asked.

"You should stay in your own cabin tonight," Darby said.

"My stuff is at Meade's, and I don't want to be alone." Justine squeezed his hand.

"Sal can keep an eye on you," Darby argued, then looked to Sal, as if hocus-pocus would determine Justine's fate for the night. The decision belonged to him and Justine alone.

"He and I need to talk. Privately." Justine lifted her chin as if daring anyone to contradict her.

Meade released her hand and stood. "I'll warm up the car."

He knew the others would talk trash behind his back, but he didn't care. Darby wouldn't retract her initial assurance to Justine: Meade Godwin was a safe guy. Justine could trust him.

For the first time in his life, Meade liked being the safe guy. The nice guy. Justine needed safety now, security, more than she needed anything else. She needed Meade's brand of heroism.

He ran into Heath in the kitchen.

"She's gotta stay off her leg," Heath muttered. "Tonight's escapade probably aggravated the injury."

Meade owed the man an apology. He'd been wrong about Heath's intentions toward Justine. He'd been jealous for no reason. "Would a wheelchair work?"

Heath had been an army medic. He might know that sort of thing.

"Yeah."

"Is there a local place where I can rent one for her?" Meade wanted to kick himself for not thinking of it sooner.

"Oh yeah. Winter sports, injuries, and wheelchairs go together. I'll see what I can do."

"Thanks. And thanks for your help tonight, too." Meade never envisioned being grateful to the other man concerning Justine. Maybe he could name his next hero after him.

"I don't like guys who hit women. I don't like guys who force women."

The lack of emotion on Heath's face, the blank hardness in his eyes, chilled Meade. Maybe not a hero.

"And I really don't like bullies. Justine better press charges."

"If I have any say, she will."

"Good luck with that."

"I'm going to marry her. If she'll have me."

"Yeah? Good luck with that, too."

"Thanks." Meade planned to seize all the luck he could get.

CHAPTER 40

Justine snuggled against Meade as he carried her from his Hummer to his cabin, as if she belonged in his arms. His bed.

But did she trust him enough to marry him?

He plopped her on the bench inside the door long enough for him to remove their boots, then he lifted her into his arms again and carried her to the bedroom.

She appreciated Meade's comfort with silence. Their conversations weren't trite or unnecessary. The drive between the lodge and Sacral Cabin had been quiet, but not awkward, allowing her to think.

He placed her on the mattress as if she were a web made of sugar glass, then stood next to the bed and stared at her. Waiting for a reaction. No, expecting an answer. He'd asked a question, and she had yet to respond. The next move belonged to her.

"Thank you," she whispered.

Meade sank to the mattress next to her. "This afternoon, I thought I'd exceeded my maximum anger point when Palmerton put his hands on you. The force of my rage scared me."

"I know."

He feathered her injured mouth with his fingertips. "Yeah. You would. You understand. You see me, not my actions. You see the man, not the romance author."

"You're not what you do. Neither am I."

"No, you're not. But you have standards."

"So do you." Even though her mouth hurt, she smiled at him.

"Then tonight. Tonight, I discovered another stratosphere of fury. I accepted the rage, partly because Heath had my back. More importantly, all I could think about was you. How dare Palmerton try to hurt you? How dare he try to take you away from me and away from yourself? One of the things I first loved about you is your confidence. How much of yourself you are."

He'd said it again. The L-word. The same word with which she'd been wrestling.

"I was only half-joking when I told Darby I would marry you in order to stay here. I had just gotten free of my ex and found myself questioning why I wanted to... shackle myself again." He made a face. "I know, rotten word. But the idea of being married to you didn't repulse me. I didn't run in the opposite direction.

"Then we were here, alone together, for almost three days. You made me aware of how much of myself I am. And you supported whatever version of me happened to show up. I never had that before, and I don't want to go back to living without it. Without you."

His palm cupped her uninjured cheek before drifting up to brush an errant strand of hair from her forehead. "I love you so much."

Oh Puck. Tears gathered in her eyes. No weepy heroines. Lenny had never made her want to cry until she'd discovered the mess he'd left for her. Meade offered nothing except everything she ever wanted.

"If you suspect my reasons for wanting to marry you, we don't have to stay here. We can go back to Manhattan. Or I can sell my apartment, and we can choose another place. Together. One where my ex never lived. Or we can relocate to London or Los Angeles or Hong Kong. Whatever you want. I can work anywhere. As long as you're with me, I'm home."

Justine's expression gave away nothing. She had the best poker face Meade had ever seen.

"Say something. Please." He needed to know how she felt about... everything. Him.

"I've never cared for the instalove trope."

"Neither have I," he admitted. "I'd call our relationship more of a slow burn. It took a whole couple of hours the first night." True confession time. "I was jealous when you were nice to

Heath while he examined you because I wanted you to be nice to me."

"I thought you hated me."

"Not hate. Suspicious and hostile. I'd just come from my lawyer where we figured out how to deal with excessive spousal support, and there you were. Listening to a book I loathe and appearing needy when I was tired of needy women. Then you tried to convince me you didn't want my help. In fact, you were going to help me by cooking dinner. You confused me."

His mouth watered remembering the simple dish she'd cobbled together for their dinner.

"You weren't needy, and you weren't helpless, only sidelined. You drove to the High Peaks during a snowstorm on bald tires." Remembering still turned his insides to water.

He leaned in and gently kissed the fading bruise on her forehead. Worked his way to the fresh injury on her mouth and jaw. He rubbed a thumb against her nipple, which responded right away. "Can I take off your top?" His voice sounded husky, even to himself.

Justine nodded.

Meade lifted the hem of her borrowed sweater. Gently tugged the garment over her head. Static electricity crackled in her hair. The purple splotches on her upper arms tempted him to throw Palmerton through the ice in the middle of Nippletop Lake. Each bruise required a kiss, as if he had a magic mouth and could heal her with his love alone. By the time he found her bare breast, her entire body strained toward him.

"Meade," she whispered.

Her nipple slipped from his mouth. "I want to make love to you, Justine." He slid his hands inside the stretchy waistband of her leggings, savoring her skin's soft smoothness as he pulled the garment down her legs. Her sighs were the love song he wanted from her.

Kissing and licking his way along the path created by his hands required no brain.

Justine flinched as his lips approached her swollen knee.

"Hush." He tried to calm her. He parted her legs. Explored with his fingers the area he intended to nibble and sip.

"Meade—"

"Shh." His breath ruffled her pubic hair. "Please trust me."

She tried to jackknife upright, but he pushed on her belly. "Relax. Let me pamper you. Let me love you."

At first, she tensed, as if no one had ever tasted her before. Gradually, she relaxed. Melted under the heat of his ministrations. Soft moans turned to whimpers. And when her climax hit, he lapped the nectar of his success.

Her legs splayed on either side of him. One last lick, then he sat up and divested himself of his jeans and sweatshirt.

Her body, warm and pliant, accepted him. "Marry me," he groaned. He lowered his forehead to hers as he gently, tenderly moved inside her. "Where we live doesn't matter, because you are my home."

"I love you," she replied as she looped her arms under his. "But be warned. I won't eat sauce from a jar, and we will always serve genuine Parmesan cheese at our table."

"Right," he agreed. "Whatever you say. I'm afraid of your knives."

EPILOGUE

(TWO AND A HALF YEARS LATER)

"My first novel debuted at number one on the New York Times bestseller list!" Meade whooped.

"Wonderful!" Justine managed to croak. She doubted Meade heard her through the closed bathroom door. A good wife should celebrate with him, and she really wanted to, but she was dealing with her own issues at the moment. Her very unpleasant issues. Issues that had her kneeling on the floor and hovering over the toilet.

"Are you okay in there?" The solid wood panel muffled Meade's voice.

"Yup," she lied.

Meade deserved to bask in his exciting news. He'd finally listened to India about his "man book" concept and wrote a thriller featuring a psychic female sleuth, under his own name. His new genre and characters were so different from Andromeda Zeus's romance novels, there was no way his ex-wife could claim part of the royalties.

Justine hauled herself upright and staggered to the sink. She managed to brush her teeth without being sick, but the cold water she splashed on her face didn't wash away her fatigue. She didn't know how much longer she could ignore her symptoms. Between her iffy stomach, her exhaustion, and her extremely tender breasts, she figured her IUD had failed. She just wasn't sure how to break the news to Meade that he was going to be a daddy—and not the kinky kind, either.

She slapped on a smile and opened the door.

And nearly gagged.

Two years of living in Salome's former cabin should have been enough to erase the smell of her incense and candle collections. The lingering fragrances hadn't bothered Justine until recently. Now she kept the windows open and frequently debated boiling eggs or cabbage to counter the aromas but feared that fix might be worse than the problem.

Meade stood at the kitchen table, clutching a sheet of paper and beaming so brightly, his grin rivaled the sun pouring through the open windows. "You just missed Heath. He brought over a fax from India with the good news."

Meade's status as The Write Place writer in residence included access to the retreat's business equipment. He and Justine had negotiated an exceptional deal with Darby, who would do just about anything to keep Justine on staff, including the two-bedroom cabin and bestowing a title on Meade.

Justine, however, feared her honeymoon with Darby was nearing its end. After all, what kind of chef couldn't stomach the smell of raw meat?

"You earned it," Justine assured Meade. She'd seen how much effort and angst he'd put into excavating a new voice after years of writing with an alter ego. "Let's frame the fax and hang it in your office."

After you move to the loft.

Meade's current office was Salome's former bedroom on the ground floor. That needed to change. Justine wanted the baby nearby.

The baby. Hers and Meade's. She placed her hand on her flat stomach. It didn't seem real. It couldn't be real.

Meade's eyes narrowed as he studied her. "I shared my good news. Isn't it time you shared yours?"

Justine started. "My good news?"

He crossed the room and drew her into his arms. "I've written enough romance novels to know the symptoms, Justine. Morning sickness, tiredness, sore boobs—yeah, I've seen you flinch every time I go near them—we're going to have a baby."

We. She wasn't alone anymore, a situation that still had the power to amaze her.

"I think so," she admitted. She closed her eyes and rested her cheek against his chest. Funny how food and other scents upset her stomach, but Meade's citrus-spice aroma comforted her. Too bad she couldn't keep him with her while she was working—not that it had worked out so well when he'd been writing Andromeda's final book. But their relationship had been different then.

"Want to run out and pick up a home pregnancy test?" He rubbed her back.

"You mean you're not going to kidnap me and drive me to Urgent Care?"

"Only if you insist."

Oh, how she loved this man. Loving him, however, didn't mean she was going to let him get away with anything. "Try tossing me over your shoulder again. I dare you."

"So you can throw up on me? I don't think so." His chuckle caressed her cheek as it vibrated through the soft cotton of his shirt.

"Smart man, but I need to get to work in about half an hour. The guests won't feed themselves." She swallowed hard. The thought of prepping raw chicken breasts to grill reignited her queasiness. She reluctantly eased out of his embrace.

"We could check with Sal. Have her read the cards or tea leaves."

She didn't know if Meade was kidding or not. Since writing *Dark Crystabelle*—their code name for his new book series—he'd started paying more attention to Salome's utterings. He'd even asked for a tarot reading to help create the main character.

Justine shook her head. Carefully. White spots salted her vision. "Let's not."

Salome had become a close friend, even standing up for Justine when she married Meade. Still, she did things that made Justine uncomfortable. Meade could tap into Salome's hocus pocus for his writing, but Justine would rather stay clear of any woo-woo, especially when it came to the baby.

Her hand went to her abdomen again.

"I think it's too late," Meade said. "Heath also brought peppermint tea that Sal insisted you needed to settle your stomach."

"Oh, Puck."

He grinned. "And I got a blend of tea to help with my throat chakra."

"Definitely too late." Justine had absorbed some of Salome's philosophies, despite her unwillingness to engage. Throat chakra was for communication, which Justine assumed meant Meade's books.

Meade corrected that impression. "Not quite. I've shared the good news, but there's more, and I'm not sure if it's good or bad."

Justine waited.

"India and Finn hired a new publicity team that wants me to go on a book tour, including guest appearances on a couple late night talk shows. Throat chakra."

Of course they did. Andromeda Zeus would remain an enigma, but Meade Godwin? Finn Upshaw, his new editor, was determined to make Meade Godwin a household name.

"Are you comfortable with that?" Justine asked.

Comfortable? Hell no. There were times Meade wished Justine wasn't so astute. Sometimes he thought she was more psychic than Sal. "I'm not sure."

"Why?"

"Because."

Justine crossed her arms, visibly wincing as she did. Her toe started to tap.

How could he explain? Marriage, a permanent move to the Adirondacks, a new publishing career, and now impending fatherhood. He'd made a lot of adjustments since rescuing Justine from that ditch. Since falling in love with her. One more change shouldn't stymie him.

Except publishing under his own name exposed him. Scared him. He'd loved the anonymity of Andromeda Zeus, the excuse to stay holed up in his apartment and focus solely on his writing. Everything else was a distraction. He didn't want to be sidetracked by critics or even readers. His life was complete now. He was writing what he wanted, living at The Write Place, married to the perfect woman, and they were starting their family.

"I need to be available for you, especially now, not galivanting around the country doing book signings, readings, and late-night TV," he grumbled. "Someone has to make sure you're taking care of yourself and the baby."

"Don't use me as an excuse."

She was right. She was always right.

"Fine. I don't *want* to be a public figure. I *want* to be my generation's version of a reclusive author, the JD Salinger or

Harper Lee of this century. I *want* to write the next book. I *want* to be available for you."

My need to take care of you is in my DNA.

"You know, you don't have to travel to be a guest on a podcast or do interviews. The COVID pandemic proved that. All you need is an internet connection and a nice background."

Whew. She'd given him an out. "And there's no internet here." He grinned.

"Oh please. Darby would love to host her writer in residence at her house. Or any venue in Lake Placid would do it for the free publicity." Justine faked an announcer's voice: "Live from the Not-A-Chain Motel in Lake Placid, New York, best-selling author Meade Godwin."

Meade inhaled deeply. Justine wasn't going to let it go until he completely bared his soul. If he didn't love her so much, he'd hate her for making him accountable to himself.

"What if I don't like the questions?"

Justine smiled. "Say you're having technical difficulties and leave the interview."

She had an answer for everything.

"You really want me to do this."

"I'm so proud of you," she admitted in a soft voice. She cupped his cheek. "You deserve every penny your publisher wants to throw your way to launch your new career. But I'm also very selfish. I like coming home to you every night."

He covered her hand with his. "I like being home for you every night."

"You are my home. I love you." She raised up on her toes and pressed her lips against his.

He dropped his hand and wrapped his arms around her. If he never wrote another word and could spend the rest of his life simply holding her, he would be complete.

If Andromeda Zeus were writing their story, she would say something appropriately mushy. Profound, but mushy. Because love was both of those things, plus a whole lot more—like not eating sauce from a jar, serving only genuine cheese, and respecting any moose that wandered onto the highway, because it could be St. Lawrence, their personal patron saint.

Sure, that sounded like an Andromeda plot, but Andromeda was no more. Meade's choice. He didn't need an alter ego to write him a happily-ever-after, because he had Justine. Their baby. Their future.

I HOPE YOU ENJOYED Meade and Justine's story.

Please consider signing up for my newsletter at my website: www.mjcompton.com

Newsletter subscribers receive exclusive content, first look at covers, and other fun stuff.

ALSO BY MJ COMPTON

PINCH OF SPICE, JUSTICE SERVED

COLUMBIA GEMS BASEBALL ROMANCES
PARANORMAL ROMANTIC SUSPENSE (Shifters)
THE WRITE PLACE RETREAT ROMANCES

About the Author

MJ Compton grew up near Cardiff, New York, a place best known for its giant—a hoax so successful, P.T. Barnum duplicated it. The tale of the "petrified man" convinced MJ that inventing stories could be a career.

Although her 30 years working in local television included such highlights as being bitten by a lion, preempting a US President for a college basketball game, giving a three-time world champion boxer a few black eyes, and meeting her husband, MJ never lost her dream of creating her own stories.

MJ still lives in upstate New York with her husband. Music and cooking are two of her passions, and she enjoys baseball, college basketball, and sitting on her patio on summer nights to count lightning bugs, but she's primarily focused on writing.